Until the Ribbon Breaks

a novel

New York Times Bestselling Author

E.K. Blair

Dedication

To my younger self

Until the Ribbon Breaks

Chapter One

"**H**ER WORRY COMES IN FRACTIONS; YOU KNOW THAT."

"Better in fractions than not at all, right?"

My eyes drift to the window to spare him having to see them roll. The mist collects on the glass in a similar way misery collects in my soul. It's never-ending, much like the clouds that hardly spare us their presence. I miss the sun at times, among other things. I'd rather be at the Sound than stuck here in this banal office that has already claimed too much of my time.

When I turn back to Dr. Amberg, my psychiatrist, he's staring at me with his legs crossed and his notepad resting in his lap. He's an older man with peppered hair and wire-framed glasses with small round lenses. They look funny on him.

I scan the room, which is void of any kind of decoration. The hours I've spent in here have been countless, yet with each passing week, this office remains just as desolate as it was the first time I walked into it. "Why have you never decorated?" I ask. "How long has this been your office?"

He fiddles with his pencil as he thinks for a moment. "Around eight years, I suppose."

"And you've never hung a single picture? Not even your college diplomas? Are you even a real doctor?"

"I never got around to framing them."

"Are they not important?"

"Not as important as my patients. So, why don't we get back to you?"

"There's nothing to get back to because there's nothing to talk about."

"Your mother is worried."

"What's new?" I scoff.

"What would you say if I told you that *I* was worried?"

"I don't want to hurt myself," I defend on the veins of irritation.

"I wasn't insinuating that you did."

I don't believe him. Everyone who knows about my incident uses it as a reason to treat me differently, as if I can't be trusted, as if I'm malfunctioned, as if I'm a ticking time bomb. It makes it impossible to forget—not that I want to forget, I only want *them* to forget.

"Triggers have a way up popping up when we least expect them, and sometimes, if we aren't paying attention, we can miss them," he adds.

"I'm not triggered."

"And what about when you hurt yourself?"

Nervously, I clasp my hands together. I think about that day often. There was nothing alluring about it—it wasn't a fantasy about to be fulfilled—even though, in a way, it was. When the attempt happened, it was all a blur.

Maybe I should tell him that.

If it weren't so hard to open up about it, maybe I would be able to be honest with him.

I want to feel better, there's no doubt, but I'm scared and embarrassed.

Information creates power that I fear could be used against me. This is why I'm selective with what I share with Dr. Amberg in these weekly sessions.

He means well. I've actually come to like him since I first met him at Hopewell, but it isn't enough for me to trust him entirely, and he knows it. It's been seven months since I was admitted to his facility, and even now that I'm back home, I still find it extremely difficult to talk about that day.

After setting his pencil and notepad on the small table beside him, he folds his hands together on top of his legs. "What happened with you is never an easy thing to talk about."

His eyes linger on me, and I know he's trying to read me, trying to find the crack in my façade. I want so badly to be fixed, but that would require me to open up and be transparent, to expose the depths of my sadness buried inside.

"How have you been sleeping?"

My hands itch to move, to fidget, to pick the last pieces of polish off my nails. I take a slow blink, conjure a little courage, and make the conscience decision to answer his question truthfully. "Restless. I've been having nightmares."

"What's happening in those dreams?"

"I'm outside of my body, watching myself in the bathroom." I pinch my eyes shut when the visions become too clear. Behind my lids, tears drip like acid, their presence burning the back of my tongue as they fall inside me.

"Can you tell me what you see?"

Turning my head, I look out the window again. "Disappointment."

"With what you intended to happen or with what actually happened?"

"Neither." He doesn't press forward with another question, and when I shift my eyes back to him, I give him one more truth before our hour is up, saying, "Disappointment with who I am."

After leaving therapy, I need to clear my head, so I drive to my favorite spot along the Sound.

Gray blankets the city as I walk across the damp parking lot. Soggy petals from cherry blossoms cover the pavement. It's blooming season—March—and yet, so many of the pink flowers have already found death. They stick to the bottoms of my shoes. The lot ends, and I take the old wooden stairs down to the vacant beach. Patches of puddles have formed in the densely packed sand—I walk right through them before settling on a large piece of driftwood. I shrug my backpack off my shoulders and pull out my notebook. The ever-present Washington mist speckles the page I started working on yesterday, but not enough to ruin the paper.

A gust of wind whips through my long, auburn hair, and I flip the hood of my raincoat over my head to keep the unruly locks tamed. I then grab my pencil, inhale a lungful of salty air, and allow the sound of lead against fibrous paper to lull me.

This notebook started about six months ago when I needed something to keep my hands occupied. I often feel restless, as if there's a constant hum in my body that rarely subsides.

It began in middle school, not long after my father announced that his job at Boeing was transferring him to the Renton office. I was so upset because I knew the promotion meant he would be traveling overseas most weeks out of the year, leaving me with my mom. I begged him not to take the job, but he accepted it anyway. His absence has increased over the past few years and so has the tension between my mother and me. But here, in the dank chill along the Puget Sound, I'm able to forget the stress at home and relax. My pencil skitters across the page and, without breaking my flow, I drag my pinky along the lines to smooth them out. I have pages filled with drawings, poetry, and sporadic journal entries.

Time is illusive as I become hyperfocused. It isn't until the sheet is filled with my feelings that I tuck it back into my bag. This spiral notebook is my only outlet where I can be utterly honest. It's my release.

I grab my cell phone and note the time. My dad's plane should've landed an hour ago. I haven't seen him in almost two weeks. I also haven't talked to my mother since I left for school earlier this morning, but it isn't surprising that she hasn't called or texted to ask my whereabouts. Lately, she swings on the pendulum of being overbearing or completely disconnected. It drives me crazy not knowing which of the two I'm getting from one day to the next.

She swings whereas I stand still. I'm annoyed when she's too busy to notice me, and I'm annoyed when she's breathing down my neck. It would probably take a cataclysmic act for her to find a happy medium.

Slinging my backpack over my shoulders, I head to my car.

From the Sound, I drive along the winding road, which is flanked by tall lush trees that canopy overhead. I've always loved this drive. It's peaceful and not littered with the city's traffic—at least not this time of year. When summertime hits, these roads will be clogged with locals and tourists alike, anxious to soak up the sunshine before the rain returns.

When I make it home, my dad is already here. The exterior lights illuminate the two-story house that's surrounded by towering pines, giving the illusion that we're tucked far away from civilization. In reality, our neighbors are just around the corner.

"Harlow?" my mom calls from the kitchen when I walk through the front door. "Is that you?"

"Yeah."

"Dinner will be ready in five minutes."

The smell of garlic and basil fills the air, and after tossing my bag by the foot of the stairs, I make my way into the kitchen to find my parents.

My father is pouring my mom a glass of wine while she stirs the pot of spaghetti sauce. "Hey, sweetheart," he says as we both walk toward each other. He gathers me into his arms, hugging me tightly. "I've missed you."

"Missed you too, Dad."

We have always had a special bond, one I've never felt with my mother. He and I don't talk as much as we used to, but if I had it my way, I would choose for my mother to be gone so my father wouldn't ever have to leave. It isn't that I hate my mom or anything. I mean . . . she's my mom. We just fight and butt heads a lot.

"Where have you been?" she questions as I grab a soda from the fridge.

I pop the tab. "At the Sound."

Silently, the two of them move about until dinner has been plated, served, and we are all sitting at the dining table.

My dad passes me a piece of garlic bread. "So, how's school been going?"

"The usual . . . boring."

My mother shakes her head as she stabs her fork into her salad.

"And the newspaper?" he questions.

"I think I have all my stuff in order for the next edition, but I'll be staying after school more until everything is ready to submit." I take a bite of the warm bread. "People are already arguing over the layout design."

"Don't talk with your mouth full, dear."

I drop my breadstick and turn back to Dad when he asks, "Did you get some good photos this year?"

"Uh-huh."

My father bought me my first camera when I was a little girl. It was a cheap one we found at a souvenir shop when we were at Disney World. I took photos of anything and everything. It sparked my love for photography, and I've found comfort behind the lens ever since.

"Emily came into the flower shop this afternoon with her boyfriend to pick out a corsage and boutonniere for the spring formal," my mother says. "He seems nice."

"I wouldn't know," I mutter while I twirl my fork in the pile of spaghetti on my plate.

Emily and I used to be inseparable when we were younger, but once middle school ended and high school began, we sort of went our separate ways.

"Has anyone asked you to the dance yet?"

Noodles dangle off the prongs of my fork when I stop mid-bite. "Seriously?" I snide. "Those dances are lame."

"How would you know? You've never been."

"Mom. Stop."

Her need for me to fit in and be okay—whatever *okay* is—is annoying. Her idea of how I should spend my high school years drastically contradicts mine, but she doesn't get it.

"I just worry that you're going to look back one day and regret not being more involved."

"Let it go, Jamie," my dad tells her gently.

"I'm serious. You should be enjoying yourself and going to dances."

"I'm fine," I exhaust. "I swear we have this same conversation every few days. Can we just drop it?"

She looks at my dad for backup, but he defends me instead. "I agree. Let's drop it. If she says she's fine, then that's all that matters."

But I know my mom, and after a minute of silence passes, she can't help herself. "I'm just worried, Harlow."

I drop my fork, and it clanks loudly against the plate as I shove my chair back and stand.

"Harlow, stop."

"Why don't you stop, Mom?"

"Harlow," my father warns.

"She does this all the time, Dad. You're always gone, so you don't see it, but it's literally *all the time*."

"That's an exaggeration," she murmurs before taking a sip of her wine. "I just think it would be healthy for you if you got out more and made some friends. You're always alone."

Heat crawls up my neck, and I cross my arms defensively as I stare down at my uneaten plate of spaghetti.

"Why do you have to be so hard on her?"

"That's easy for you to say, Jonathan. You're never even here, and with the little time that you are, you act as if you're the parental expert," she snaps at my dad while I shut down. "I think I know our daughter a little better than you do."

"That's a low blow. I work my ass off to provide for our family."

"I work too! I've built that flower shop from the ground up. You have no idea about the stress of owning your own business. I only wish I could fly all over the world like you get to."

"You act like I'm on vacation."

"You pretty much are while I'm stuck here. I never get a break, unlike you."

They continue to sling their words back and forth, each jab fueling the next. They don't even notice when I turn and stomp up the stairs.

Slamming my bedroom door behind me, I toss my backpack onto the floor and pull out my cell phone. I sit at my desk, lean back in my chair, and text my brother.

Me: Please tell me you're coming home for spring break.

Tyler is four years older than I am and away at college on the east coast. Lucky him for getting out of here. When he told me he was going to college in North Carolina, I was upset. I had hoped he would go to school somewhere around here. The last thing I wanted was to be left here alone. Not that we are incredibly close or anything like that. To him, I'm probably just his annoying little sister. But to me, he's someone who I can actually talk to—more like complain to.

Tyler: Sorry. I'm actually going down to Florida with a few friends.
Me: Dad just got home and the two of them are already fighting. I wish I could go to Florida with you.
Tyler: You only have one year left. Have you started thinking about what colleges you want to apply to?
Me: Yeah. Ones that are far away from Mom.
Tyler: Try to go easy on her. You know she just worries about you. We all do.

I hate when they say that. I hate that they all know what I did when they have the privilege of hiding their deepest secrets. It makes me feel weird—abnormal. As if I'm some poor, pitiful girl who can't take care of herself.

Me: That's so annoying. You guys act as if I'm broken, but I'm not.

It's a lie.

The thing is that I often find myself trying to pinpoint the moment in my life that broke me, but I'm beginning to think that I was born broken. It would be so much easier if there were an event that caused the fracture. At least then I could have something tangible to work through, to mend the pieces and get better.

Unfortunately, that doesn't exist for me.

<h1 style="text-align:center">Chapter Two</h1>

HARLOW

THE BELL RINGS, AND I GROAN, MIFFED THAT I'M BEING forced to eat lunch in the cafeteria today. I typically hide in the photo lab where the newspaper staff meets, but Mr. Duncan had to leave school early, and he locked the room.

Taking my time, I shove my laptop into my backpack while the other students flee the class. As I drag my feet through the halls, I consider spending my lunch in the library, but my stomach has been grumbling for the past hour. Apparently, the candy bar I got from the vending machine earlier wasn't enough to fill me up.

I stop short of the entrance to the cafeteria and stare in. Loud voices fill the space. The jocks are at one table, the emos at another, and the stoners are in the corner. Each clique has their designated spot, leaving a few tables scattered about for the loners like me.

I've known most of these kids since elementary school. Back then, I wasn't the outcast I am now. There was a time when I used to be friends with most of them, but then middle school hit. Everyone began branching off into their small cliques. At the time, it was Emily, Kassi, me, and a few other girls.

Around eighth grade, things started to change. I can't say exactly what, but, slowly, I felt myself drifting from them. Not intentionally. It isn't as if they ever did anything wrong; it kind of just happened. My friends that once felt like sisters to me eventually became the girls I could no longer relate to. It was as if some unexplainable force picked me up and dropped me down in the middle of nowhere, and ever since, I haven't been able to find my way back.

Then high school came and image was everything. Emily, the free-spirit who I used to have sleepovers with, became obsessed with her social standing. Fitting in and being popular was her biggest concern while I was simply lost.

I've spent the better part of these past few years trying to figure out where my old self went. I haven't seen her in a very long time, so long that I forgot how it even feels to be her—to be *me*.

Rumors started to spread when I was gone last semester. Since after Christmas break, I've become privy to the gossip that was circulating about why I had vanished for the first half of junior year. Pretty much the consensus was that I got knocked up and went away to have the baby in secret.

So, not only am I freak, but now a slut. Little do they know, I've never even kissed a boy, except for that one time when Alex, who now sits at the emo table, kissed me under the monkey bars in fifth grade. Apart from that, I doubt I've ever been on any guy's radar. Not that I'm unfortunate in the looks department. At least I don't think I am, but it doesn't matter how pretty you are, it only matters how popular you are.

I resign a heavy breath as I stroll in, hoping to go unnoticed, and head straight to the snack bar to grab a bag of chips and a soda before making my way over to the loser's table. Out of nowhere, a package of M&Ms flies through the air and nearly sideswipes my face, but I duck in time to dodge the impact.

"Watch out, Cricket," Sebastian barks from the table to my right.

He's a jock, but mostly, he's just an ass.

"Thanks, dude," his buddy across the way says, already ripping into the bag of candy.

"Why don't you watch where you're throwing things?" I mumbled beneath my breath, but it's loud enough for him to hear.

He slings his arm around his girlfriend's shoulders and throws me a cocky smirk. "Why don't you stop being a freak?"

A few kids laugh at his lame insult.

"Gross," Kassi, his girlfriend, says. "Why are you even talking to her?"

My eyes flit from her over to Emily, who's sitting next to them.

She looks up at me but doesn't speak. Not that I expect her to. She's barely said two words to me since middle school.

"Mooo-ve, Cricket," Sebastian taunts loudly, mocking the sound of a cow.

Shaking my head, I walk away and take a seat a few spots down from a lanky kid who's sipping his milk and reading an old copy of *The Chrysalids*.

A loud eruption catches my attention, and when I look over my shoulder, Sebastian is high-fiving Brent, his lacrosse teammate. Emily and Kassi smile at whatever has them amped up. I turn back and shove a chip into my mouth, dreading having to be around them tonight at the game I'm in charge of photographing. If it weren't for being on the newspaper staff, there's no way I would subject myself to high-school events. For the most part, I go unnoticed—a wallflower, if you will.

Lanky boy looks up from his book, and we awkwardly catch eyes.

"Are you new here?" he asks, leaving me to assume he's the new one since I've lived here my whole life and everyone should, at the very least, know *of* me. Plus, I've never seen him before.

"No." I crunch down on another chip. "You?"

He nods. "My family just moved here from Kansas."

"What's in Kansas?"

"Absolutely nothing," he says with a hint of laughter.

I smile, appreciating the small interaction.

"Why aren't you sitting with your friends?"

"Because everyone here sucks," I respond with a hint of laughter.

"So, you're saying I shouldn't waste my time?"

Another loud uproar sounds from behind me. This time, it's a bunch of guys cheering on Brent as he attempts to shove an entire slice of pizza into his mouth. The crust is bulging out from between his over-stretched lips when he pumps his fists in victory.

Turning to the new kid, I shrug. "Case and point right there."

He closes his book and scoots down a couple of chairs to sit right in front of me before extending a hand. "I'm Noah."

His formality amuses me, but I shake it anyway. "I'm Harlow."

"Nice to meet you." He shoves his book into his bag. "What do you do for fun around here since you detest everyone?"

"You make it sound like I'm nothing but a hater."

He smiles. "Aren't you?"

I quirk a brow before responding to his question. "Sometimes I like to drive to Seattle. This town has a way of feeling small when you've lived here your whole life."

"What do you do in Seattle?"

"Nothing really. It's just nice to be surrounded by fresh faces. But there is this local book and record store called Spines that hosts small concerts and stuff. It's pretty cool."

"Any bands I would know?"

"Maybe some. But most are indie, which I prefer. Nothing worse than an artist who sells out commercially for a paycheck."

"I couldn't agree more," he says. "I hate when one of my favorite songs winds up on the radio. Ruins it for me."

"Oh my god! Me too. I mean, I get it, they want to be rich and famous, but once they hit the radio, all their music turns to crap."

"Like you said—commercialized."

"It's like people are scared of originality. They all claim to be original, but they're really just like everyone else."

He laughs, quipping, "Clones."

"Exactly."

The bell rings and groans fill the cafeteria as everyone throws away their trash and heads to their next class.

Noah stands and grabs his backpack. "It was nice meeting you," he says before picking up his small milk carton and tossing it into the garbage. "I'll catch you later."

"See ya." I idle in my seat as I watch him file out of the cafeteria with the rest of the herd. I pop the last chip into my mouth right before someone bumps into the table, causing my soda to knock over.

It spills onto my lap, and when I jump up, Sebastian is laughing.

"Why are you such a jerk?"

He doesn't say anything as he and Kassi snicker at me.

"Dude," Brent announces loud enough for everyone to hear, "Cricket pissed herself!" He then takes Emily's hand in his as they walk out.

Embarrassment flames my cheeks, turning them hot while everyone stares and laughs as they pass me on their way out. I pick up the can, throw it into the trash, and make a beeline to the bathroom.

Wadding up a handful of paper towels, I soak them under the faucet before blotting my pants. My whole crotch is soaking wet when Emily enters. She looks at my pants as she walks over to one of the other sinks.

"I don't think he did that on purpose," she says as she pulls out her lip gloss.

"I don't know why you hang out with them."

I go to the hand drier as she looks at herself in the mirror, rubbing her lips together. "They aren't that bad."

"Whatever."

After she leaves and the door closes behind her, I punch my palm against the round silver button that brings the drier to life with a loud hiss.

There's a light mist in the air tonight while I snap photo after photo of the players on the field. It's nearing the end of the fourth quarter, and we're up by one, not that I care. I keep behind my camera as I stand on the sideline. When the clock runs down, I capture the final moment when Sebastian makes a last-minute goal, securing the team's win.

Everyone cheers from the stands, the team celebrates like the obnoxious boys they are, and I pack my things. As I make my way through the stands, I run into Phoung, who's on the newspaper staff with me. We chat about nothing in particular for a few minutes, and when the bleachers have practically emptied, we say a quick goodbye before I head out.

As I'm walking, I fumble around in my bag for my keys. When I can't find them, I grow frustrated and stop next to the concession stand so I can dig through my backpack. My hand is still blindly searching for my keys when I hear Kassi whining about something. Peeking my head around the corner of the concession building, I see her and Sebastian, and I eavesdrop.

"Why can't I ever come over?" she asks.

"What's the big deal?"

"I just don't know why you won't introduce me to your mom. Are you embarrassed of me or something?"

"God, you're annoying," he gripes. "You act like we're getting married or something. Who cares that you haven't met my mom? It's not a big deal."

"Well, if it isn't a big deal, then let me come over."

"I'm not even going home."

"All we ever do is party with Brent. Why don't you want to spend alone time with me?"

"We were alone after school," he says suggestively, running his hand along her cheek and back into her hair.

She isn't amused, and she shoves him. "Sometimes I think that sex is all you want from me," she snaps before walking away.

"Come on, Kassi. Don't be like that."

She flips him the middle finger, and I shake my head at their stupid spat as I duck back behind the wall.

"Finally," I whisper when I find my keys.

As I turn the corner to leave, I bump right into Sebastian, who looks at me in annoyance. "Watch where you're going, Cricket."

Hoisting my bag over my shoulder, I stopped in my step once again when I see Noah. In an attempt to go unnoticed, I quickly turn, giving him my back, and pick up my pace as I walk to my car.

"Harlow," he calls out from across the way, and when I look over my shoulder, he's jogging toward me. "Hey," he huffs, slightly winded.

"Are you that out of shape," I tease, to which he laughs.

"Just slightly. I didn't think I'd see you here."

"I'm on the newspaper, so . . ."

"Cool."

"What are you doing here?" I ask "Did you come alone?"

He shrugs. "Trying to blend in and make friends." I give him a nod and when the conversation comes to a stall, the interaction, or lack thereof, turns awkward. "So, hey," he says, breaking the silence. "You want to go grab a burger or something?"

"Umm," I hesitate, not expecting him to want to hang out. Someone should warn him, that if he's wanting to fit in and make friends, he should probably steer clear of me.

"Are you trying to think of a reason to say no?"

He hits the nail on the head, and it gets a chuckle out of me as I admit, "Kinda."

"Come on. I haven't eaten since lunch."

Even though I'd much rather go home and call it a day, I would feel bad if I told him no with how excited he seems at the prospect of hanging out. And I'd be lying if I said that a part of me didn't want to hang out as well. There isn't much in my life to fill in the gaps of space and distract me from myself aside from school. So, I take a step out of my comfort zone, and say yes instead of making up an excuse to say no.

"Yeah, sure."

He smiles. "Great. So, what's good around here?"

"Dick's Drive-In has the best burgers." Plus, it's a drive-in and not an eat-in restaurant, so I'm not locked into this lasting a long time. "I need to get gas in my car first, so I'll meet you there."

"Sounds good."

We go our different ways before I get into my car and head toward the closest gas station. While I wait for my tank to fill, I lean against my car and send a quick text to my mom.

Me: Grabbing something to eat and then I'll be home.

When the pump clicks and I pull the nozzle out, I catch my mom walking out of the convenience store with a cup of coffee in her hand. But it isn't her car she walks towards . . . it's an SUV. I try to hide myself behind the large concrete pillar as I watch her from across the lot. The SUV backs up and when it turns my way, I see her laughing from the passenger side next to a man I've never seen before.

I tuck myself back into my car as confusion sparks a multitude of questions. My thoughts immediately go to the worst-case scenario, but instinct has me creating excuses to make that scenario implausible. I mean, it isn't as if I saw her doing anything bad. The guy could be an old friend of hers, somebody she knows from work, or he could be . . .

My cell phone vibrates in my hand, pulling me out of my thoughts.

Mom: Okay. I'm working late with a new vendor, but I should be home in an hour.

There, that makes sense. He's a new vendor. They're working late and she wanted a cup of coffee. It's a completely reasonable explanation, so why can't I shake the unease in my gut?

Chapter Three

HARLOW

"How much longer are you going to be?" Noah questions as I click and drag photos of the cheerleading team around on the computer screen. "I really want to get through this next page of layouts."

The deadline to have everything submitted for the newspaper is quickly approaching, so the staff has been staying after school more than usual to get it wrapped up.

"If you're that impatient, just download the album," I tell him. Noah's favorite band just released a new album and it's all he can talk about. I agreed to go with him to the record store after school so he can buy it, but I need to finish up my work first.

He scoffs. "Digital downloads have ruined the whole experience. Vinyl has been, and always will be, the best way to listen to music."

"Vinyl is for old people."

"Clearly, you've never listened to your favorite bands on vinyl, because you wouldn't be saying that if you had."

"You're wrong"—I click the save button and look over at him—"the best way to experience music is live, not listening to some scratchy record."

He shakes his head. "You disappoint me, you know?"

I shoot him a plastic smile as I continue to work.

"Low, were you in charge of the student council banquet?" Annie, the newspaper editor, asks from across the room.

"No. I think that was Theo."

After dropping the team lacrosse photo into place, I go back to my camera file and start weeding through the pictures. I select a few and drag them around the page, trying to decide exactly how I want the layout.

"Those guys are douches," Noah mutters, and I agree with a nod.

It's been a couple of weeks since we met, and it's turned out that he's a pretty cool guy, even though he borders on the edge of weird, but that's what makes him interesting. He's nothing like most of the boys at school, which is refreshing.

His phone chimes, and he reads the text. "That's my mom. She wants to know if you're staying for dinner tonight."

I met his parents last week when he invited me over to hang out. His mom is nothing like mine. When we walked through the front door, she was baking cookies for a fundraiser for his little sister's school. When I was in elementary school, I was always the one who showed up with store-bought sweets. My mother wouldn't even bother to take them out of the plastic containers to try to make them look like they were homemade.

Maybe that's the difference between a working mom and a stay-at-home mom.

"What's she making?"

"Lasagna."

After another click on the keyboard, I tell him, "I'm in."

"Can we go now?"

"Yes," I sigh, stretching out the word.

I save my files and email them to Annie before disconnecting my camera and packing it into its case. School got out around an hour ago, so the halls are empty as we make our way through the building. When we push through the double doors that lead to the parking lot, a few guys from the lacrosse team are lingering around. They must have just finished with practice.

I keep my head down as one of them calls out, "Looking hot, Cricket," right before something pelts my shoulder. I look down at the pacifier that lands on the ground next to my feet while they all laugh at me.

I cringe. Sometimes I wish I were invisible.

"You're an asshole," Noah shouts, which only makes them laugh louder.

"Just ignore them," I mutter.

As we make our way to our cars, he asks, "Why do they call you Cricket, anyway?"

"Don't ask."

"I just did, so spill it."

"In eighth grade science, our teacher had these lizards and we had to take turns cleaning their cage and feeding them these nasty crickets." We stop when we get to our cars, and I slip my bag from my shoulder to fish for my keys. "I didn't want to draw attention to myself so I never told my teacher that I was deathly afraid of insects."

"What happened?"

"I was able to keep my cool while scooping them out with a cup from the tank they were kept in. But, before I could transfer them to the lizards, I tripped over a book that was on the ground and the crickets went flying. They literally got tangled in my hair, and I freaked."

Noah starts laughing.

"Like, screaming and flailing around like a maniac. By lunchtime, the whole school had heard about it, and that's when they started calling me Cricket." I find my keys and click the fob to unlock the doors.

"I would've paid good money to have seen that."

I slap his arm. "You're so mean. Seriously, it was traumatizing."

"They're just crickets," he says with a shrug, as if they were harmless cotton balls.

"Yeah, nasty, brown crickets that have more legs than I do."

We get into our cars, and I follow him to the record shop so he can buy the album he won't stop talking about. After we arrive, he finds it quickly, but we linger, flipping through the records.

"I love this album," I say, holding up the vinyl from an old nineties grunge band.

""Garden" is my favorite song from that one."

I slip it back and continue exploring. It's been a long time since

I've hung out with a friend like this. These past few years have been really lonely, and I'm enjoying the distraction that Noah is able to offer me.

"Check out that one up there," he says, pointing to a bootleg that's displayed on a shelf. "I wonder what tracks are on it."

Reaching up, my fingers barely graze the bottom, and I have to stretch farther, lifting onto the balls of my feet. Finally, I'm able to pluck it from the shelf, but when I turn to hand it to Noah, there's a look of shock written on his face. As I'm holding out the vinyl for him I notice the sleeve of my sweatshirt has ridden up, exposing my horrid scar that I'm always so careful about hiding.

I shove my sleeve down, gripping the hem between my palm and fingers as a current of heat spirals around me.

The moment he opens his mouth, I'm quick to shut him down. "I have to go."

Shoving the album against his chest, I bolt.

"Low," he calls after me, but I'm already pushing through the door.

When I'm in my car and throwing it into reverse, I look up to see him staring at me through the large windows of the store, con-fusion clear in his expression. I step on the gas and pull out of the lot, leaving him to wonder about the freak I am.

Turning right instead of left, I head to the beach. Embarrassment floods me, causing my breathing to grow uneven as I speed away. But beneath that lies the sadness, and before I know it, my eyes are puddled with tears. When they spill over, I wipe my face with my sleeve, all the while panicking.

What if Noah tells someone at school and then everyone finds out about it, that it wasn't because I was pregnant that I missed last semester but because I was locked away like the mutant I am.

By the time I park, the mist has thickened, and I reach into the backseat to grab my raincoat. Stepping out of the car with my note-book in hand, I flip the hood over my head and walk down to the sand. A strong wind kicks off the water, sending a light sea spray my way as I sit on a big piece of driftwood, close my eyes, and allow the salty water droplets to collect on my face. After a moment, I pull the pencil out from the wired spiral of my notebook and open it to the last page I was writing on.

It's a rambling poem I scribbled down a few nights ago after my father left for London. My bones were heavier than normal that day, and I'd given up on feigning strength.

I cried silently while words poured out and onto the page. Words that expose my truth, a truth that's so enigmatic that it's entirely unexplainable. So, I wrote, not in sentences, but rather, in fragments that don't connect in a way that would make sense to others.

But they make sense to me.

With my pencil in hand, I mindlessly start scribbling at the bottom of the page. Lines link with curves that blend into shapes, and soon, the image of an eyeball appears. A single teardrop slips from the inner corner as it peers up at me, but it's a hollow connection. I look into the empty pupil, but I have it all wrong.

It's me who's empty.

Slipping the pencil back into the spiral, I close the notebook on my lap and slowly pull up my left sleeve. With my wrist upturned, I stare down at my failed attempt at freedom. I run my thumb along the dark pink line of scar tissue.

My brother was the one who found me that day. It was summertime and he was home from college. Tyler was supposed to be out with one of his old friends from high school while Mom was at work, but he came back early because he thought it would be nice to take me out to lunch and spend some time together before he flew back to North Carolina.

If he hadn't come home, I would've been free.

I was unconscious when he discovered me on my bathroom floor. The doctor said I hit my radial artery. They gave me a blood transfusion and kept me in the ICU for two days before moving me to a floor room until my wound was stable.

I thought I'd be able to go home, but that didn't happen. They put an EOD on me, an emergency order of detention, and I was forced into a private facility. It was horrible. I begged my parents to let me go home, but they refused. I could tell that my dad was conflicted, but my mother was adamant that I stay.

Things only got worse while I was there. It was a brutal downward spiral, and I just wanted to die. I wound up staying for almost three months before they released me.

When I got home, it didn't really feel like home anymore.

Since the semester was already halfway through, my mom thought it would be best to continue the homeschool program I had been doing at the mental health facility.

My thumb continues to drag along the four-inch scar, and I wonder about what the kids at school would say if they ever found out. With the way I ran out of that record store, I'm positive Noah has come to the correct conclusion about how that scar got on my wrist, and I can only hope he keeps that knowledge to himself.

I'd rather be teased than pitied. I get enough of that from my family. It only reminds me that I'm messed up, that I can't be trusted, that I'm incapable of knowing what's best for myself.

If only they knew the truth.

But they don't.

Because they can't.

They don't know what it feels like to be a prisoner to this suffering. Despite taking my meds every day, there's still an incessant ache I can't escape. I've tried and failed to get better, yet, here I remain—trapped.

Some days are better than others.

I have my ups and downs, but the ups are still downs, just not as far.

Tugging my sleeve, I cover my botched effort before wrapping my arms around my body as the chill kicks up a notch. Thank goodness the dank climate here lets me get away with wearing oversized sweaters and long-sleeved shirts almost all year.

Another gust of wind blows off the water, forcing me to find warmth in my car. After tossing my raincoat into the back, I start the car, but before I shift into drive, my phone chimes with an incoming text.

Noah: Is everything okay?

I want to ignore him, but then I fear that, if I don't say anything, he might go fishing for answers elsewhere. Not that he has any other friends at school aside from me. As much as I want to hide and pretend this away, I go ahead and respond, doing my best to squash this.

Me: Everything's fine. Sorry I overreacted. See you tomorrow.

Chapter Four

HARLOW

"You still haven't texted me the hotel information," my mom nags as she stands in the doorway to my bedroom. "Can you just stop for a second and do that before you forget again?"

"Ugh, fine." I drop my toiletry case into my bag and grab my phone off the bed so I can text her the information.

"And remind me again who you're going with."

"Mom," I groan, drawing out her name, "I've told you like a million times already. Her name is Annie. She's the newspaper editor."

"What's her cell number?"

I stop mid-zip of my bag and turn to face her. "No way, Mom."

"What's the big deal?"

"You're hovering again."

"What if I can't get ahold of you?"

"Then you'll know I'm busy and I'll call you back when I have time, but I'm not giving you her number. That's just embarrassing."

Welcome back, overbearing mom.

Ever since I told her I had to go out of town to shoot the lacrosse state championship, she's been up my butt. I didn't bother mentioning this trip when it was assigned to me because our team has never been good enough to make it to state. So, when they qualified, I had no choice.

Truth be told, I don't even want to go, knowing I'll be riding on the bus and staying at the same hotel as the team. When I tried bailing, Annie got annoyed, so I made her promise to tag along. Luckily, she agreed. It isn't as if people at school are blind to the fact that several of the guys on the lacrosse team are jerks to me.

"Okay, fine," she concedes. "But I expect you to check in."

"You're doing it again." I walk over to my desk and grab my phone charger. "I'm not about to fall off the edge of a cliff. I'm fine."

"I can't help it. I'm your mother; I worry."

A honk sounds from the street below, and when I peer out of my window, I see Annie parked along the curb.

"That's her. I have to go."

Slinging the bag over my shoulder, I head out, but she stops me to give me a hug. I tense in her arms, but she doesn't care. She acts this way to make *herself* feel better, not to make me feel better.

"Okay, Mom." I sigh when I pull away.

Another honk has me hurrying down the stairs and out the door. Annie pops her trunk, and I toss my bag in before slipping into the passenger seat.

"Thanks again for coming with me."

"It actually turned into a lifesaver," she says as she drives to the school.

"Why?"

"I kind of went behind my parents' backs and accepted a scholarship from UCLA when they thought I would be staying in state. They found out last night."

"What did they say?"

"They flipped. I couldn't get out of the house fast enough this morning."

Annie's a senior and lucky to be graduating in a couple of months while I'm stuck here for another year.

"It isn't *that* far. I mean, it could be worse."

"That's what I said."

We arrive at the school to find the guys standing in the parking lot next to the charter bus, so we toss our bags into the luggage bay and settle into one of the front seats. My earbuds are already in when the team boards, so if there are any comments coming my way, they're muffled behind the music blasting in my ears.

When the bus pulls out, Annie opens her physics book and studies during the two-hour drive down to Olympia. The trip is uneventful, which I'm not upset about, and I go unnoticed as we file into the hotel. Coach passes out the keys, and then Annie and I head up to our room. We only have a handful of hours before we have to be back on the bus for the four o'clock semifinals, so we decide to order lunch and watch an old movie. I'm soon distracted when I receive a text from Noah.

Noah: You want to catch a movie when you get back?

Since the record shop last week, I've been ditching lunch to hide out in the library. I'm nervous he's going to want to talk about what he saw, so I've been avoiding him. But I like Noah; he's a cool guy, and I like having him as a friend. Unless I want to lose that, I know eventually I'm going to have to face him. At least at a movie, we won't be talking.

Me: Sure. I'll be home on Sunday around lunchtime.

For the first time ever, our high school takes the state championships. I want to bail on the celebratory dinner, but Annie makes me go. Fortunately, the boys are too amped up to even sense my presence. It's only when we return to the hotel that someone finally notices me.

"Low."

Across the lobby, I find Emily turning from Brent and walking my way.

"What are you doing here?" she asks.

I hold up my camera. "I had to take pictures for the school paper."

I'm surprised that she's even talking to me. From over her shoulder, I see Kassi with her tongue halfway down Sebastian's throat, and I cringe.

Emily turns and follows my line of vision. She shakes her head and shrugs before saying, "A few of us are heading up to the rooftop pool. You should come."

"Fun," Annie says, appearing out of nowhere.

I don't share her enthusiasm, which is clear in my expression, so Emily adds, "It'll just be us girls."

"I don't know . . ."

"Oh, come on, it's not like we have anything else to do," Annie encourages.

"I didn't bring a bathing suit."

"So, dip your feet in," she says, and when I look at Emily, she's nodding in agreement.

I'd rather hide out in the room, but I reluctantly give in. "Okay, sure."

As Annie and I head up to our room, she keeps oh-my-goshing about hanging out with the girls I try to avoid. Emily and that whole crowd are super popular, something Annie is clearly impressed by even though she's a senior.

"How do you know Emily?" she asks as she changes in the bathroom.

"We used to be friends in middle school."

Sitting on the edge of the bed, I wait nervously as I contemplate different excuses to get out of having to go hang out with my old friends. But when Annie emerges with a huge smile on her face, I bail on any potential escape plan and head up to the pool with her.

Anxiety piles as we take the elevator to the roof. It's all I can do not to think about how badly this evening could go.

What if this is some mean girl's setup?

It's the age-old story of the cool kids pretending to like the loser in order to humiliate them. Like in *Carrie*. That poor girl seriously thought that she was elected prom queen. For a moment, she felt as if she were finally being accepted by the popular kids, only to end up on stage covered in pig's blood.

Okay, maybe they won't throw blood on me, but they could do a lot of other things that would be equally mortifying.

The elevator doors open, and we make our way down the long corridor that leads out to the pool where the girls are already in the water. It's clear by Kassi's ick face that she wasn't in on Emily's idea to invite me.

"You made it!" Emily exclaims. She looks genuinely happy to see me, but in the back of my mind, I'm still questioning the intent behind this invite.

Annie tosses her towel over a chair and quickly slips into the heated pool that's expelling a cloud of steam into the chilly night. Tugging off my shoes and socks, I push my pants up and over my knees before sitting on the edge of the pool and sinking my feet into the water. Somehow, the warmth soothes my insecurities as I lazily swirl my legs around.

"I ran into your mom the other day at her flower shop," Emily tells me.

"Yeah, she mentioned that."

"Are you going to spring formal this year?"

I have to stifle my laugh. "No."

She swims closer to me and farther from the other girls, who are yapping about their boyfriends.

"Remember when we were younger and we couldn't wait to be in high school so that we could go to all the dances?"

When I nod, she adds, "And that one time when we snuck into my mom's closet and stole her high heels—"

"Yes!" The memory brings a smile to my face. "We were dancing in your room when she busted us. She was so mad because they were her designer shoes."

Emily laughs. "It wasn't our fault we had good taste in fashion." Our smiles slowly fade, kind of like our friendship did. "We used to have so much fun together."

It only takes a second to remember all of the good times with her, but the commiseration ends when her boyfriend busts through the door with an obnoxious, "State champions!"

He runs and cannonballs into the pool, splashing all of us. I jump to my feet and back away as Brent kisses Emily before grabbing her hips and tossing her into the air. She squeals until she hits the water and goes under, only to pop up and slap his arm. "I didn't want to get my hair wet."

All the guys head for the water except for Sebastian, who flops down on one of the lounge chairs and takes a swig from his water bottle. I sit on another chair that's a decent distance away. Kassi steps out of the pool, wraps a towel around her hips, and settles herself next to him.

"What the fuck are you staring at?" he sneers, and I quickly dart my eyes elsewhere. "Who invited Cricket?"

"Don't be a dick," Emily defends from the water, and Brent reacts with a mocking laugh, teasing, "What, are you two girlfriends now?"

She slaps his arm again.

I look to Annie, who's chatting with one of the other girls, and wonder how much longer she's going to stay because I'm ready to leave.

"You smell like alcohol," Kassi whispers loud enough for me to hear.

Glancing over from the corner of my eye, I watch Sebastian grow irritated with her. "Are you my babysitter?"

"No, I'm your girlfriend."

He tugs her arm to bring her down to him, and when he tries to kiss her, she pushes against his chest. "Stop," she warns under her breath. "You're wasted."

Her attempt to keep their spat on the low backfires because he just gets louder. "Why do you always have to be a buzzkill? It's annoying."

"Lay off the guy," Brent calls out. "He's just celebrating our win."

"You want to take this celebration to my room?"

Kassi huffs and turns away from him. In the pool, the other guys are being extremely loud, roughhousing and disturbing the peaceful night with their bellowing cheers, still reveling in their win. My attention turns back to Kassi just as she takes a sip from Sebastian's water bottle and then immediately spits it out.

"Are you kidding me?" she screeches, wiping spittle from her chin. "Why didn't you tell me this was vodka?"

He laughs, but everything falls silent when one of the hotel's staff walks out with Coach Lipscomb.

"Coach!" Brent exclaims, shooting his arms in the air. "Let's celebrate!"

"We need to shut it down, boys. A couple of guests have complained about the noise."

Everyone groans.

"Come on," Coach tells them, "everyone out of the pool."

"You've got to be kidding me," Sebastian complains. "We're just having a little fun."

He stands and stumbles a bit before catching his balance. Coach walks over to him and grabs the clear plastic bottle from his hand. Unscrewing the lid, he takes a whiff and then shakes his head in disappointment.

"It isn't a big deal," Sebastian says.

Coach, however, disagrees. He looks pissed as he shoves a finger against Sebastian's chest and grits out a soft but angry, "You made me a promise."

"I know . . . I'm sorry."

"You're coming with me."

"Come on," Sebastian groans.

"Shut it down," he announces, pointing at the guys. "I want all your asses in your rooms for the night!"

He then grabs Sebastian's elbow and pushes him toward the door, tossing the vodka into the trash can on the way.

Chapter Five

"**D**ID YOU HEAR ABOUT THE PARTY AT JUSTIN'S THIS next weekend?" Brent asks from the desk next to me. "Yeah, I'll be there. Are you going?"

"Emily has been complaining about how I don't take her out anymore, so I promised her dinner and a movie that night, but if I can get away, I'll stop by."

"Yeah, Kassi's been giving me crap too," I tell him. "Honestly, I'm getting tired of her constant nagging. She used to be cool, but lately, she's been on me about everything."

Brent shakes his head and sighs. "Girls, man."

"Quiet," Mrs. Powell warns from the front of the room. "Have you boys finished reading the chapter?"

Looking down at my United States History book, which is still open to the first page of chapter twelve, I respond, "Almost, Mrs. Powell."

"No talking until you've answered the review questions."

A few people turn my way, including Low.

"You should tap that," Brent jokes from beneath his breath.

"Who? Low?"

He chuckles quietly and nods.

"You're fucked. That girl hates me."

"That girl hates everyone."

I've known Low since the fifth grade when my family moved here from Shoreline. She used to be part of our circle of friends. That was when she was fun and talkative, not the quiet recluse she is now. Brent would never admit to this, but he used to have a crush on her in middle school. One Halloween, we were all at her house for a party her parents threw. His goal was to kiss her, but when he finally got her alone in the backyard, she totally rejected him, which was a sucker punch to his ego.

The memory humors me. "You two really would've made a cute couple. Does it still burn?"

His eyes narrow. "Does what still burn?"

"Knowing that she'll never kiss you the way you wish she would."

His fist barrels into my bicep. "Fuck off."

Rubbing my hand over where he hit me, I laugh, only to be scolded once again.

"If I have to get on to you boys one more time, you'll be spending lunch in detention."

"Mrs. Powell," the office calls over the intercom.

"Yes?"

"Could you please send Sebastian West up to the office with his belongings?"

My gut sinks, wondering if this has anything to do with the alcohol coach caught me with this weekend. I toss my textbook into my bag and tell Brent that I'll catch him later. As I walk through the empty halls, I pass Coach Lipscomb's English class, but he doesn't see me. Saturday night wasn't the first time he caught me drinking. Earlier this year, I came home from a party completely wasted. My mother's boyfriend, Kurt, was at the house, and we wound up getting into a fight. He knocked me around, took my car keys, and threw me out.

It was freezing as hell that night, and I was trashed and had nowhere to go. My eye was swelling shut, so I couldn't crash at any of my friends'. They'd only ask me questions I wouldn't be able to answer, so I called Coach.

He let me stay in one of his spare bedrooms, and the following morning while I was nursing a killer hangover, I made him promise that he wouldn't tell anyone about my situation at home if I promised to stay away from the bottle.

It was a bluff on my end.

When I walk into the main office, the principal's secretary approaches. "You can go on in to Mrs. Wilcox's office," she tells me.

When I enter, she stands from behind her desk and motions to the chairs.

As I take a seat, I silently pray that, whatever this is about, it won't affect my standing with the lacrosse team next year.

"Well," she begins after she situates herself at her desk, "I've been trying to get ahold of your mother this morning so she could join us for this meeting, but I haven't been able to reach her."

"She's probably still sleeping," I respond, which is most likely the truth, but I cover for her shortcomings when I explain, "She's been sick the past couple of days."

"Oh, well, I'm sorry to hear that, nonetheless, I still need to speak with her."

"Why? What's going on?"

She gives me an eyeing look as if she wants me to tell *her* what is going on, but I play dumb and stay quiet. I'm not stupid enough to rat myself out if this so happens to be about anything other than this past weekend.

"The reason I called you in was to talk to you about an incident that happened this past weekend."

Shit.

Mrs. Wilcox goes on to explain, "I was informed that you were caught with alcohol at the hotel after the state championship." She folds her hands on top of her desk. "Is that true?"

The intensity in which she says this is laughable, as if I committed an armed robbery or something. I consider lying for a split second, but I'm not going to throw Coach under the bus and go against him. My standing with the team, even though the season is over, means too much to me, so I'll own up to it in hopes she'll respect my honesty and go easy on me. "It's true," I admit with a slight nod.

"Where did you manage to get alcohol?" she asks.

I shrug my shoulders, and this time, I go with a lie. "A friend."

Her lips purse for a moment, unsatisfied with my vague answer. "Who else was drinking?"

Brent was, but I keep that to myself. "Just me."

She leans back in her seat and there is a silent understanding between us, that we both know I've royally messed up here. The longer the silence spans, the more nervous I become. I wait for her to cut the tension and speak, but she keeps me waiting, and I eventually cave, pleading, "Am I in trouble here or can we please just let this be a lesson learned? I mean, if this goes on my record, no scout is going to recruit me."

"Well, I spoke with Coach Lipscomb. He sees a lot of potential in you, and since this is the first issue we've had, he and I have decided to make an exception."

"What kind of exception?" I ask.

"You'll be suspended for five days, but I won't put this on your record."

"Five days?"

"Five days," she reaffirms. "But it's important that I get in touch with your mother."

"I'll let her know that she needs to call you."

"I would appreciate that."

Relieved that she is cutting me a little slack by keeping this off of my record, I give her a sincere, "Thanks," but I'm not thankful to be suspended.

I'm sure most kids would love to get out of school for a week, but home is pretty much the last place I want to be. Coming here every day is a vacation in my eyes. Hell, it's one of the few places I feel safe these days.

"Let this be a warning," Mrs. Wilcox adds. "Next time, there won't be any leniency, understood?"

"Understood."

"I hope you'll learn from this. I would hate for you to jeopardize any college opportunities because of this foolish behavior."

"It won't happen again," I tell her even though I doubt that it won't. Next time I will just have to be more careful about not getting caught.

When the meeting concludes, I head out and drive home. I'm

already sick to my stomach before I pull into the driveway. Knowing what's waiting inside that house has me hating my life. There's nothing I can do to avoid it, so when I step out of my car, I erect all my defensive walls because I refuse to expose my weaknesses.

I walk inside and find Kurt sitting on the couch, drinking a beer. It's only ten in the morning, but he's a loser, so it's to be expected.

"What are you doing home?"

I ignore him and head into the kitchen to grab a soda from the fridge.

"I asked you a question."

"Where's my mom?"

"I asked you a question, boy!" he barks as he stands from the couch.

My patience is shot today and it's taking a lot of self-control to keep myself in check, but I'm boiling beneath the surface. His attention diverts away from me when my mother comes out of her bedroom.

"What's going on?" Her voice is groggy as she drags her feet into the kitchen and secures the tie around her robe. "Why aren't you at school?"

"The principal has been trying to call you this morning." I tell her as I pop the tab on my soda and take a drink.

"Why? What did you do?"

Her accusation annoys me. The fact that her immediate assumption is that I did something wrong hurts even though it's the truth.

"I got suspended for the week."

"Why?"

"Alcohol."

I take another swallow of my soda as Kurt shakes his head as if he's disappointed. But to be disappointed in a person, you have to actually care. All Kurt cares about is the free ride he's getting, mooching off my mother and sucking the money and life out of her.

"I've tried telling you that he has a drinking problem, Miranda."

"I know," she agrees as she walks over to pour herself a cup of coffee as if she can't even be bothered by the fact that I got in trouble.

"Look in the mirror," I mumble beneath my breath.

"What did you just say?" Kurt's tone comes out hard and loud.

Righting my spine, I set the can down and strengthen my voice. "I said, look in the mirror."

He stalks over to me, and I want to cower, but I refuse. Instead, I brace myself for the inevitable. In the background, I catch my mother scurrying away back to her bedroom.

"You think you're a tough guy, huh?"

"You said it, not me."

My demeanor only serves to piss him off more. He steps up to me and gets in my face, seething, "You're nothing but a shit stain." His breath reeks of beer and cigarettes. "Nobody cares about you, not even your mom. She doesn't give a rat's ass, which is why she's enjoying her morning cup of coffee in her room instead of dealing with you. If she cared at all, she'd be in here, but all you do is remind her of your father and the crap life she had with him."

Heat erupts beneath my skin, and when my hand clenches, I throw my fist toward him, but the asshole dodges and sucker-punches me in the gut. Hunching over, I heave against the spasm of pain that's rippling through me. It takes a second before I'm able to suck in a decent breath and straighten. When I do, Kurt's gone, leaving me with so much hate boiling inside.

I reach for my keys, but Kurt must've swiped them because they're no longer on the counter. With too many pent-up emotions, I lose control and punch the marble countertop so hard I hear bones crack.

"Fuck!" I scream through gritted teeth as fire pierces my knuckles, scorching them in a current of agony.

I drop to the floor and lean against the cabinets, cradling my hand against my chest as I take controlled breaths that sound more like hisses as I attempt to alleviate the throbbing ache. My face burns as I fight not to break. I can take a lot in life, but the mere mention of my father cuts deep, but what cuts even deeper is the fact that my mother allows Kurt to degrade him—her dead husband.

Although this woman remains, it's as if, somewhere along the way, my mother died too.

When my dad was alive, my mom and I had the best life. It was nothing like the one we have now, which is utter chaos. We weren't perfect, but we were happy.

I never wanted much because my father worked hard to make sure I had everything. I remember elaborate holiday parties and spending our summers traveling the world. As soon as I turned fifteen, I had a brand-new Audi waiting for me in the driveway.

"What's this?" I ask when he opens the front door and I see the black sports car sitting in the circular drive.

He claps his hand on my shoulder. "You're going to need something to practice in, right?"

That was my father.

He was a surgeon who had been working several twelve-hour shifts in a row at the hospital. One night, on his way home, he fell asleep at the wheel. His car was found wrapped around a tree the next day. He was dead. That was two years ago, and our lives have never been the same since.

At one point, I begged my mom to sell this house because it was too hard being surrounded by all of the memories of him. She refused. While I fought the heartache, she gave into it.

It isn't her fault my father died, but it is her fault she allowed the devastation to take over her life, rendering her needy and weak.

It started with alcohol. She began drinking heavily, which only made her lonelier, so she turned to men. She doesn't go after clean, hard-working guys like my father though. It's as if she's drawn to losers who see her as a golden ticket, but they give her the attention she's desperate for so she doesn't care that they're bottom-feeders.

She quit her job when the life insurance settlement came in. The interest off that money is more than enough to live off of.

For a while, it was just the two of us, but now there's Kurt who shares in her dependency. I thought life couldn't get any worse after my dad died, but this past year has proven me wrong. She's thrown me aside because the only things that matter to her are Kurt and alcohol. She's completely spiraled out of control, leaving me to fend for myself.

The last place I want to be is stuck in this hell, but I'm at a total loss with how to help her because she refuses to listen to me or admit that she has an alcohol problem.

So, yeah, I drink to numb myself, but she knows this. She just doesn't care.

I have one more year until I'm out of here. My only hope is for her to clean herself up before I leave, but those hopes are disintegrating with each passing day.

Chapter Six

HARLOW

M Y ALARM WENT OFF A FEW MINUTES AGO, BUT I WAS already awake with the same blue devils that have been tormenting me for the past few days. They were gone for a while, but they're back.

To get out of going to school this week, I told my mother I was coming down with something. I don't think she believed me, but she didn't call me out on it.

She's smart not to.

She's gone from hardly caring to checking in on me too often, calling too often, and texting too often. It's overbearing, but I keep my mouth shut because it would only cause her to call and text even more.

It isn't as if she would understand even if I did tell her the truth. Plus, she'd panic and smother me when it's the last thing I need. When I think about what has triggered this mood shift in me, it sounds so trivial. Who gets upset about the school year ending?

I do.

School keeps me busy and provides a purpose for my days. It's something I can focus on and distract myself with. It lessens the consumption of everything else in my world that chips away at me. But knowing it's coming to its end, I feel empty and listless.

See? It sounds stupid, doesn't it?

I don't expect anyone to understand how lost . . . how hollow I feel. But it isn't just school. It's any change. I don't like it, and with summer about to begin, I should be happy and excited, but I don't feel things like I should—like a normal person would.

There's a light tap on my door, and I groan. "I'm still sick, Mom."

When the door opens and Noah steps in, I shoot up in bed. "What are you doing here?"

"Dragging your butt to school."

"How did you get in?"

"I pulled up when your mom was leaving for work," he says, walking over to me as a hint of a smile grows on his lips. "She seemed excited when I introduced myself, and now I'm wondering if you've been talking to her about me."

I sling my pillow at him, but he catches it and chuckles. "Are you crushing on me, Harlow?"

"In your dreams. Seriously, what did you tell her?"

"That I'm your friend and that I'm here to take you to school. She seemed happy enough with that alone, and she let me in."

"Is she still here?"

"Nope." He sits on the edge of the bed and gives me *the look*. The same look my mother gives when she's trying to see past my walls to the truth, because to the ones who know that I tried to end my life, there's always a degree of skepticism. "You aren't sick, are you?"

I cock my head and narrow my eyes.

"What?" His voice pitches in defense. "I'm just saying. You don't look that sick."

I shake my head and then tense when he covers my hand with his. Oh, God. I can see it in his eyes; he's about to say something sentimental and serious. On the inside, I'm already cringing.

"You know you can always talk to me, right?"

I roll my eyes, and when I toss the sheets aside, he pulls his hand back.

"I'm serious, Low. You haven't been at school for days, and you've been ignoring all of my texts."

"So?"

"So, I've been worried."

The word I hate. Just what I need, another person in my life who's worried about me. I try to shrug it off, but it sticks like glue.

It was a month ago when Noah saw the scar on my wrist. Noah's a smart guy, and with my reluctance to address it, he knew exactly what had happened without my having to spell it out for him.

Yeah, I'm the nutcase who tried killing myself. How do you even begin to explain that situation to someone you've just met?

You can't.

But now there's this weird, unspoken thing between us.

"Well, you have no reason to worry."

"So, you're coming to school then?"

I rock my head back, dreading having to go.

"Come on," he nags. "It's the last day. There is no way I'm going alone."

It isn't just the idea of going that has me in a silent panic. It's everything leading up to it. It's having to move, to get dressed, to brush my hair, to fake a mood, to simply exist. These may be simple things for him, but to me, they're painfully difficult. The very thought of leaving this room is agonizing. It's a paperweight in the pit of my stomach.

"Don't let me down," he adds, pressing the issue. "I need you there."

Looking at him from over my shoulder, I release a defeated sigh. "Fine."

I drag myself over to the closet, grab some clothes, and lock myself in my bathroom while Noah waits for me to get ready.

The sun is shining today, and I squint against its brightness as we walk onto the front porch. Everything illuminates under the rays of light making the plants appear greener. Funny how a little light can make things prettier—happier. So, why doesn't it have the same effect on me?

The day goes by in a synthetic blur of slow motion. In a sea of excitement and celebration for summer to begin, I stand on a sinking island. Surrounded by hundreds of people, I'm alone, wondering why I can't feel a particle of what they feel but wishing I could. I should be happy that I don't have to come back to this place for three months, that I won't have to face the ridicules and side-eyes. But, strangely, I'm not.

I'm sad, and that breeds confusion because I don't want to leave even though these people make me miserable.

I'm still trying to unravel the mess of emotions inside myself when Noah pushes his way through a hoard of kids with a huge smile on his face. "There you are," he shouts above the ruckus. "Come on, let's get out of here."

He takes my hand and navigates us to the parking lot. Once outside, he dramatically throws his hands toward the sky and rejoices, "Free at last!"

I should laugh at this point, but it's lost somewhere inside me. "You act like it's a torture chamber in there."

"Isn't it?"

There's an overwhelming urge for me to hug him and thank him for being my friend for these past two months. To tell him that he made my days a little more bearable and to release the tears I've been barricading. The desperation to cling to him in hopes that it'll pull me out of this gloom is irrational, so I keep my mouth shut.

"Let's go to Taqueria El Sabor and get wasted on nachos."

I want to go. More than anything, I want to believe that spending time with him and filling my belly with carbs will pull me out of this funk, but I know better. There's no faking my way out of this. "I wish I could, but my brother comes home tomorrow, and I need to help my mom around the house."

"Don't you have a cleaning lady?"

"She's sick and cancelled this week, so . . ." I shrug, but he still pushes.

"You're kidding? It's the last day of school; you can't just ditch me."

"I'm sorry. Another time?" I offer.

Disappointment presses down on his shoulders. "Yeah, sure."

He doesn't say anything else as he turns and walks to his car.

"Noah, don't be mad."

"I'm not. It's cool." His words are just as fake as my own. "I'll catch you later."

I toss my backpack into my car before sliding behind the wheel.

The anarchy inside the building has now funneled out into the parking lot. Shifting into reverse, I look into my rearview mirror to back out of my space and find Sebastian, Brent, and a handful of other students clumped together. Sebastian has a cast on his hand as he lifts a flask to his mouth and takes a sneaky sip.

That guy is such a douche. Not even a month ago, he got suspended for drinking, and now he's at it again—on school property.

I ease my foot onto the gas pedal and back out, but when I get a tad too close to their group, they get loud and flip me off before I drive away. After pulling to a stop at a red light, I grab my cell and text my brother.

Me: Can't wait to see you tomorrow!

Before the light turns green, he texts back.

Tyler: Same here. Hey, will you make sure Mom has those frozen bagel pizzas I like?
Me: No problem. Anything else you want?
Tyler: You know what I like.

When the light turns green, I toss the phone aside and head to my mother's flower shop so I can grab some cash to run to the store. I decide to bypass the perky girls she employs and pull behind the building to let myself in through the back entrance. I'm getting out of my car when another text comes through.

Tyler: Oh, and don't forget to get a case of Dr. Pepper!
Me: Gotcha!

When I look up from my phone, I spot my mother getting out of the passenger side of a familiar SUV.

"Jamie," a man calls.

I duck behind the dumpster and then peek my head out enough to see my mom walking back to the SUV, the same SUV from the gas station the other week. The driver's window is rolled down, revealing the same guy. But it's when she leans her head in and the two of them kiss—like *kiss*, kiss—that my heart drops, hitting every rib on the way down. Horrified, I freeze, and when he drives off, my mom turns to walk into the building.

She comes to an abrupt halt when she catches sight of me.

"Harlow," she says as naturally as she can, but her voice flits nervously. "Honey, what are you doing here?"

I open my mouth, but all I can think about is my dad.

"Is everything okay?"

Is she seriously pretending that she didn't just kiss a man who isn't her husband?

My hands have a death-grip around my phone, and the reality of what just happened has me choked up. I watch her neck flex as she takes a hard swallow, and wish I could turn and run so I didn't have to look at her any longer.

"Tyler texted me and wanted some things from the store," I tell her, my voice also trembling. "I came by to grab some money."

"Oh, well that's nice of you to go to the store, but I can do it if you need me to."

"No, it's fine. I'll go."

She's already digging in her purse when she walks over to me. "Here," she says, handing me several twenties. "Is that enough, dear?"

I shove the money into my pocket, and without another word, I bolt. My hasty departure should be enough to clue her in that I saw and that I know.

Chapter Seven

HARLOW

Anger festers but shock prevails. I literally can't believe that my mother kissed another man. How could she do this to my dad? To our family? I don't want my parents divorcing, I don't want any of this.

I put the last of the groceries away, thankful that, in less than twenty-four hours, my brother will be here. I've already called my dad, but he didn't answer. Since it's seven in the morning in Singapore, he's probably busy getting ready for work. I sent him a text, asking him to call me when he had some time. I need to talk to him, to let him know what Mom is doing.

After I finish in the kitchen, I head up to my bedroom and pull out my notebook from under my mattress. Tingles begin radiating through my left hand as they often do—permanent nerve damage from cutting too deep. I shake them out as best I can before I open to the page I'd started yesterday as I tried to work through my current low. But all the thoughts are trivial in comparison to how I actually feel.

Worthless, damaged, lonely, loser, outcast, hopeless . . .

The list goes on and on until I can barely see the white paper beneath all the black ink that's scribbled across it.

I flip to the next clean page and sketch out a broken heart with sand pouring out of it.

It's my heart.

Closing my eyes, I think back to the day I got brave with the blade. A part of me wondered what I would see when I dug it into my vein: blood or sand.

It should've been sand.

As minutes collect and form hours, my shock begins to evaporate, allowing the anger to rise to the surface. My hand aches, and when I push up my sleeve, I take the pen and trace it along my scar. The black ballpoint rolls over the pink line, and in an indefinable way, it soothes. I drag it back and forth, back and forth, inking my wrist until my eyes fall shut and the pen slips through my finger. Peacefulness washes over me, and I keep my eyes closed for fear that it will vanish if I open them.

So, I don't.

Sitting in the center of my bed, I relish in the darkness and absorb the quietness. My muscles slacken, and I send up a silent prayer for me to live in this forever.

"Harlow."

Another forsaken prayer.

"Harlow," my mom calls out again. "Can you come downstairs, please?"

My eyes open, dumping me back into the harsh hands of reality. The sound of her voice punctures straight through me like a rusty nail.

I drag myself off the bed and down the stairs where my mom is sitting in the living room.

"Why don't you sit down?"

"I'd rather stand," I respond defensively.

She isn't quick to speak as she fidgets in her spot on the couch. When she finally opens her mouth, she hesitates before noting, "You seem upset."

"You think?"

"I feel it's important that we talk about this."

"Talk about what? Your new boyfriend?"

"Harlow," she cautions, but it only fans the flames of my irritation.

"I mean . . . that's what he is, right? That's why you kissed him?"

"It's a little more complicated than that."

I shake my head. "You're unbelievable. How could you do this to Dad?"

"I know this is confusing for you—"

"No, it isn't confusing at all," I tell her. "You're cheating on Dad. All I want to know is why?"

"Marriage isn't easy, and things . . . well, things have been strained between your father and I, and—"

"And what? You're bailing on us?"

"No," she says quickly. "I would never bail on you. And you need to know that I love you."

"What about Dad?" I ask as my throat tightens. "Do you love him?"

"Of course I do. I'll always love him, but sometimes in life, love shifts." She leans forward and folds her hands together. "Your father and I have been dealing with a lot lately."

"You mean me?"

"No." She stands and approaches me. "This has nothing to do with you, and I need you to believe me when I tell you that." She reaches out to touch my arm, but I shrug it away. "This is between your father and me."

"I called him."

Her eyes widen. "You what?"

"I called him to tell him what you did."

"You told him?"

"He didn't answer."

She releases a breath of relief. "I need you to let me tell him."

"You should've already told him," I snap.

"I know, but I have to find the right time. I still care deeply for him, and the last thing I want to do is hurt him. But it's best that it comes from me, not you. The two of us need to be able to sit down and talk face to face."

Emotions build, making it difficult to speak without breaking apart, but I force the words out anyway, asking, "Are you leaving Dad?"

She shrugs. "That isn't something I can really answer right now."

"I can't believe you." She reaches out once more, and I snap. "Don't touch me! Don't try to kiss my ass to save your own!"

"Watch your tone."

"Are you serious?" I stride angrily across the room before turning back. "How can you say you love me when you're throwing this family away for another guy?"

"I'm not throwing this family away."

"I hate you!" My words come hard and fast. "All you care about is yourself!"

"That is not true."

"This isn't fair," I mumble before strengthening my tone. "It isn't fair that I'm stuck here with *you*."

Her shoulders drop, and I can't stand to look at her anymore, so I stomp up the stairs, grab my phone and keys, and head back down.

"Where are you going?"

"Just leave me alone!" I yell before slamming the door behind me and heading straight to my car.

The moment I drive away is the same moment my tears fall. With my heart pounding out of rhythm, I drive through the night with nowhere to go. But nowhere is better than being at home— with her.

Truth is, all I want right now is my dad, but he's halfway around the world and won't be back for another three weeks. I would go to Noah's house, but the last thing I want to do is talk to him about how I caught my mother cheating on my father. In the end, I decide to go to my favorite spot at Marina Beach.

The moon glows behind a veil of clouds, painting everything in a silvery hue. I sit in my usual spot and stare out into the rippling water. Gravity presses down, and the weight of it pains me. It's in my heart, in my lungs, and in my bones. I ache all over, and when I think about our family being divided, I fold over my knees and cry. It was hard enough when Tyler moved out; I don't want to imagine losing my dad too. Because that's what will happen. I'll be stuck with my mom, the last person in this family I would choose to live with, and there won't be anything I can do about it.

My phone rings, and when I lift my head and blink back the

tears, I see it's my dad calling. With a sniff and a hard swallow, I answer, doing my best not to sound as if I've been crying.

"Hi, Dad."

"Hey, sweetheart. I'm between meetings so I don't have much time, but I wanted to call you back quickly. Is everything okay?"

Nothing is okay. Nothing at all, but my mother's words echo in my head, and as much as I hate to admit it, maybe she's right. Maybe my telling him will only serve to hurt him more. Perhaps I should let my mom be the one to do it, let her impale that dagger into his heart and not me.

"Are you there?"

"Yeah, I'm sorry. I just really miss you," I tell him.

"I miss you too. It isn't easy being away from you and Mom so much," he says, and I grit my teeth when he mentions her. "Are the two of you getting along?"

"Yeah, everything's fine."

"Wasn't today your last day of school?"

"Uh-huh."

"Are you excited to finally be a senior?"

I force a smile, unsure of why or for who. "Yes. I'm so over high school."

He laughs, and I hang on to the sound as hard as I can. "One day, when you're old like me, you'll look back and miss these years."

"Doubtful."

"You say that now, but you'll see." He pauses. "You'll never believe what I ate for dinner last night."

"What?"

"Reza, one of the higher-ups here invited me to his home for dinner with his family . . . I had no clue what I was getting myself in to."

"What do you mean?"

"One of the dishes came out, and I couldn't tell what the hell it was. It was white and kind of looked like a brain. I didn't want to be impolite, so I took a bite. The texture was all wrong. When Reza saw the look on my face, I asked what the dish was."

"What was it?"

"Shirako."

"What's that?"

"Are you ready for this?" he asks and then tells me, "It's fish sperm."

"Ugh, are you serious? People actually eat that?"

Through his chuckles, he says, "You'd be surprised by the things people around the world eat."

"No way. That's flat-out nasty."

"You aren't the one who had to be polite and eat it!"

"You mean you continued to eat it after you knew what it was?"

"I didn't want to be rude," he defends, and I laugh—like, a real laugh, and it feels good.

"I can't believe you ate fish sperm."

"Remind me never to complain about your mother's cooking again."

And just like that, the laughter is gone.

"I really miss you," I tell him once more.

"I'll be back as soon as I can. Promise."

"But then you'll just turn around and leave again."

He sighs in the background. "I know my being gone so much isn't easy on you. It isn't easy on me either."

"I know. I just wish I had more time with you."

"Same here, but your brother will be there tomorrow. I know you're excited to have him back home."

"I am, but it isn't the same as having you home."

"Three weeks," he reminds me, and I repeat, "Three weeks."

"I have to go now, okay?"

"Okay. I love you."

"Not as much as I love you, sweetheart."

Somehow, he manages to balm the wound my mother inflicted. Not entirely, but it's enough to ease some of my anger. I know I should probably head back, but I'm not ready to go just yet. So, I remain and soak in as much solitude as I can, knowing that it'll be short-lived once I leave.

When I return home and walk inside, all the lights are off. I don't dare call out for my mom—no need to stir the beast. Still, I peek down the hall that leads to her bedroom as I pass it and see the stream of light from under her door, telling me she's awake. I tiptoe up the stairs and into my room, keeping as quiet as I can.

After I throw on my pajamas, I lift the corner of mattress to grab my notebook.

It isn't there.

I walk to the other end of the bed where I never leave it, but it isn't there either.

I stand and turn in place, looking at my desk, looking on the ground, and looking at my nightstand.

It's gone.

My pulse catapults, and before I know it, I'm ripping through my backpack, yanking out folders, papers, and books, but it's nowhere to be found. Heat scorches my neck, and fury locks my jaw. The nerve of my mom to sneak into my room and take the one thing that helps me cope.

She has no right!

If I thought I hated her before, I truly hate her now.

Chapter Eight

HARLOW

I BEGIN STIRRING AS SLEEP DISSOLVES, BRINGING ME CLOSER to consciousness, but it isn't until I feel someone touching me that I jolt awake and snap up. It takes a second for the fog to clear, and when it does, I jerk my arm out of my mother's hand. She sits on the edge of my bed with doleful eyes that are rimmed-red. Either she hasn't slept or she's been crying.

"What did you do to your wrist?" she questions softly.

I flip my hand over to see what she's talking about and remember tracing my scar with a pen.

"It's just ink, Mom."

Her eyes fall from mine and well with tears. When I shift to sit up more, her gaze comes back to mine and her hand brushes along my cheek as a tear falls down hers. She doesn't move to wipe it away, and as much as I hate her, a part of me feels bad. No one wants to see their parent cry.

"Why are you in my room?" I ask, and when I do, she finally wipes her hand across her face, erasing the sadness that just slipped down it.

"There are muffins downstairs. I thought you could throw on some clothes and we could talk."

"I don't feel like talking."

She gives an understanding nod. "Okay. No talking. But you've got to be hungry," she says while trying to gauge my reaction. When I show no interest, she adds, "They're banana nut; your favorite."

"Fine." I sigh, giving in. "But only because I'm hungry."

She pats my leg tenderly, and her smile reveals itself for only a split second before vanishing. "I'll wait for you downstairs."

When my door closes, I crawl out of bed and drag myself into my bathroom to scrub my wrist clean. I then trade the T-shirt I'm wearing for a long-sleeved sweatshirt to hide my scar from her nosy eyes. When I open my bedroom door, a trill of unease swims through me when I hear hushed voices. I pause for a moment to eavesdrop, but I can't make out what's being said. The mere fact that someone else is here has me returning to my room and putting on a bra.

When I head down and reach the last step, I see Dr. Amberg in the kitchen.

I freeze.

"There she is," my mom announces, but not in a joyful way. No. There's something else behind her tone that I can't lay my finger on, but it doesn't sit well with me.

"Good morning, Harlow."

I stare at my psychiatrist as he sets his muffin onto the plate. "What are you doing here?"

"Why don't you get a bite to eat, dear?" my mother suggests.

My doctor's face gives nothing away, but when I glance over at my mom, she hides nothing.

Fear snuffs out the suspicion, and my fight or flight instinct kicks in. My brain yells for my feet to move, yet I stay paralyzed as Dr. Amberg stands.

Finally, I'm able to take a cautious step back.

He holds up a hand meant to calm, but it only sparks more worry, forcing me another step away from him.

"Harlow." My mother's timid voice echoes through a tunnel.

"What's going on?"

"I think we should sit down."

I look between the two of them, and I know for certain that my mother didn't invite him over here for muffins.

"Just tell me what's going on," I demand, my voice wavering.

"Your mother called me with some concerns—"

My eyes fly to her, and she cowers. "You did what?"

She shrugs and shakes her head, muttering, "I-I didn't know what to do. I found your notebook—"

"You had no right!"

"After looking at what was in it, your mother did the right thing by calling me."

My eyes widen. "How could you? That's private!"

"Harlow, please."

"You have no right to invade my privacy like that, Mom!"

"I was worried when you stormed out last night." Her justification is weak, and she knows it. "I wasn't snooping to be mean, but I'm your mother. It's my job to protect you."

"Protect me from what? From getting my feelings out?" I glare at her. "That notebook is what protects me—not you!"

"I understand your anger, but your mom is only looking out for your wellbeing, and so am I," Dr. Amberg says, taking her side. "The two of us spoke last night, and she told me about what happened yesterday and what you saw. This situation would be difficult for anyone to handle, but—"

"This is bullshit!"

"Harlow," my mom scolds harshly.

"It is! You cheat on Dad, and suddenly, it's all about *me*? You're only spinning this to get the attention off you!"

"Look at her wrist," she blurts out while stalking over to me in quick strides. "Look at what she's done."

I stand in place, thankful that I scrubbed the ink away, and allow her to yank up my sleeve, exposing nothing.

"Why don't you give Harlow and me a moment?" he suggests, and she drops my arm before leaving the room. "Come on, take a seat."

"This is what I've been trying to tell you," I say as I walk over to the bar, but I don't sit. "She's always doing this. Taking the smallest things and blowing them up into something they aren't. That notebook was *your* idea."

"What you filled the pages with alarmed her."

"What I fill the pages with is no one's business but my own."

"I understand you feel as if your privacy has been violated, but she isn't the enemy," he tells me. "We're all on your side."

"Are *you* alarmed by the notebook?"

It takes a moment before he gives a subtle nod. "Getting our feelings out can be therapeutic, but some of these thoughts you are having need to be addressed." He shifts in his seat and then asks, "Can you tell me what she saw on your wrist that scared her?"

"I have no idea what she's talking about." If I tell him, it will only heighten his concern.

His brow lifts in skepticism. Before he can say anything else, a loud bump from upstairs catches my attention.

"What is she doing up there?" I ask, and Dr. Amberg immediately stands, but I'm already out of the kitchen and running up to my room. "What are you doing?"

She has a duffle bag on my bed, and it's already filled with my clothes as she looks at me in alarm.

It's in this moment I know exactly what's going on. Adrenaline combusts, and I turn on my heel, ready to run, only to find Dr. Amberg standing in my doorway. He grabs my arms, preventing me from escaping, and I begin to fight against his hold. "Let me go! You can't do this!"

On the other side of the room, my mother cries as I flail, trying to rip myself away from this ambush, but they have me. Dr. Amberg gets his arms around me, and I continue to cry out, repeating, "You can't do this!" over and over while my mother scurries around my room to pack the rest of my things.

"Harlow," my doctor says in a soothing tone that doesn't soothe at all. "I need you to come with me out to the van, but if you can't calm down, I'm going to have to bring in Marcus who's waiting outside."

Looking into his eyes, I beg, "Please, don't do this."

I hear the zipper to my bag closing, and I want to scream at my mother to stop.

"Can I trust you to walk with me, or do I need to call in Marcus?"

I remember Marcus. He's a nurse at the facility, and although he's nice and friendly, he's also intimidating. As much as I want to, there's no use putting up a fight. They have me outnumbered.

"I didn't do anything wrong."

"No one said you did," he assures. "But your mother thinks it's best if you come back for treatment."

From over my shoulder, I glare at her as she cries while keeping one hand on my bag, and when I turn back to my doctor, I ask, "For how long?"

"Well, that depends on you and your progress." His grip on me loosens, but he still keeps a strong arm around my shoulders. "Can I trust you to walk with me to the van?"

I want to scream and fight my way out of this house and run away, but I give in, nodding, even though it goes against everything that's screaming inside of me. As we head downstairs with my mother following behind us, I feel like a prisoner. I pretty much am. When the front door opens to reveal Marcus standing in front of the facility's van, I crack even more. Everyone who drives by will know that a mental case lives in this house.

Marcus slides the door open, takes my hand, and helps me in. Dr. Amberg sits next to me as Marcus gets the bag from my mother, who's sobbing on the front steps.

"I hate her," I mutter under my breath.

The door slams shut, Marcus hops into the driver's seat, and we drive away.

Happy first day of summer.

Pressing my forehead against the window, I close my eyes, but tears continue to seep out. No one talks. There's nothing to be said.

My mother, for no reason, is locking me back up in the loony bin I never thought I'd return to, and my not having any say over this situation is terrifying.

When we pull up to the private facility, my gut roils in anxiety for what's to happen next. It's a routine I'll never forget because it's so beyond humiliating. They lead me into the left wing of the building and into a private room where a couple of nurses I recognize from my last stay are waiting.

They smile and greet me warmly, but it does nothing to quell the myriad of emotions colliding inside me. When you live in a place like this, you get to know the staff well. I remember Nurse Leslie and Nurse Shanice. I also remember this exam room. It's just as cold as it was the first time I was here, and it comes as no surprise when the door closes and Shanice instructs, "Go ahead and remove your clothes."

Mortification scorches my modesty as I undress, bashfully trying to cover myself with my arms and hands as I do. When I slip my underwear down my trembling legs and am entirely naked, she examines me. In an attempt to distract myself, I watch Leslie search through my belongings for "contraband" as the chill of the tile floor bites into the soles of my bare feet.

"Sorry," Leslie says, holding up a random pencil my mother must've tossed in during her rush. "No personal items or sharp objects."

"It's only a pencil."

"There are crayons and markers in the rec room for you to write with."

Misery gathers in my throat, forming a painful lump that's nearly impossible to swallow against. Piece by piece, my dignity crumbles as I stand here—an unclothed captive.

"I need you to jump up and down a couple of times and cough, okay?" Shanice asks as if I have a choice.

I do what is asked before she does a mouth check. Once they conclude that I haven't snuck in drugs, razors, or anything else they deem to be harmful, I'm allowed to get dressed.

"Here," Shanice says, handing me a sealed urine cup. "Are you able to go?"

I nod as I hold back tears, take the cup, and walk into the bathroom.

After I hand over the filled cup, I'm taken to the lab where they draw several vials of blood. I feel distant as I sit here with a needle shoved up my arm. Somehow, I've gone numb. After the nurse secures a cotton ball down with a Band-Aid, Shanice escorts me through a series of locked doors that lead to the right wing of the building, which houses some of the patients. All the common areas are co-ed except for the rooms we sleep in. As I walk down the girls' hall, memories come flooding back—memories I wish I could forget but can't, and now I'm here to make more.

"Here we are," Shanice says when she steps into one of the rooms and sets the stack of clean sheets she'd been carrying onto the end of the bed. "Everyone is outside for morning exercise, so you'll meet your roommate later."

Staring down at the small twin bed that's bolted to the floor, my heart slips a few inches down.

Hopeless.

That's the only word to describe what I'm feeling.

How is this happening? How is this my life?

"I'll take those," she says after unlocking the closet.

I hand over the armful of clothes I'm holding and let her put them away. When she's done, she locks the door again.

"Would you like me to help you settle in?"

Through teary eyes, I shake my head. There's no settling in when you're locked up. We're given nothing but a laundry basket to toss our dirty clothes into. The rooms are bare and everyone is stripped of all personal items. We can't even have books in our rooms for the fear that we'll use the edge of the paper to cut ourselves with. The staff makes sure there's no contraband when they do their daily morning and evening room sweeps. All anyone can have is a few changes of clothes, which the staff keeps locked up along with our freedom.

Shanice tilts her head and encourages, "You're going to be okay, Harlow."

Her statement is a lie—untruths she probably says to everyone who walks through these caged halls.

She steps out into the hallway and takes up post against the wall. If I was allowed to close the door, I would. I don't even know why there are doors in the first place because no one is ever to be left alone—ever. All of us are monitored constantly, even when we go to the bathroom. I sit on the edge of the bed and, within the stillness, I go from numb to utterly desolate. The sensation washes over me, and I cling to it like a child would to a blanket. I gaze at my shoes, which have been stripped of their laces, and zone out. Everything around me fades away, and when I close my eyes, I wish myself to the driftwood on the beach. My eyes pinch tighter, and I swear I can almost hear the waves.

I try to lose myself more in my search for escape but the sterile smell of this place won't allow me. It only reminds me that I'm diseased, that I'm not like the others who are out enjoying the freedoms of summer. Instead, I'm here, sad, lonely, and filled with so much anger toward the woman who gave me life. I want to call my brother or my father, but cell phones aren't allowed and I doubt my mother has added names to my call list yet.

My eyes open, and I kick off my laceless shoes before lying on the bare mattress. Wallowing in what I'm powerless to change, I throw in the towel and surrender to the infestation of my own suffering.

Chapter Nine

"Renata wet the bed."

My tired lids open, and when I lift my head, the frailest girl I've ever seen is sitting on the bed that's against the opposite wall from mine.

"What?"

"The girl who was here before you," she says. "She peed in her sleep."

At the speed of lightning, I jump off the bed and look at the mattress, but I don't see any stains. I lift the edge to take a peek underneath, but it appears just as clean.

"They must have replaced it," she says as I drop the mattress and sit back down. "Did you touch my things?"

I shake my head as I try not to stare, but I can't help myself. This girl has an eating disorder, no question about it. I could easily wrap my hand—with overlapping fingers—around her bicep. Her collarbone protrudes, her cheeks are sunken, and her hair is brittle and limp. She's on the edge of death. It's painful to look at.

"Don't touch my things," she warns.

"I didn't."

She frowns as she picks up her pillow and hugs it.

"What's your name?"

"Harlow."

"Are you messy?" she asks, still hugging the pillow.

"Um . . . no."

"Good," she says before standing and setting the pillow on the bed, adjusting it a few times until it's at just the right position for her. "I like things neat."

My eyes drift down the edge of the wall where she has her shoes lined up meticulously next to each other.

Great. She's OCD.

"So, what's your name?"

As she moves around her space, touching everything, she responds, "Maxi."

What a travesty to be named after a feminine hygiene product.

"You can call me Max, though." She turns to face me and leans against the wall. "What're you in for?"

My last roommate didn't speak—like, ever. It annoyed me to no end, but, right now, I kind of miss her. Even in a place like this, a place where we're all messed up in one way or another, I still want people to see me as normal. It's never easy having to admit the truth—that I've been diagnosed with major depressive disorder.

"Well?" she pushes.

Knowing it's only a matter of time before she, along with everyone else, finds out during group therapy, I tell her, "Depression."

"What type? PDD, MDD, bipolar, seasonal affective—"

"MDD," I answer, cutting off her rambling, and her eyes bulge slightly as if she's in awe.

"How bad?"

Subconsciously, I tug my left sleeve down over my hand, gripping the fabric between my fingers and palm.

She notices the movement. "You tried killing yourself?"

Man, she's blunt.

Heat slithers up my neck, but I'm saved from having to answer when someone taps on the open door. "Harlow?" Marcus steps in. "Dr. Amberg is ready to see you for your intake assessment."

As I slip on my shoes, Max asks the nurse, "Did you talk to him about the Colace?"

"I already told you that he denied your request."

"But I'm constipated," she whines. "Tell him that I haven't pooped in four days and my stomach is killing me."

"Your stomach hurts because you need to eat."

"I have been."

"A few sips of Pediasure isn't enough."

When I stand to follow him out the door, she hollers in agitation, "I want my Colace!"

"There weren't any non-verbals you could've put me with?"

"Not this time, kid."

Marcus is one of the more decent nurses here. During my last stay, he would often sneak me candy bars when he'd come in for his shifts. Let's face it, the food here blows, so the treats were much appreciated and made me feel a little more human.

"Have a seat," he tells me when we enter the administrative wing. "I'll let him know you're here."

I take a seat, the same seat I used to take twice a week when I was last here. Ever since I was deemed sane enough to live beyond these walls, I have my sessions at Dr. Amberg's secondary office that's on the other side of town and closer to my house. If I had to come back here for my appointments, I'd go crazy.

Bad choice of words.

"Harlow, come on in," my doctor says from the open doorway to his office.

The room still smells the same as it did before. It's a mixture of cinnamon and leather, reminding me of the spiced pinecones all the stores sell during the holidays.

When I situate myself on the plush couch, he sits adjacent to me in his oversized chair with my file in his hand. "Have you had a chance to meet some of the residents?"

"I don't plan on staying long."

The stillness in his expression tells me he isn't amused. "So, your lab work came back. Everything looks good." He scribbles something in my file and then closes it on his lap before looking back to me. "How are you feeling?"

"Like this is entirely unfair. I did nothing, and now I'm locked up against my will."

"You make it sound like a prison sentence."

"Isn't it?"

He crosses his legs and leans back. "I see it as an opportunity for self-reflection and growth."

That is so easy for him to say since he isn't the one stuck here and being told that he's not normal enough to be free.

"Do you understand why you're here?"

I fold my arms defensively across my chest. "I understand that you and my mom are against me."

"No one is against you. I'm in your corner, Harlow."

If that were true, he would've seen straight through my mother.

"That's a load of crap. You took my mom's side without even hearing mine. I mean . . . it's so obvious what she's doing."

"And what's that?"

"I catch her cheating and in less than twenty-four hours, she sends me away. How can you not see through her?"

"I don't feel like these two situations are linked."

"Of course they are!" My voice pitches up a few octaves. "My mom only cares about herself."

"I understand that you're angry with her right now, so why don't we shift a bit?" he suggests. "Why don't we talk about the journal?"

"You mean the one *you* suggested I keep and then used it against me?" I bite.

"What concerns me most is what I saw in that book. It doesn't reflect what I'm seeing and hearing from you in our sessions. I realize now that there are things you haven't been telling me, and in order for me to help you, I need you to be honest at all times."

"Why should I bother? You lied to me! You told me that I could trust you!" I dig my nails into my arm, trying to scratch the itch beneath my skin. "I did everything you've asked of me, and for what? For you and my mother to twist it all around and lock me back up in this place! Why? Why would I bother talking to you about any of it now?"

"I still stand by you using the notebook to express yourself. But it would be negligent not to address what you've put in it. This is something we should talk about because, if those drawings and poems are a reflection of your thoughts, then it's important that we discuss it."

"I'm not talking to you about this because I don't trust you, and I don't need to be here," I fume as I push off the couch and stalk over to the window that overlooks the entrance to this black hole.

I continue to claw my skin, but the irritation crawls far beyond just my arms. It's my whole being that radiates with angry tingles, which drives my agitation even further.

"Have you even called my dad? Does he know I'm here?"

"Isn't he out of the country?"

I pace a few steps as I grow anxious to talk to my father. "She did this behind his back, I know it."

"Regardless, you're here now, and we should use this time to your advantage, don't you think?"

My left palm prickles in throbbing annoyance, and I shake it out, but it doesn't wane. I want to rip the skin off my bones. It's as if my veins have become electrical wires that are zapping against exposed nerve endings. I quicken my pace and start scratching again, but the irritation becomes too much, and I snap, "I want my dad! Let me call him!"

"I'm not sure that's a good idea right now."

"This is bullshit!"

"Why don't you sit and take a few deep breaths?"

"Why won't you let me call him?" I yell as my nails find their way to the back of my flaming neck. "Why are you taking my mother's side?"

"The only side I'm on here is yours."

Acid-soaked needles drive into my palm, and before I know it, I'm slamming it into a small table, sending a potted plant crashing to the floor. I stare down at the clay fractals that are scattered about the soil, and the ringing in my ears becomes too much. "None of you care about me!" I shout.

Dr. Amberg sets my file on the end table and stands. I rush over to him, and when I swipe the file, he yanks it right out of my hand.

"Give it to me!"

"I need you to back away," he warns, but it only fuels my anger.

"That's my file. I want to read the lies you've written about me."

He turns to walk to his desk, and when he does, I try for a second time to snatch the file out of his hand, but I fail. He turns on his heel and cautions, "If you threaten my space again, I'll have you removed from my office. Now, please, step back."

"My dad is the only one who cares about me! If he were here, none of this would be happening."

The moment he touches the phone, I reach across the desk and slam my hand over his, knocking the receiver out of his hold.

"Back away, Harlow."

"I haven't done anything wrong!" I snap, trying to grab the phone when he picks it up again, but he pulls away from me.

Fury churns, and I swing my hand against a cup of pens as he calls for assistance. I lose all control, yelling and clawing at the papers and files on his desk in a storm of rage I've never felt before.

"I want my dad!" I pound my nagging palm against the wood to kill the current that's radiating through it. "This isn't fair!"

"Code gray," Dr. Amberg bellows into the phone, and my full attention is caught on those two words, sending a rush of panic through me.

"No!"

He drops the receiver and holds up a hand. "Harlow, focus on me, okay?"

"I hate you!"

The door busts open, and when I see Marcus and two other nurses rushing my way, I freak. "Stay away!" I shoot my arms out in front of me, and when he launches toward me, I lunge to the right and try to bolt. He's too quick and too powerful, tackling me to the floor. "Get off me!" I cry, kicking and fighting to escape. "No! Stop!"

Heedless of my shrieking pleads, the three of them pin down my ankles and wrists long enough for Marcus to uncap the syringe.

"No, please! Don't!" I beg as I continue to jerk my body beneath their hold, but I'm powerless.

The waist of my pants is yanked down, and Marcus painfully squeezes my thigh in his hand. "Everything's going to be okay."

My eyes fill with terror when he shoves the needle into my hip, shooting the drugs into my body. Within a matter of seconds, my screams evaporate into silence as my muscles go limp. Everything fades into a distance, and the next thing I know, I'm being lifted. My head dangles lifelessly until everything loses meaning and my focus dissolves into negative space.

Chapter Ten

SUMMER BLOWS. IT'S BEEN SEVERAL WEEKS SINCE THE FINAL bell of the year rang and everyone erupted in cheers, including me. Too bad it was bullshit on my end. The thing is that those walls keep me safe from the dysfunction at home. Last summer wasn't as bad as this one since Kurt wasn't living with us. He's a total shit show and has managed to drag my mother even further away from who she was. Because of him, our wrecked lives have become more mangled. My mom is always too drunk to see it, but I know what is going on. I see it for everything it is, but if what I say to her poses a threat to her drinking or her scumbag boyfriend, she won't listen. She'll shut me out. The woman is terrified of losing the only two vices she has. I just wish she could see how those vices are destroying her—destroying us.

I'm drowning too. I don't want to be, but I am.

It feels hypocritical to blame her crutches when I have my own, but with each new bruise, with each blow to my happiness, I care less and less about that hypocrisy. Kurt has managed to rip me apart relentlessly. He's found my weak spot and preys upon it.

Sand sticks to my damp skin, and I take another swig of beer as I stare into the blazing fire. The music helps muffle the voices of everyone that showed up tonight, and it all combines to mute the crashing waves. I look around at my friends, who don't truly know a thing about me other than what I purposely choose to show them, most of which are lies anyway. A few buddies sit around the beach fire with me while Kassi is off dancing with her friends.

Someone tosses their beer into the flames, sending embers spraying out.

I'm gone at this point—drunk and slumped in my chair. This beer is child's play next to the whiskey I finished off a little while ago. The bottle dangles from my fingers, and when Kassi flops down next to my feet, the jolt causes it to slip out of my weak grip and spill into the sand. I don't care because the beer had already turned warm.

I stare lazily into her eyes, which boast nothing but her disappointment in me. I should break up with her, but with so much lacking in my life, it's hard to walk away from the one person who loves me, so I stay when I know I shouldn't because I don't share her feelings.

I'm not sure I even know what love is.

What she cares for is only an illusion. She thinks she knows me, but she doesn't. I lie to her, more so than all the others, to protect my reputation. For our whole relationship, I've been feeding her fabrications. Hell, the girl doesn't even know where I live because the last thing I need is for her to pop by and see the disgrace. To her and everyone else, I have the perfect life. In reality, it's in shambles.

It's so much easier to live in people's false perceptions, so that's what I do.

Kassi runs her hand up my calf and gives a soft squeeze as she smiles. She wants my attention, but I can't do more than stare down at her with a sloppy grin that causes her expression to drop.

"How much have you had to drink?"

I shrug.

"You promised," she whispers so no one around us hears.

"Sorry." Even though I did promise her earlier that I wouldn't get drunk tonight, here I am, completely hammered. Reaching down, I tug her to sit in my lap, saying, "Come here," but she pulls back.

"Just stop."

She stands and walks away, and when I get out of the chair to follow her, my head spins, causing me to stumble and fall, nearly landing in the fire.

"Shit, man."

I lift my head from the sand to see Brent standing above me laughing. He offers me his hand and helps me to my feet.

"What did you say to Kassi?"

Looking over his shoulder, I see she's crying and talking to Emily.

I sigh and head over. "Kass, don't cry." I pull her into my arms, but she keeps hers folded across her chest.

When Emily walks back to Brent, Kassi shrugs me off.

"Babe, don't make this a big deal."

"Why do you always do this? I have every right to be pissed," she snaps. "And it *is* a big deal."

"Everyone here is drinking." My defense is weak.

"They're drinking, but they are not wasted. Look at you! You can hardly stand."

"Then chill and let me go sit back down."

Her eyes narrow. She's fuming mad.

"Baby, I'm kidding." I try to soothe her anger with a lopsided grin. "Come on. Don't ruin a good night."

"I didn't ruin anything. You did. You always do." She turns toward the water and takes a few steps away, pauses, and then turns around. "Do you even love me?"

"Didn't I show you earlier today how much I love you?"

Her mouth falls open in disbelief. "Are you kidding me right now?"

"Can we talk about this tomorrow when I can think straight?"

"You always do this," she complains. "You always want to talk later, but it never happens and nothing ever gets solved."

In the corner of my vision, the moon swirls lazily in the sky, throwing my equilibrium off and causing me to sway before I regain my steadiness.

"Are you even hearing me?"

I return my attention to her. "Okay, then. Tell me what you want to solve."

"This," she stresses. "The constant drinking. I feel like all you ever want to do is drink, have sex, and hang out with *your boys.*"

"I'm not hanging out with my boys right now, am I?"

"I want more. I want you to stop pushing me away every time I ask you to open up to me. I want to see where you live and meet your mom. I want to go out on dates, and—"

"And what?" I question, growing annoyed. "You just want me

to be the opposite of who I am? Has it ever occurred to you that I like my privacy?"

"Why do you need that from me? I'm your girlfriend!"

Her voice pitches higher, gaining the attention of my buddies, and even though a part of me doesn't want to push her away, an even bigger part of me doesn't want to look like a chump in front of everyone.

"Maybe the problem is *you*," I throw back. "The fact that you're too needy."

Her jaw tightens, but I'm over the ridicule. She used to turn a blind eye to my shit, but that hasn't been the case lately. Since summer began, she's been riding my ass more and more.

"Why are you so uptight? You used to be chill."

"Because nothing is changing," she exclaims.

"You mean me?"

She gives a bitchy curt nod that stabs through the insecurities I keep buried down. "If I'm such a piece of shit, then walk," I spit harshly. "No one is forcing you to be with me, so if you want to go, be gone."

"You're such a jerk!" she shouts, throwing her hands against my chest before walking away at the same time Brent starts in my direction.

"Dude, what the fuck?"

"Not now," I exhaust under my breath as I head back to the fire, clipping his shoulder with mine.

I flip the lid to one of the coolers and grab another beer as one of the guys says, "Girls. They're nothing but drama."

"No joke." I pop the tab and chug the whole can before crushing it in my hand and tossing it into the sand. Turning to Brent, I say, "I'm out, man."

"Are you sure you should be driving?"

"Yeah, Mom. I'm sure." I snicker, shaking my head as I start to make my way up the beach toward my car.

Slipping into the driver's seat, I fumble as I try to land my finger on the push button, missing a few times before I'm able to hit it and start the car. In the rearview mirror, I see Emily hugging Kassi, and I hesitate, but a second later, I shift the car into drive and speed away, squealing my tires as I do.

Streetlights paint the night sky, and somehow, my bleary eyes and numb arms get me from one stoplight to the next. Piece by piece, my worthless heart breaks into shards that stab me from the inside out, ripping a giant hole inside this wound I can't rid myself of no matter how much alcohol I consume. A tear slips out, and I brashly wipe it away. I'm sick and tired of living with these emotions no one should ever feel.

But I do.

I feel them all.

When the light turns green, I slam down on the pedal and speed away to nowhere because I have no one. Burning tears stab my strength in the back, which only pisses me off more. Lights blur into watercolors, bleeding out of focus as I fly. It's a desperation to escape, but knowing I have nowhere to escape to has my heart pounding in anguish.

Red lights streak in front of me, a car honks, and tires squeal, but when I turn my head, I'm blinded by my own misery. I veer down another road as I contemplate going back to the party to find Kassi, to finally be honest, to reveal the ugly truth that is my pitiful life. I shut the idea down just as fast as it comes.

"Fuck!"

The steering wheel nearly snaps under the intensity of my grip, and I scream out in frustration. It's only when a spiraling of red and blue from my rearview mirror catches my attention that I ease off the gas.

The cop flashes his brights, and I wonder how long he's been trailing me.

This is bad.

I'm seventeen, drunk out of my mind, and driving like a maniac. But I can't run when there's no place to run to, so I slow the car and brace myself for whatever is going to happen next.

Chapter Eleven

"I don't want to be fat," Max says as tears stream down her face. "I'd rather die."

"But if you continue to allow this disease to take charge, you will die," Dr. Benson, the psychiatrist who leads our morning group therapy, tells her.

"I'd rather die thin than live as a lard-ass whale."

From across the circle, I stare at my neurotic roommate and feel sorry for her. It was just last week when Dr. Amberg put his foot down and admitted her to the hospital because of her refusal to eat. She returned two days later with a feeding tube running up her nose. Every day when the nurses come in to inject whatever it is they have in the large plastic syringe, Max flips out. It's a storm of screaming, crying, and tears, and each time, the staff wins.

"And what about you, Harlow?" Dr. Benson asks, drawing everyone's attention away from Max. "How are you feeling today?"

Without any inflection in tone or change in facial expression, I respond, "Fabulous," but he isn't pleased with my attitude—the one I've had ever since I woke from being sedated after blowing up in Dr. Amberg's office.

It's been a month since I got here and, because of my refusal to participate, I'm no closer to leaving. I don't even bother calling home. My mother has made several attempts to visit me, but I refuse each and every one of them.

I've seen my brother twice so far, but the last time, he sided with my mom's decision to have me here. The visit didn't end well. I wound up coming unglued and screaming at him until Marcus and another nurse intervened.

My body runs on resentment's fumes, and I barely recognize the cold and bitter girl I've become in here.

"Would you like to share anything with the group today?"

"Nope."

He crosses one leg over the other in frustration. I don't blame him; I have yet to speak in these daily group therapy sessions, which is a total contrast to my last stint in this place. But things were different then. I understood why I was here. This time . . . this time, it's completely unwarranted and nothing more than a punishment for my mother's mistakes, not my own.

"This is bullshit," Kevin complains. "We all come to group and talk. We do what we're supposed to do. We don't want to do it, but we do it."

I glare at Kevin who thinks he's so cool. He's sixteen with an opioid addiction that, according to him, makes him above the rest of us.

"That's the problem," I tell him. "I've been here before. I've sat in this very room and did everything I was supposed to do. And when I was released and went back home, I *still* did everything I was told, but they used it against me, twisted it around, and now I'm back again." A few eyes widen. "I'm starting to wonder if this place is nothing more than a money scheme."

Dr. Benson uncrosses his legs and leans forward. "I can assure all of you that there's no money scheming going on here."

"Of course you would say that." Max's suspicion is written all over her face. "It's not like you would admit the truth."

Everyone begins chattering as paranoia spreads through the group, pulling the attention away from me as Dr. Benson tries to calm everyone down. A menagerie of voices fills the room, so much so that it sounds like nonsense, which it is. I don't actually believe what I just accused this place of, but at least, for now, Dr. Benson isn't focusing on me as he attempts to regain control of the group. So, I sit back and stifle the grin that's tugging on my lips.

"Harlow," Marcus announces when he steps into the room. "You have a visitor."

"I don't want to see anyone."

"It's your father."

Sitting up in my chair, a wave of excitement comes over me. "Come on. Let's go."

A smile stretches across my face as I stand and rush out. Anticipation sizzles through my entire body as Marcus walks me out of the unit and over to the visitation room. I've yet to talk to my dad or see him since I got here. But now that he's back from his trip, I can get out of this place and go home.

"I don't think I've ever seen you this excited," Marcus notes with a grin, and it takes effort to stifle the eager bounce in my step.

"I finally get to leave," I tell him as we approach the room.

He stops in front of the door and looks at me. "It won't be a private visit today."

"Why not?"

"Because of the outburst you had with your brother, Dr. Amberg wants your visits monitored."

I roll my eyes, but who really cares because I'm getting out of here. "Whatever."

The moment he opens the door, my dad stands, and I can't run into his arms fast enough.

"Sweetheart." He breathes the word the instant I'm safe within his hold.

Nestling my head against his chest, I feel like I just might burst with relief. "I'm so glad you're here."

Taking my face in his hands, he angles me up to him. "I've missed you, baby girl."

"I've missed you too."

"Come sit with me."

We settle on the couch, and he takes my hand in his. My smile feels obnoxiously big.

"How are you doing?"

"Better now that you're here and I can finally go home."

There's a subtle shift in his grip, and a slight cinch appears between his brows.

"Harlow—"

"You came to get me, right?"

His eyes drop away from mine, instantly snuffing all the joy I just held.

"Dad?"

Lifting his head, he says gently, "Why don't we talk?"

"Talk about what? This is a mistake," I tell him as bubbles of anxiety start popping inside me. "I don't need to be here."

"Your mother thinks otherwise."

I pull my hand out of his. "She's lying."

"I saw the notebook."

"It's just a notebook." My voice pitches, and Marcus takes a step away from the wall he'd been leaning against. Calming my tone, I explain, "Dr. Amberg suggested I keep it as a tool to get my thoughts out. That's all. Mom is just overreacting."

There's a slight shake of his head when he gives an uncertain, "I don't know." He takes my hand again. "Seeing everything that was in it scared me."

"Dad—"

"Look, I'm not home enough. I don't get to see you as often as your mother, so I have to rely on what she says. And if she says that she's concerned for your wellbeing, then I have to listen."

"I'm fine," I stress.

"Your doctor feels differently. He told me about your erratic behavior and that they had to sedate you. That doesn't sound like a girl who is fine."

"No, you have it all wrong," I tell him as panic blooms.

"He says you've been shut down for weeks and refuse to cooperate in the daily therapy sessions."

"Dad, listen to me," I beg. "It isn't how he's making it seem." There's so much to say that it all gets swept up into a tornado in my head as I try to explain to him that this is a huge mistake. Quickly, I tether my thoughts and blurt, "Mom lied."

"What do you mean?"

"She's lying."

He tilts his head, perplexed.

"Didn't she talk to you?"

"Talk to me about what?"

She said she was going to be honest with him about the affair when he got back, but my gut is telling me that she hasn't done that.

"What is she supposed to talk to me about?"

I want to tell him, but I hesitate. There's confusion in his eyes, and suddenly, this all becomes too real, and I don't know if I can hurt him like that. None of this is my doing—it's hers—but if I tell him, then it's me stabbing the sword of truth into him when it should be her.

"Sweetheart?"

I can't hurt him.

"Nothing. Never mind." I drop my head for a moment and gather my thoughts before returning to him. "Dad, I really need you to trust me when I tell you that I don't belong here. I promise, you have nothing to worry about. I'm fine."

His hand cups my cheek when he says painfully, "I want to believe you."

"Dad, please."

With furrowed brows, he presses his lips together, and I watch as he fights back his emotions, which only deflates my hopes of going home.

"Dad, I swear to you."

He shakes his head, and his lack of trust stirs my frustration. "I love you." His eyes begin to water. "I love you so much, but . . ."

"Please."

"I almost lost you once, I can't . . . I can't risk it again."

"You're not."

"Just use this time, okay? Use it the best you can."

I yank my hands out of his. "Why are you doing this? Why don't you believe me? I thought you loved me."

"I do love you."

"Then why aren't you on my side?"

"Your side is the only side I'm on."

But it isn't. He's taking Mom's word for it, having no clue that she's been lying to him for I don't even know how long while I'm left here to suffer in this place. Anger eclipses frustration, flaming my skin and sending a current of heated tingles through my bones. I get up from the couch and pace a few steps, but distance does nothing for the burn of outrage boiling inside me.

"Harlow—"

"Why are you doing this?" I lash out. "It isn't fair!"

He stands, but the glare of outrage in my eyes keeps him in place.

"You can't leave me here!"

He glances across the room, and when I look over my shoulder, Marcus takes a cautious step closer. "Harlow," he warns in a tone meant to calm.

I turn back to my dad and plead, "Don't leave me here. I swear to you that I'm fine."

"I'm sorry, sweetheart."

Fisting my hand to dull the unrelenting needling, I lose it. "This isn't fair!"

In the slip of a second, Marcus has my wrists locked in his hands and pulled behind my back.

"Let go!"

His grip tightens, and I thrash to try to break his restraint, but he's too strong. "I need you to calm down."

But I won't. I ignore him as I yell, begging my dad, "I want to go home! Please, don't leave me here!"

Tears slip down his face as Marcus drags me out of the room, but I don't stop kicking and screaming.

"Don't leave me here, Dad! Don't do this! Please."

"I love you," is all I hear before the door slams shut.

"Dad!" I cry out before Marcus shoves my chest against the wall.

"If you don't calm down, I'll call for backup."

"No, don't!"

"I need you to breathe for me, okay? Just breathe."

"I want to go home," I cry.

"I know you do, and I want that for you too, but you need to calm down," he says. "Don't make me sedate you."

Fury pops into a thousand pieces of devastation that rain down over me, and as Marcus continues to do whatever he can to spare me from another sedation, I give up.

In his hold, I go limp against the wall and begin sobbing.

"You're going to be okay."

"Do you need assistance?" a nurse asks from down the hall.

"No, everything's fine. She's calming down." Then Marcus leans in, cautioning me quietly, "You have to pull it together, Harlow."

I give him a compliant nod, knowing all too well how some of the other staff members are quick to shove their needles into our hips.

He holds my wrists for a minute longer before slackening his grip. "Can I trust you to stay calm if I let you go?"

"Yes."

Once his hands are off me, I turn and press my back against the wall while staring at him in defeat. His expression is soft, but it doesn't matter if he's sympathetic. It isn't as if his feeling bad for me is going to get me out of here.

I'm stuck until my parents or the doctor says otherwise.

"Are you okay?"

"What do you think?" I scoff at his stupid question. Of course, I'm not okay.

"I'm just trying to help."

Dropping my head, I rub my wrists, muttering, "I know."

"Do you need to go to the breathing room?"

"No."

"Well then, I'll walk you back. It's almost lunchtime."

"I'm not hungry," I tell him as I retreat into the comfort of desolation.

"You know the rules."

I keep focused on the floor, repeating once again, "I'm not hungry."

I watch his feet as he steps over to me, and when he places his hand on my back, he tosses a favor my way when he asks, "You won't cause any trouble if I take you in the rec room, will you?"

I shake my head.

"Okay then."

He leads me back over to the right wing, the metal double doors automatically locking behind us when we enter the patient unit. We pass the cafeteria where everyone is eating lunch, and when we arrive at the rec room, I split away from Marcus, leaving him at the threshold.

"No trouble," he warns.

I take a seat in a chair in front of the wall-mounted television and curl into myself. Resting my head on my knees, I turn to look out the window and away from Marcus, who's babysitting me from across the room. The television drones in the background as I hone in on the faint pitter-patter of the rain hitting the window. Beads of water collect, and when the weight becomes too much, they give way, sliding down in haphazard rivers. I lose myself in watching them fall, wondering if the pane of glass is shatterproof, wondering if I'm brave enough to find out.

"And this is the recreational room," Nurse Leslie says to someone from across the space, but I don't turn to see who she's talking to. "When you aren't in group or participating in other activities, this is where you'll be."

Great, a new freak.

"Harlow?" she calls out. "Why aren't you at lunch?"

Not wanting to move, I respond bleakly. "Bad visit with my dad."

"We have a new patient I'd like to introduce you to."

"Spare me."

"Maybe you could show him around?" She sounds closer than she was before, but I still don't turn to look at her.

"Isn't that your job?"

"Harlow," she lightly scolds.

"Just leave me alone."

"At least say hi."

Another drop slips down the rain-speckled pane before I lift my head and turn around with a dull, "Hi."

The moment I see who's standing next to Nurse Leslie, my eyes widen in shock.

"Hey, Cricket."

Chapter Twelve

HARLOW

EVEN AT THE HOPEWELL RECOVERY CENTER, THE CAFETERIA dynamics are similar to what you would find at any high school. The room is on a smaller scale, yet everyone still cliques up at their tables. Maybe it's habitual, and no matter who or where you are, you seek out your comfort zone. For weeks, I've sat at the same table, in the same chair, alongside the same people—Max and Wes.

I scoop up a bite-sized piece of chicken with my spoon and stare at it for a moment before putting it into my mouth. The meat here comes pre-cut since the freaks of the world can't be trusted with plastic forks or knives.

As I chew, I watch as Max stares off, anxiously rocking back and forth.

She's terrified.

The poor thing can't bring herself to take a bite, much less look at the food. Even though she refuses to eat, she's still required to sit here, in what must feel like a torture chamber, and make an effort.

I've never seen her actually eat anything, but I wish she would because the fear and sadness in her cries when they restrain her and attach the plastic syringe to her feeding tube are heartbreaking.

"I doubt this has very many calories," I tell her when I scoop up another piece of chicken. "It doesn't even have the skin on it."

Her reluctant eyes meet mine.

"Maybe just a tiny bite tonight?"

Her restless fingers itch the side of her neck as she continues to rock.

"You're going to have to get the calories in one way or another, you know that," I tell her. "Wouldn't it be better if you just took a bite yourself instead having to deal with the nurses pinning you down?"

"They put oil on it."

"It doesn't taste like it."

"They did," she says. "I can see it."

It's hard to see her like this, tense and afraid. "The oil will help you poop, and I know how exciting that is for you."

"I doubt that's even true."

"Eat a piece and find out," I dare with a smile as I take a bite of my dinner roll, and she cringes in disgust.

"Come on, Max," Wes encourages.

He arrived a week after I got here, and the two of them became instant buddies. He's quirky, with long blue hair and a diagnosis of factitious disorder. He claims to have a different ailment every day.

"There's the new guy," Wes whispers, and when I look up, Sebastian is grabbing his dinner tray. "He's so hot."

"Gross," I mutter under my breath.

Wes turns to me and drops his jaw.

"What?"

"He's the best-looking dude in here, and you know it."

I roll my eyes.

"Max," he says, "look at him. Don't you think he's cute?"

On the sly, she checks him out as he walks over to an empty table in the corner and takes a seat. She blushes.

"See, even Max thinks he's hot."

"Seriously?"

"What?" she defends. "He's cute."

"He's an ass."

"Wait, you've talked to him?" Wes questions. "I thought he was in intake with Amberg all afternoon."

"He was." I set my spoon down and sit back, having lost my appetite. "He goes to my high school."

They stare at me in surprise.

"Do you know why he's here?"

"Aside from having a severe case of assholery, no." I take my tray and get up from my seat, needing some space.

"You didn't eat much," Marcus notes when I throw out the other half of my dinner.

"Not hungry. Can I go to rec?"

He nods his approval. "Nurse Shanice is already down there."

Without a glance back, I duck out of the cafeteria and head to the rec room. As if my day couldn't get any worse, I'm now living with a person I despise. If this were any other situation, I would just bail, but I can't, and neither can he. We're stuck here together. It's beyond humiliating. No doubt he'll tell everyone back home about me being locked away in a loony bin while he spins *his* reason for being here. They will buy it because they look up to him as if he's some god or something.

"Already done with dinner?" Shanice asks when I walk in.

"Yeah." I grab a deck of cards and situate myself at one of the tables before shuffling and starting a game of solitaire.

The room is silent apart from the soft background noise coming from the lame cooking show Shanice is watching while she waits for everyone else to arrive.

Flipping three, I play the four of spades, but I can't distract myself from Sebastian. There's no way I'm going to be able to avoid him in a place like this.

I can't believe this is happening, as if this day didn't suck enough with my father refusing to take me home. I swear the world is plotting against me in the cruelest of ways.

"Olympics!" Wes announces enthusiastically when he enters the room ahead of the crowd from the cafeteria. "Shanice, change the channel."

The summer Olympics recently started, and every night after dinner, they all huddle around the television to watch. It's the highlight of their day, seeing athletes live out their hopes and dreams. Too bad it only serves to remind me that I have none of my own.

Wes squeezes my shoulder as he passes, asking, "You joining us tonight?" He doesn't stop to wait for my response though.

"Can I play?" Max asks when she takes a seat next to me.

"It's solitaire. Not really a two-player game."

"Oh, okay. So, how did the visit with your dad go?"

"Peachy." The bitterness of pessimism stains the back of my tongue, and I flip three more cards. "He doesn't believe me."

"About your mom?"

"About me being okay to go home."

"I'm sorry. But he knows about what she did, right?"

"I didn't tell him, and I don't think she did either."

"Why didn't you say anything?"

I look at her, and when I do, Sebastian strolls in. He stands awkwardly with his hands shoved into his pockets as he glances around the room, which is filled with noisy chaos. When Max turns to see what has caught my attention, I shift my focus to her. She blushes again and coyly places her hand over her nose in an attempt to hide the feeding tube.

"I'm serious," I say, drawing her back to me. "He's not a nice guy."

Timidly, she shrugs and asks again, "Why didn't you tell him about your mom?"

"I guess I got scared. I don't know . . . I couldn't hurt him like that."

"But he left you here."

"I know." The game comes to a stall, and I can't make any more moves. "He totally took her side."

"Parents suck."

Gathering the cards to shuffle, I nod. "Tell me about it."

"Max," Marcus says as he and two other nurses walk toward our table.

She turns in her chair, shaking in fear, but before I can say anything to her, she's already crying. Lurching out of the seat, she scrambles to make a run for it with nowhere to go. Max only makes it halfway across the room before they get ahold of her and drag her out while she begs them to let her go. It's a nightly disturbance we've become immune to—well, everyone except Sebastian, who looks on in shock.

I won't see her again until it's lights out, so I decide to deal another game.

I don't even realize that Sebastian is now standing next to my table until he says, "What's up with that girl?"

Why is he talking to me?

"Go bother someone else." I flip three and score an ace.

"Who am I supposed to talk to?" he questions, and I peer up to see him scanning the room as if he's surrounded by wild animals.

"Why not your roommate?"

"That guy?" He nods to Jeremy, who's currently talking to the floor. "What the hell is he even doing?"

"He sees rats . . . big ones."

He cocks a brow. "You can't be serious."

"He's schizophrenic."

"What?"

"Relax, he's harmless."

He pulls out a chair and takes a seat, but I wish he wouldn't. It's beyond mortifying for him to see me in this place. If only a force of nature could scoop me up and drop me somewhere else—anywhere other than here.

"What are you doing?" I ask, irritation heavy on my words.

"What does it look like? You're the only normal person in this place for me to talk to."

I roll my eyes. "You sure about that?"

He reaches over, swipes the Jack of diamonds off the top of the stack and places it on the queen of spades before smiling at me like the prick he is.

"You having a fun summer?"

"Seriously, dude," I snap. "What's your problem?"

"Just trying to make small talk. You don't have to be a bitch."

"Hey!" Nurse Shanice scolds loudly, snapping her fingers at him from across the room.

Raising his hands in defense, he stands and walks away from my table to busy himself over by the shelves filled with puzzles.

No one else bothers me for the rest of the evening, and when we're dismissed to our rooms, there's a collective groan from the Olympics watchers.

"You can catch the recaps in the morning," Shanice tells them as she leads the girls into our private hall while Marcus takes the boys to theirs.

When I walk into my room, I find Max sitting on her bed, weeping against the pillow she's hugging tightly to her chest.

"Are you okay?"

She doesn't acknowledge me, and I don't push. It has to be hell to be injected with the thing you fear most. I'm actually surprised she holds herself together as well as she does.

I kick off my shoes before placing them against the wall in the order in which she approves. After sharing a room with Max for the past month, I've gotten used to her OCD and have learned that it isn't worth it to dismiss her rules. The chick may be the size of a toothpick, but her temper is downright crazy.

Once Shanice unlocks my closet and hands me my pajamas, I change, slip into bed, and wait for the nightly head count before the lights are shut off.

As I stare at the ceiling, I think about what everyone beyond these walls is doing. Sebastian mentioned summer, but I've yet to see a minute of it. Noah and I had talked about spending some of our days in Seattle, catching a concert, and possibly taking a day to hike at Rainier. Not that I like to hike, but he seemed excited about it, so I agreed to go.

I wonder how many times he's tried calling or if he's shown up at my house. I wouldn't put it past my mother to have actually told him where I am. My eyes close at the embarrassment of it all.

She wants to fix me so badly, but all she's doing is breaking me more. I finally made a friend, but no doubt, once I return, he'll view me as the plague—just like they all do. God only knows what the lies will be this time.

No, this time will be different because it won't be lies. There won't be any need for them because they'll have Sebastian telling them the truth.

I'm not even sure it matters since I'm never getting out of here. There's no way I'm opening up in group with him sitting there, which means I'm stuck.

The beam from a flashlight spears into the room and shines in my eyes. Squinting, I look over to the door to see Rosie. Night staff is the worst, and she's the worst of the worst.

"Check," she says as if I need to be reminded of the fifteen-minute safety checks, and then she moves along to the next room.

"You should tell your father," Max says quietly.

I lift onto my elbows. "What?"

"He should know what your mom is doing behind his back."

I drop back down. "I doubt he'd believe me. No one ever does."

Chapter Thirteen

HARLOW

"So, how was everyone's weekend?" Dr. Benson asks once we're situated in our seats.

Group therapy, I loathe it, but today, with Sebastian sitting across the circle from me, I'm extra tense.

"I see we have a new face." Dr. Benson looks down at the files on his lap and pulls one out of the stack. "Sebastian West, welcome to the group. How are you settling in?"

"Fine, I guess."

"I know it can be a difficult transition for some, perhaps a little scary, but I assure you that we don't bite."

"Okay," he responds wearily.

"Okay then, why don't we start by you introducing yourself."

Sebastian is slumped in his chair with his arms crossed over his chest and a smug look on his face as if this is a joke. Unfortunately, for all of us, this is very real.

"Umm, I'm Sebastian. I'm seventeen, and I live in Edmonds."

The group gives a collective, "Hi, Sebastian."

"What do you like to do for fun?"

He shrugs. "Typical things . . . hang out with my friends, play lacrosse, go to parties."

"Do you party a lot?"

"I guess."

"Does that ever get you into trouble?"

"I'm here, aren't I?"

My ears perk because, until this moment, I've had no idea why Sebastian landed in this facility, and I'm obviously curious to find out.

"Well, let's talk about that." Dr. Benson crosses one leg over the other and gets his pencil ready to take notes. "How did you wind up here?"

He gives another careless shrug. "I got arrested."

I stare at him from the corner of my eye, but he keeps his attention on the doctor.

"What for?"

"Drinking and driving."

"Dude," Wes remarks, "that isn't cool."

"Whatever."

Dr. Benson scribbles something in his file. "That's a pretty reckless choice. What led you to get behind the wheel?"

"Just in the mood for a drive, I guess." His arrogance isn't surprising, but it's still irritating.

"You could've killed someone," a girl comments.

"Could've, but I didn't."

"You're lucky," Dr. Benson says.

"I wouldn't consider this lucky."

"No?"

He scoffs. "Hell, no."

He reads something in Sebastian's file. "It appears you were suspended from school last semester for drinking at a school function, which leads me to believe that this behavior is a common occurrence. Would my assumption be correct?"

"Everyone drinks. We were just having a good time. Ask Cricket, she was there too."

All eyes skitter around the room, unsure of who he's talking about, but when they notice him staring right at me, everyone's attention comes my way. My face scorches.

"Cricket?" Wes questions.

I glare over at Sebastian. "Stop calling me that."

He chuckles beneath his breath.

"The two of you are friends?" Dr. Benson asks, and I quickly respond, "No. He's not my friend."

"But you two were partying together," Wes says as he tucks a lock of his blue hair behind his ear.

"We weren't partying. I was photographing the state championships for the school newspaper. We were just hanging out at the hotel afterward," I explain. "It wasn't a party, and no one else was drinking."

The doctor nods and turns to Sebastian. "Let's assume that what you're telling me is the truth and the others were drinking as well. Why is it that you were the only one who got suspended?"

"Don't know," he says flippantly.

"Sometimes people use substances as a way to cope. It provides an escape to help alleviate emotions tied to a particular event or situation they're struggling with."

"Is this you trying to therapize me now?"

"This is me trying to understand so I can help you."

Remaining slouched in his chair, Sebastian's arrogance doesn't wane. "I don't need help."

Dr. Benson nods. "Okay then; we'll come back to this tomorrow. Let's move on." He closes Sebastian's file and pulls another one from the stack. "Harlow," he states, and I cringe. "How do you feel like you're progressing?"

What he's really saying is that I'm not progressing at all and he wants to see if I'll admit that I'm actually regressing. The gloom has thickened over this past month.

"How did the visit with your father go on Friday?"

He knows exactly how the visit went because Marcus would have reported to him about it. I'm still so angry with him for taking my mom's side over mine, for not trusting me. Just thinking about it has my irritability awakening.

"Harlow, a simple good or bad is all I'm looking for," Dr. Benson says, but I'm unwilling to give him either of those because I don't trust him. I don't trust anyone anymore.

"Just tell him the truth," Max encourages, but I shake my head, keeping my eyes downcast.

"Harlow?"

"I don't want to talk," I state.

Dr. Benson smacks my file shut before heaving a sigh.

"What are you doing?" His tone is stern. "This isn't the same Harlow I remember from last year."

I sneak a fast look at Sebastian, who is entirely too focused on this conversation.

"Don't you want to get out of here? To see your family? See your friends?" Dr. Benson adds.

There's a faint snicker, and a second later, Wes whispers harshly, "You're an asshole, Sebastian."

Ducking my chin a little more, I curl into myself.

Dr. Benson softens his voice when he addresses me again. "Where's that fighter I saw in you last time. Where has she gone, Harlow?"

She's faded away.

How can they expect me to fight when not even my family is willing to fight for me? Maybe the reason they aren't is because I'm not worth it to them. And if I'm not worth it to them, am I even worth it to myself?

There's an urge to tremble and cry, but I'm too broken to function like I should, like everyone wants me to. The effort it would take is overwhelming—impossible even.

"Harlow, look at me." I don't want to, but I do, and when my eyes meet his, he tells me, "I'm not giving up on you."

Maybe you should.

After a second, he nods and writes something in my file before slipping it to the bottom of his stack. "Jeremy, how are you feeling, buddy?"

I don't need to look to know Sebastian is staring at me, examining me, questioning me, judging me. It makes my skin itch, but I'm too scared to draw any more attention to myself by scratching, so I suffer in the discomfort. Eventually, Sebastian diverts his attention to Jeremy, who's now upset, and I relax a fraction.

"Gus is back, and I'm really trying to ignore him, but I can't," Jeremy says. Last time he mentioned Gus was two weeks ago.

Apparently, whatever the evil rat is saying this time has Jeremy freaking out and unable to sit still.

I'm not going to lie, a part of me feels bad that Sebastian has to share a room with him—a very microscopic part.

"You don't think they took Jeremy to isolation, do you?" I ask Wes while we stand in line to get our meds.

"Doubt it."

While Dr. Benson was trying to calm him down in group earlier, Jeremy wound up losing it and got a code gray called on him.

"They probably took him to the breathing room," Wes says.

After Wes gets his anxiety pills, I step up to the window. Shanice finds my name on the clipboard, hands me the small white paper cup that holds my two pills and another one filled with water, and watches while I swallow.

"Check."

I open my mouth, stick out my tongue, and then lift it.

"Cough." After I do, she marks my name before announcing, "Next."

I rejoin Wes and we walk to the rec room.

"So, do you think pretty boy is going to break any time soon?" he asks about Sebastian.

"Doubtful."

"What's his story?"

"Aside from drinking, I have no clue."

"I wonder if there's something deeper than just a substance problem," he says, and when I look at him, he shoots me a wink before dipping out and running over to the television to get the latest update on the Olympics before we have to go to art class.

"Harlow," Max calls out as she hurries over to me. "Did you hear?" she asks with a smile on her face.

"Hear what?"

"We have a guest instructor for art today."

"And?"

"Umm," she says, uncertain about my lack of enthusiasm. Her eyes shift back and forth a few times while she tries to hold on to her smile, which drops slightly in her confusion. "Aren't you excited?"

"Ecstatic."

She shakes her head and walks off to share her elation with someone else. I used to find her childlike qualities endearing until she broke down in group last week and told everyone about some gut-wrenching things her uncle did to her when she was a little kid. Dr. Benson explained that suffering extreme trauma at a young age has the ability to stunt a person's development. Now, I just see her behaviors as tarnished. They don't come from a place of joy, but of trauma, and that sours them.

"Line up!" Marcus calls.

When we enter the large art room, there are canvases on easels that are stationed in front of each stool. I pick a spot as far away from Sebastian as I can. All the seats are fairly spread out, so none of us are too close.

Last time I was here, we didn't get to do many classes like this since it was during the school year and we were busy with curriculum, but since it's summer, curriculum hours are shorter, leaving more time for activities. They might be fun if they didn't all come with a hidden agenda.

"Good afternoon," a woman says from the small platform at the front of the room. "My name is Juniper."

Of course it is. The woman looks like she just crawled out from beneath one, with her ankle-length brown cotton skirt and—I lean to the side to see her feet—her woven Teva sandals.

She goes on to give us a little background information about herself as if I care that she's spent most of her life traveling around the United States as a therapeutic art instructor.

Max, however, has an obnoxious smile on her face as she listens attentively. Apparently, she cares.

"Today, I'd like for all of us to dig deep within our souls to find our places of tranquility. So, if everyone could close your eyes with me."

The woman closes her eyes, and when I look at the people sitting around me, they all have theirs closed as well—all, except Wes, who smirks at me while mimicking the jerking off motion with his hand. I stifle a laugh as I turn back to the front.

"I want you to take a deep breath and imagine yourself surrounded by serenity. It doesn't have to be a place you've been to before. It doesn't have to be real. It can be whatever you wish it to be."

I tilt to the side, curious to see if Sebastian has his eyes closed, but his easel blocks my view.

"Has everyone found their place of Zen?"

Murmurings of yeses and uh-huhs sound from around the room.

"Wonderful. Now, open your eyes." She tucks a lock of her frizzy hair behind her ear. I bet she smells like patchouli. "In front of you is a canvas in which you're going to give your special place life by painting it. Go ahead and use the brushes and paints that are there for you," she tells us. "It doesn't have to be perfect, that isn't the goal. This is an exercise in personal expression and positivity. So, pick up your brushes, relax, and have fun."

Once she's satisfied that we are all getting to work, she takes out her phone and starts playing weird meditation music.

I try not to groan as I reach over, pluck a brush out of the holder, and dip it into the cup filled with gray.

It's these very activities, which I'm sure are designed to make us feel human, that reinforce the fact that I'm different. How many seventeen-year-old kids spend their summers painting places of harmony? None—that's how many. Only the ones who are so unstable they too can't even be trusted within these walls of confinement. We're constantly babysat and treated like toddlers, coaxed throughout our days and spoken to like morons.

I can't take this activity seriously as I move the brush along the blank canvas, creating a mockery of the intended purpose. My place of serenity doesn't need my ill-skilled hand disgracing its beauty. It doesn't need to be brought to life because it already lives inside me. I can still feel the cold, rough driftwood on the backs of my thighs, the wind blowing through my hair, and the frigid sea spray sprin-kling my face. The smell of salt embodies my nose and fills my lungs. It's more than what a stupid painting could encapsulate. And if I did paint it, it would forever be tainted by the memory of this place, this unfortunate woman—this hopelessness.

Time creeps along slowly as Juniper meanders around the room, praising everyone's efforts. When she makes her way to my side and observes my creation, she says, "Wonderful work."

It's all the proof I need to know she's a crock.

Sitting back, I waste precious moments of my life, literally watching paint dry.

"It seems everyone is finished," she says when she steps back onto the platform stage. "How are you all feeling?"

Again, more positive murmurings.

"Great. Now, what I would like you to do is share your creation with a friend."

Oh god.

"I'm going to pair you up, and one at a time, I want you to re-veal your painting to your partner and tell them one thing about it that you find to be a symbol of peace. Remember, only one thing. In return, your partner will say one compliment about your picture."

She begins pointing to people, randomly pairing us off. As ev-eryone moves around the room to sit next to their partners, she aims her finger at me, saying, "You there." She scans the room to find who's left, and to my misfortune, she selects Sebastian. "You two."

Gritting my teeth, I watch as he stands and walks over. I kick the easel to angle my painting away from him when he sits next to me.

"Ladies first," he suggests, and I roll my eyes.

"Fine," I mutter beneath my breath, thankful that I don't have to subject my actual happy place to the likes of him.

I flip my canvas around and prop it on my knees.

An unforeseen laugh busts out from his lips, and a few speckles of his spit fly out of his mouth and land on my picture.

"Gross," I complain. "I just painted that."

"It's scary as fuck."

"No, it isn't." I actually think I did a decent job considering. I pretty much nailed the giant, hunched-over troll with his lanky fingers, stringy hair, and one eye.

"What the hell is it?"

"It's the Fremont Troll."

"The what?"

"You seriously don't know what the Fremont Troll is?"

"You mean you didn't make this mutant up?"

I look at my painting and lift a subtle grin. "It's a sculpture under the Aurora bridge in Seattle."

"And *this* is your place of tranquility?"

I shrug and get on with the assignment, telling him, "It is, and the thing I find most peaceful about this is the troll's bulging eye."

He can't hold back his smirk, which causes me to smirk too, and before I know it, we are laughing.

"This is what you spent the last hour doing?"

I shrug. "It was a stupid assignment anyway."

His smile lingers for a moment longer as if my making a complete joke out of this class is entertaining. His attention drifts back to my painting, and he looks it over for a moment before shaking his head at the absurdity of it all. "His eye looks possessed by the devil."

"We're supposed to be practicing positivity, remember?"

"Okay," he says, stretching out the word as he tries to conjure one nice thing to say, and I take pleasure in how difficult this task is for him. It takes a moment, but he finally gets there. "Your, um, brush strokes are . . . well, they're smooth, and the paint doesn't look goopy."

My brows quirk. "You're horrible at this."

"Well, you did me no favors by painting"—he gestures toward my canvas—"*that.*"

"Your turn," I say as I place it back onto the easel, but he hesitates. "Come on, show me."

He picks up his work and passes it over to me facedown, muttering, "I didn't think we were going to be sharing these."

When I flip it over, I have to bite my cheek to keep myself from smiling. He's fidgeting so hard that I get the feeling he actually took this seriously.

"I've never been really good at art," he defends.

Gee, I couldn't tell.

It legit looks like the drawings I used to do in kindergarten. He's painted the Puget Sound, with brown wooden boats and tiny black stick figure people standing on them. But the kicker is the bright yellow sunshine that has an actual smiley face. *A smiley face.*

"Can I ask one question?"

"I'd rather you didn't?"

"Okay cool," I respond. "Why is the sun smiling?"

"I don't know. Because we never see it, so it's exciting when we do."

I nod because I get it. "What do you find most peaceful about this place?"

He shrugs as if it's no big deal, but he's still fidgeting, giving himself away. "I guess it reminds me of my dad."

I scan his painting once more before piggybacking off the compliment he gave me, saying, "I like your use of brush strokes and how the paint *is* super goopy. The texture gives it more dimension."

"Whatever." He swipes the canvas out of my hands and places it on the easel. "You need to throw *that* away," he says, pointing back to my picture. "It's creeping me out."

Chapter Fourteen

HARLOW

Brushing my teeth, I stare down at the sink, watching the minty blue toothpaste being washed away into the drain.

There's a heaviness today.

I can feel it inside me, like someone dumped a barrel of bricks into my hollow body. It's an ache that's impossible to ease; an agony to be weathered, not subdued.

The day has just begun, and I'm already wishing it would end.

I cup my hand beneath the running water—slurp, swish, spit. Morning routines are simple enough, but when they feel like climbing mountains, the effort doesn't seem worth it. I want to crawl back into bed, but that isn't allowed here at the Hopewell Recovery Center.

Hopewell.

A well of hope.

If only someone in this place would lead me to it because my hope is blood on broken glass.

"Harlow, check," Leslie calls out from the other side of the door after fifteen minutes have passed.

"I'm going to the bathroom now."

As I sit on the toilet, I zone out at the white cinder-block wall. They couldn't be bothered to paint it any other color. This place is dank and cold—much like I am. My empty gaze travels to the light switch next to the plastic mirror. It's dirty and the safety cover over it has a big chunk cracked out of the corner of it. One of the screws is loose, and I wonder who's been loosening it.

"Harlow, I have to pee, and all the other bathrooms are being used," Max says when she knocks on the door.

"One second."

Quickly, I finish up and as soon as I flush, she barges in.

"Can you not wait?" I complain as I wash my hands.

"You've been in here forever." She rips down her pants and starts doing her business.

"One at a time, girls," Leslie reprimands as I grab my shower caddy and head to the hygiene supply station. The nurse behind the counter checks in all the items before I return to my room. Sitting on the edge of the bed, I slip out of my flip-flops, and put on my shoes. There's a ray of sunlight cast across the room, illuminating the speckles of dust in the air. I watch them mindlessly float around, free to go where they may. I'm jealous of the dirt particles, jealous of the sun, jealous of whatever you want to put in front of me. It doesn't matter what it is, I want what it has so that I can use it to fill everything I don't.

The tides of gloom are high today with no reason at all. Not that there ever is a reason. Some days are like that—dark and pointless.

"Can you believe it?" Max says when she walks into the room.

"Believe what?"

"We're finally having a heat wave." She looks out the window and closes her eyes as if she's trying to feel the warmth from inside this icy cold purgatory. "I love the sun."

With a smile on her face, she moves to her bed, straightens the blanket, and then fluffs her pillow before repositioning it at least five times until she's satisfied.

"It's bright," I mutter.

"How can you complain about the sun?"

"Because." I squint against the blade of light that hits my face at just the right angle when I stand. "Come on, I'm hungry."

We head toward the cafeteria, and all the while, Max's steps bounce as mine drag.

"Why are you so chirpy?" I grumble. It's just another thing for me to be jealous of.

She doesn't bother responding as we walk into the cafeteria. Max goes slightly rigid as we make our way over to the food trays, but breakfast isn't as bad as dinner is for her. They give her three chances to eat, but they'll only feed her through her tube if she fails to make an effort throughout the day.

She's getting better though. She actually ate a couple of vegetables off her last tray. I was so happy for her, but she only cried.

"Finally, something good," Wes says when I step in line behind him and see they're serving pancakes.

Maybe if I shove enough of them into my mouth it'll make me feel better.

Sebastian is already sitting at our table when we get there. Apparently, in the boy's unit, they did some dumb team bonding a few days ago and now Sebastian and Wes are friends. He's been sitting with us ever since. I still do my best to keep my interactions with him limited.

"This shit isn't half bad," Sebastian says around a mouthful of food.

"Did you hear about family day?" Wes rips the foil top off his syrup. "We're going to have a cookout."

It amazes me how the stupidest things get people excited.

"Is your family coming?" he asks Sebastian.

"Doubt it. What about you, Cricket?"

I glare his way, but he only grins, satisfied to know I'm annoyed. "When are you going to start calling me by my name?"

"When you start being nice to me."

"Seriously? When was the last time you were nice to *me?*"

"I gave you my dessert last night," he defends.

"Yeah, only because you're allergic to cherries."

"Still, I didn't give it to Wes."

"He had already gone to rec."

Sebastian dips another piece of pancake into the syrup while shaking his head. "There's no winning with you, is there?"

He's so irritating.

I pick up my carton of chocolate milk, only to have it splatter all over me when I open it too hastily. The three of them attempt to hold back their laughter as I wipe my face with my napkin.

The remainder of breakfast is spent with Sebastian enthralling Wes and Max with a story of how he and his lacrosse friends snuck into the girls' locker room and tossed dead fish in the showers while the cheerleaders were practicing out on the field. They all laugh while I take bites of food, which only feeds my somber mood.

After we finish, everyone heads outside for our daily dose of exercise. Sitting against the wall in the shade, I watch the boys toss around the basketball on the court, even Jeremy is out there with them. A couple of girls sit on top of a picnic table with their heads tilted up to the sun as if they're going to get a tan. Maybe they like the warmth on their skin. Max is off picking dandelion weeds and making wishes before blowing the seedlings into the air to spread their infestation.

Days here drag on. Minutes feel like hours that hold me hostage to these emotions that never leave. They only get worse, breeding on infinite time. All they do is multiply beneath the surface, pulling my skin taut and stretching my fibers too thin. It's overwhelming, and I'm trapped, bound to their relentless power.

There's no escaping this suffering.

I think about the light switch, the loose screw, the possibilities.

"Here. Make a wish," Max says as she extends a dandelion out to me. "Come on."

I pluck it from her fingers and stare at the ball of white fluff.

"You have to blow for it to come true."

I wish something could fix this shattered hole inside me. Inhaling a deep breath, I pause for just a beat, and then I blow. The seedlings fall around my feet, and when I peer up, Max is smiling as if she's done the Lord's work.

I often wonder if He's real. If there's a Heaven and a Hell, and if so, is it true what they say about people like me—the forsaken?

I used to pray.

I was so desperate to be saved last time I was here that I started talking to God. For a moment, I thought He was listening, but here I am again, drowning in the same misery. Now, I just feel stupid.

Are souls even real? And if they are, why was mine folded up like a paper doll and cut into a million pieces? Because that's how it feels. So many parts of me are missing, and no matter how much I try to find them, they simply aren't there, so why even bother?

Not even my family is trying. They dumped me here and left me to rot.

If I'm not the one thing they can't stand to lose, then what's the point?

The boys erupt in cheers when Sebastian dunks the ball.

How has he managed to win these people over? He doesn't even belong here.

I'm sick of this: the feelings—the *unfeelings*.

Needy for relief of any kind, I stand and walk over to Marcus, who's with one of the other nurses.

"You should be enjoying the sunshine," he says as I approach.

I don't bother acknowledging his statement when I ask, "Can I use the phone?"

"Exercise time isn't over."

"Yeah, I know. I was hoping to call home."

His brows lift. Rarely do I use my phone privileges, and he knows it, so even though it's bending the rules, he nods. "Come on. I'll take you inside."

I follow him into the common area. There is usually a staff member stationed behind the desk to monitor all calls, but it's empty when we get there. Marcus takes a seat and opens the binder to my approved list of numbers. "Who's it going to be today?"

"Tyler."

He picks up the receiver, dials the number, and hands it to me when it starts ringing.

I drag the phone's long cord over to one of the chairs and take a seat while I wait for my brother to answer.

"Hello?"

"Hi, it's me."

"Low, hey, how are you?"

"Oh, you know, living the dream."

He chuckles. "I was wondering when I'd finally hear from you. I tried calling you last week."

"Yeah, I heard. Sorry, I was kind of tied up with something." Truth is, I've been harboring so much anger toward my family that when they call, I often refuse to take it.

"It's cool."

"So, what have you been up to? Tell me something good."

I'm desperate for you to help distract me from this mood I'm stuck in.

"Just been hanging out with old buddies from high school. You know how it is," he says, but I don't know. I don't have friends like he does. "Last night, a bunch of us went and saw *Pulp Fiction* at the Mural in Seattle."

"Were there a lot of people there?"

"Yeah, it was packed. Afterward, we all went bar hopping before catching the train back home."

I close my eyes and fictionalize myself there with them, smiling and laughing and having a great time—whatever that feels like.

"We wound up at this retro arcade. They had all these old-school Atari and Nintendo games and there were a couple of bars inside."

"That sounds like fun."

"Yeah, it was, but I'm paying for it today."

"Too much to drink?"

"Oh man, you have no idea." He groans. "Then Mom had me up early this morning to help her fix the stove."

"What's wrong with the stove?"

"Who knows? She thinks because I'm a dude I should know how to fix everything around the house."

I let go of a breathy laugh, but it doesn't feel right. I thought talking to my brother would help me feel a little more human again, but it's only making me feel worse.

"Hey, I wanted to ask you something."

"What's up?"

"Next week, they're having a family day here. It'll be a cook-out or something like that," I tell him. "You think you could come?"

"Next week?"

"Yeah."

"I can't."

I twirl the phone cord around my fingers. "Why not?"

"I'm heading back to UNC early. A couple of friends and I snagged a small house right off campus and we move in next week."

"Oh, that's cool."

"Does Mom know about the cookout? She hasn't said anything."

"I don't know. I haven't told her."

The line goes silent for a moment before he says, "She's trying, Low. You shouldn't be so hard on her."

I clench the cord in a tight fist and swallow my annoyance. "Easy for you to say."

"She cares about you. We all do."

I shake my head because it's all lies. "If any of you cared, I wouldn't be here."

"That isn't fair. It isn't like I have any say in this."

"And if you did?"

He sighs and then goes quiet. Silence tells me he agrees with her decision, and I can't do this anymore. Dropping the phone from my ear, I walk over to the desk and hand it to Marcus, saying, "I'm done."

Tyler's voice calling my name on the other end is audible, and when Marcus gives me a curious look, I tell him, "Just hang up," and he does.

"Is everything okay?"

Why does everyone keep asking me that?

From down the hall, voices echo as everyone comes in from outside.

Marcus stands and nods toward the door. "Come on. Rec time."

"Hey, where did you run off to?" Sebastian asks when he sees me step into the rec room.

"Phone call." My response is clipped as I pay him no real attention.

"Everything okay?"

Again, with the question.

I shoot him a glare.

"Damn, you're a moody girl."

"Whatever," I mumble as I turn away from him and go to the cubbies to grab a deck of cards.

The day passes as it always does—uneventfully. It's a daily rotation of meals, three groups a day, rec time, curriculum, art and meditation, and one-on-ones. Every minute is accounted for and scheduled.

Some days, we have special activities or guests that come in to offer classes or give stupid motivational talks. It's all a pointless waste of time when you're a pointless waste of space. When each breath is more meaningless than the one before.

Lying in bed, staring up at the ceiling, I try to think of a reason to hang on.

A flashlight pierces my eyes as it does every fifteen minutes until I fall asleep.

"Check."

Lights out was hours ago, but sleep refuses to find me.

I'm restless.

Resigned.

Empty, aside from dread.

It's the fear of having to go another day, enduring the weight of this indefinable hopelessness that's slowly sucking the life out of me.

My heart hangs above me as the darkness takes hold of the vacant space in my chest. It fills me like the landfill hole I am, burying itself in my bones, decomposing me. Slipping out of bed, I pad over to the door and quietly get Rosie's attention.

"Rosie, I have to go to the bathroom."

She drags herself down the hall and motions, silently giving me permission to step out of my room. After she escorts me to the bathroom, she tells me, "Make it fast."

When I close the door behind me, I slowly drag my open palm along the bumpy surface of the wall. My eyes close as I concentrate on the coolness of the painted cinder until my hand reaches the cover over the light switch. I don't turn it on though. The moon casts enough of its silvery glow through the small window near the ceiling for me to find the loose screw. I use my thumbnail to slowly back the screw out, and the light at the end of this proverbial tunnel begins to brighten.

When the thread ends, the screw falls to the floor next to my bare feet with a light *clink*.

I lower myself, pick it up, and sit with my back pressed against the wall. I've been here before. Last time I was in my bathroom at home and it was a razor between my fingers, not an old rusty screw. My body turns numb just as it did the time before, and as I stare at the sharp tip, my head goes foggy. It's a peculiar euphoria of sorts.

Upturning my left wrist, I look down at my scar. I ghost the point of the screw along the pink line that leads to my radial artery. It's a straight shot that I hit once before.

Phantom heart palpitations *thunk* in my vacant chest, which begins to rise and fall as my breaths turn shallow.

Just do it.

Pressing the point against the scar tissue, I take a deep inhale and then dig it into my skin, ripping the flesh open as I pull it along the length of my wrist. The screw slips out from between my blood-coated fingers, and I stare up into a blur of sparkles as my body fills with tingles. The breath that escapes my lungs is heavy with relief, but I hear nothing aside from a distant ringing in my ears.

I sense the door flying open, but I'm too deep in this trance to move.

"Harlow!"

The screaming of my name blows into the glittery fog like a gust of wind clearing a path of visibility. There's more yelling, and when the light turns on, I look down, confused as to why there isn't more blood.

My hand trembles as I hold it in front of my face.

No!

Adrenaline explodes inside me when I realize I didn't cut deep enough. Looking up, I see it's Max who's screaming for help, but Rosie isn't in sight.

"Max stop!"

In a bolt of panic, I scour the floor to find the screw so I can hide it. My anxiety has me freaking out as an explosion of noise stirs chaos, which forces my hands to search faster. The moment I grab the screw, there are too many hands on me to count.

"No!"

The small space fills with my hysterical screams while nurses bark incoherent commands and I struggle to get away. I don't even realize I'm still holding the screw until someone pries it out of my fingers. Kicking, I shriek in a storm of fear for what's going to happen.

"Let go of me! Let go!"

Pandemonium blurs everything as people flood the room, and the next thing I know, my feet are no longer on the ground. In a slip of a second, I'm forced into a wheelchair. A fear I've never known rips through me when leather cuffs fasten around my wrists and ankles, restraining me in the worst way imaginable.

Tears spring from my eyes as I'm rushed out of the bathroom and into the brightly lit hall. Everything happens in flashes I can't grasp as my senses fail. I'm being pushed so fast that the air whips through my hair, and all I can hear are my pleading screams, but they can't possibly be mine because I don't recognize the sounds barreling out of me.

They wheel me down one locked hall and into another, and I'm finally pushed in to a small room. Horror strikes when the lights go on and I see the restraint bed.

"No!" I scream. "Don't do this!"

They continue talking to me, but nothing filters in with four people holding on to my limbs. I'm unstrapped from the chair and hoisted onto the bed as I fight with every ounce of strength I have, but I can't break free.

Balling my hands into fists, I thrash violently while bloodcurdling screams tear through my vocal cords.

I attempt to kick but can't get more than an inch of movement as they secure the straps, locking my legs and arms down so tightly I can't move.

"Please, no! Let me go!" I continue to wail, but there is no one to save me.

A sharp sting spears into my hip, sending a cold current of ice through my bloodstream. I look up to a male nurse hovering over me, but he dissolves into vapor as my muscles slacken and my voice fades until nothing is left but silence.

Chapter Fifteen

THERE'S A STRANGE VIBE IN THE CAFETERIA THIS MORNING. Almost everyone is already eating when I walk in and grab my tray. Whispered chatter fills the room, but it's so subdued that it piques curiosity.

"Why's everyone acting so weird this morning?" I ask when I sit in my usual spot next to Wes.

"You didn't hear?"

"Hear what?" I scoop a spoonful of rubbery eggs into my mouth.

"Harlow tried killing herself."

A cannonball smashes right into my chest.

What the fuck?

I must've misunderstood him, but when my eyes flick to Max, my stomach coils. She's visibly shaken, swaying back and forth.

"What happened?"

She doesn't respond, but I'm too struck in utter disbelief to care about her mental state. "Max," I state firmly, "tell me what happened."

"It was so scary." Her voice trembles. "I heard her crying from the bathroom in the middle of the night . . . it woke me up. There was no staff outside the door, so I ran to check on her, but she had already slit her wrist."

"Holy shit."

Max's eyes fill with tears, and Wes consoles her. I can't comprehend the idea of Harlow doing that to herself—or anyone doing that.

"Where is she?"

"Isolation," Wes says. "Or as they call it here 'the quiet room.'"

"What's that?"

"A safe room where she can't hurt herself."

My appetite vanishes, and I sit back. Max wipes away a tear as I try to unscramble my racing thoughts. It's nearly impossible to grasp a single one, but there's no denying that each of them hold a common denominator of guilt. It consumes me. I've been nothing but a dick to that girl, giving her so much crap over the years, and never once considering what that could do to a person.

What if this is my fault?

"Can we see her?"

"No, man," Wes says. "She's locked down."

"Where's isolation?"

"You know the hall to the left of where we get our meds?"

I nod.

"Down there."

I start considering ways to sneak in there to make sure she's okay, but it all seems so distant, as if this is a horrible joke they play on the new kids here. I think back to yesterday, and she seemed fine. She was quiet and moody, but that's how she always is. There was nothing out of the ordinary, so what the hell happened?

I can't fathom the type of pain she must've been in for her to actually try killing herself.

"What did she even use?" I ask because everything in this place is so closely monitored. Hell, we can't even be trusted with our own shampoo. The staff squirts a little into a paper cup for us so people don't try to drink it.

"A screw from the light switch."

"It's so sad," Jeremy murmurs, and I nod, completely disturbed by the visions playing in my mind.

I'm shocked that something like this could happen. I mean, I know it does, I hear about it on television, but this is way too real. It's weird, but somehow, over this past week, I've been able to convince myself that I'm not locked away in a mental ward. In just seven short days, I've become so used to seeing Max's feeding tube that I almost forgot it was there. Being stuck in a place like this, even for a short period of time, has made me sort of immune to all the oddities and the reasons these people are here. This is a brutal wake-up call.

"Marcus said that they're moving group up this morning," Wes tells us.

"To when?"

"I think right after outdoor exercise."

Looking across the table to Harlow's empty seat is haunting, sending a visceral chill straight through my chest, forcing my eyes down to my eggs.

"You okay?"

It's a total sham when I nod at Wes.

I'm sucked inside a daze of festering self-reflection that does nothing but create regrets. It makes me sick to my stomach, and I wind up throwing away almost my entire breakfast before we head outside.

There's a somberness hanging over this place today. Everyone knows about what happened last night, and they're all gossiping about it. Little do they know that I'm the one to blame.

Jeremy tosses me the basketball, but I bounce it right back to him before turning over my shoulder and calling out, "Yo, Marcus."

He steps away from Shanice as I walk over to him. "What is it?"

"I need to go to the bathroom."

"Why didn't you go before you came out?"

"Didn't have to," I tell him, and when he hesitates to take me inside, I urge, "Come on, man. I'm pinching it off here."

"Let's go." He sighs.

After we get inside, I'm in luck when he veers to the left to take me over to the bathroom by the med station.

"It's a deuce, so it might take a while."

"Didn't need to know all that," he says, unlocking the door and pushing it open for me.

As it slowly swings shut, I catch a glimpse of him walking off, and a trill of energy spirals through me. I'm not sure what the hell I'm doing or how I'm going to get down that hall, but I have to at least try.

After waiting a minute, I crack the door open to find Marcus sitting in the med station, talking to another nurse. As quietly as I can, I sneak out of the bathroom and rush over to the hall Wes told me about, but the moment I peer through the small window, I see Dr. Benson and duck back into a corner to hide.

A loud buzz sounds a second before the double doors open, and the moment he turns in the opposite direction, I slip through the doors before they close and lock behind me. Once I'm in, I look around, but it doesn't appear that anyone is down here. It's eerily quiet, and I start walking the short stretch of hallway. There is a small square window on each door that I peek in to as I pass—each one empty. The rooms are small with nothing but a bed, and there are no outside windows at all.

When I hit the third door, I look inside and stop when I see her long brown hair strewn across the white pillow. My chest constricts painfully as I try to digest what I'm actually seeing. It's like a horror movie. Her wrists and ankles are bound to the bed with heavy straps. She wears nothing but a white hospital gown, and she's staring lifelessly up at the ceiling.

A part of me wants to knock, but I don't—I'm too scared. Nothing about this feels right.

She blinks slowly, and a thick tear slips down the side of her face and into her tangled hair. The pit in my chest expands, and I resist the temptation to scream out for someone to unstrap her. It's beyond frightening to see a person tied down like she is.

She turns her head in my direction. Her red, swollen eyes meet mine, and I freeze.

I want to look away, but I can't.

I want to yell at her through the door and tell her that I'm sorry, but I don't.

She's expressionless as she stares at me like a ghost. After a beat, her face slowly crumples before she turns back to the ceiling and begins crying loudly. Tears freefall down her temples while she lays there bound and helpless and sobbing.

Rattled to my core, I step away from the window. My hands shake at my sides, and when the heel of my foot hits the wall, the harsh buzz sounds again, and I jump.

"Hey!" Dr. Benson calls as he rushes toward me. "How did you get in here?"

I open my mouth to say something, anything, but nothing comes.

"This is a secured unit. You aren't allowed to be here."

I give him a nervous nod, and when he sees how shaken I am, he puts his hand on my shoulder and leads me away from Harlow's room. "Are you okay?"

I nod again.

"Do you need to talk?"

I can still hear her muffled cries as I shake my head. "No."

He gently squeezes my shoulder, and I swear it feels as if he's squeezing emotions out of me.

"I won't tell anyone you snuck in here," he says before tipping his head toward the doors. "You need to go."

"Thanks," I mutter as I manage to put one foot in front of the other.

When I punch the large button on the wall, the doors buzz and open. Not wanting to get into trouble, I'm cautious as I make my way back to the restrooms. Marcus is still distracted, so I kick the bathroom door open, and when he looks up, I walk over to where he's sitting.

"You ready?"

"Yeah."

My heart rate remains spiked as I follow him back outside. For the next hour, I stick to myself, unsure of how I should feel. It doesn't seem real, but I know that it is, and it's messing with me.

When we are called inside for an early group session just as Wes had mentioned, I can't shake my restlessness. I'm a bundle of anxiety with sweaty palms and fidgety hands. I press my fingers against my opposite hand to crack my knuckles, only to remember that I just popped them less than thirty seconds ago. The lack of release charges me up more. I can't sit still.

Dr. Benson takes his seat, but he doesn't have his files with him today. When everyone quiets, he clears his throat before saying, "I thought it would be good to come together this morning to have an open discussion."

"About Harlow?" Jeremy asks.

Dr. Benson leans forward and folds his hands together. "Yes. About Harlow."

"Is it true that she tried killing herself?" another guy questions.

Everyone but me stares at the doctor as they wait for his answer.

"Yes," he states matter-of-factly.

"Is she okay?" I look to Max, who's sitting next to me. "I mean, is she going to . . ."

"I just got done visiting with her. Right now, she's just very tired." His answer couldn't be any more vague.

"Is she still strapped down?" I ask when I find my voice.

"How do you know she's strapped down?" someone asks as I keep my focus on the doctor.

"Because they always strap you down when you try to off yourself," another person responds.

My throat goes thick when I think about how she looked in that bed, but he manages to relieve a miniscule amount of my tension when he shakes his head. "No, she isn't." He then addresses the group. "Look, when something like this happens, it can stir up a lot of emotions and confusion in us. So, I'd like to take this time to talk through how we feel about the situation and answer any questions I can for you."

Across the circle, Kevin shakes his head. He's a chubby kid who's in my afternoon substance abuse group. He has an ego complex, and he straight up pisses me off when he sneers, "What she did was selfish. People like that only want attention."

"Are you kidding me?" Max snaps, lurching forward in her chair.

I stretch my arm out to stop her. I've seen her lose it before, and I know how feisty she can get. She senses my caution and settles back into her seat.

"I can understand why some people believe that," Dr. Benson responds, and I open my mouth to cut him off at the same time he adds, "After visiting with her earlier, I can assure you that she didn't do this for attention or to be dramatic. We have to keep in mind that her depression is extreme and that it's an illness—an illness that's invisible, which makes it very challenging for us to know what is going on inside her and how to properly treat her."

This is the first time I've gotten an explanation as to why she's in here. After I was admitted and saw her in the rec room, I thought about possible reasons, depression being one of them.

"But isn't it your job to keep us safe?" Max is still distraught over it all. I can't even imagine what last night must have been like in that bathroom.

"It is, and I take that responsibility very seriously. But on the same token, I can only do so much to help you guys. I do what I can to teach each of you different strategies to cope with your illnesses. I can offer you the tools, but it's ultimately up to you to use them." He pauses and releases a heavy breath. "None of us knew she was thinking about harming herself. She suffers in silence, and that's important for all of us to be aware of. You never know what the person sitting next to you is going through or struggling with, and I'm not just talking about in this room. People with depression are often very good at masking it."

"I was so scared she was going to die," Max weeps, and Sally, the girl sitting on the other side of her, slips a comforting arm around Max's shoulders.

Leaning forward, I brace my elbows on my knees and hang my head. God, the issues these people are dealing with are so much deeper than I ever imagined, and here I've been, making Harlow's life more hellish than what it already was for her. I had no idea that I was hurting her with her own broken pieces.

I'm scum for what I've done, and it's no wonder she despises me so much. I feel awful for the part I've played in all of this. Remorse collides with grief, sending a tidal wave over me. It fills to the brim, and I find myself having to blink back the tears that surface.

Max places her hand on my back, probably meaning to comfort me, but it only makes me feel shittier. This poor girl is dying a slow death, and here she is, offering me support. I can't even look at her because truth is, I'm so undeserving. If she knew the part I played in dragging Harlow down, she would rip me to shreds. And rightfully so, because I've been doing nothing but looking down on everyone in this place since I came, thinking I was better than all of them.

Clearly, I'm not.

"Sebastian?" Pinching my eyes, I shake my head before righting myself and looking up at Dr. Benson. "What's going through your head?"

I shrug. How do I even begin to put all these thoughts into words? "It's just . . . I don't know how to make sense out of all this."

"How does it make you feel?"

I give him the simplest answer. "Confused."

"About?"

"How anyone could do that to themselves."

"Let me ask you something," he says. "Why were you driving drunk on the night you got arrested?"

I don't know what one has to do with the other, but I already don't like what he's insinuating. "I wasn't trying to kill myself, if that's what you're trying to get at."

"So, what *were* you doing?"

Crossing my arms over my chest, I slump down in the chair and drift my focus to the floor. "I don't know. I guess I was just trying to get away."

"From what?"

"Things."

Lifting my eyes to him, I find he's nodding. "Perhaps Harlow was trying to get away from things too." He acknowledges the group, saying, "You see, in one way or another, if you open your eyes wide enough, you'll find that all of us share similarities. It's what connects us and what helps us understand each other a little better."

"How can we be expected to understand Harlow if she never talks?" Kevin says. "All of us participate except her." He looks at me and adds, "Same with you."

I shake my head at the prick.

"Sebastian is participating today," Dr. Benson responds in my defense. "And I have hope that Harlow will find the strength to open herself up with time. The thing is, just because we want her to talk, it doesn't mean she's going to. Right now, she has to fight extremely hard against her illness to do that. And to her, it feels like an impossible feat—debilitating even. For some, it's easier to give up and drown. But we will keep encouraging her, and we will keep encouraging each other."

The discussion continues for a while longer, and when we're released to rec, Dr. Benson stops me.

"She's going to be okay," he assures once the room has emptied. "I know you're worried."

"I, um . . ." The weight of this guilt has been tormenting me all morning, and I have to get it off my chest, but it's hard to admit what I've done.

He gives me a few seconds to pick up my words, but when he realizes that I'm not going to, he tells me, "If it were meant to be, it would've been. She's still with us because she has a purpose."

Chapter Sixteen

HARLOW

Sitting in the corner of the room with my knees to my chest, I hug my legs.

I feel stupid.

I feel weak.

I feel like a parasite.

It's freezing in here and smells like bleach. There are no windows to the outside and there is nothing to distract myself with other than white walls and worn laminate floor. This room could drive a sane person mad. This is my second day, and I'm already going stir crazy.

Shanice stopped by earlier to drop off my breakfast tray. After refusing all my meals yesterday, I finally ate, but now my stomach hurts. Maybe it's from the food, or maybe it's because my mother is coming today.

I'm scared of her *I told you so.*

Yesterday, I could have sworn I saw Sebastian standing on the other side of the door, looking at me through the small window. When Dr. Benson came in a handful of minutes later to do an eval on me, I wanted to ask him if Sebastian was here, but I was too scared. If he hadn't been and I'd imagined him, there is no telling where they would've put me next.

When one of the first things the doctor had said to me was, *"Your friends are worried about you."* I relaxed a bit. Maybe Sebastian had snuck into this wing of the facility and found me, but I wouldn't go as far as to call him a friend. It was more likely that he was looking for dirt to sling about me when we get back to school.

"What friends?"

"Sebastian."

"He isn't my friend."

"I think he might feel differently."

No, I am very aware of how ruthless Sebastian is. It is far more likely that he got caught in the hallway and made up some excuse about being worried about me.

The door unlocks, and I lift my head from my knees when it opens.

Dr. Amberg steps in. "Good morning."

He holds a handful of my folded clothes and sets them onto the bed.

"What are those for?"

"You get to go back to the group today."

It's a mixture of emotions when he tells me this. The thing is, I don't want to be in isolation, but I also don't want to face everyone. I want to be alone, just not in this room.

"Also, your mother is here. So, when you're ready, we can go to my office."

As he moves to leave, I stop him. "Wait."

He turns around.

"Is she mad?"

"No one is mad at you, Harlow. *No one.*"

He steps out and closes the door behind him.

Once I'm changed, I knock to let him know I'm ready, at least on the outside. On the inside, I'm brimming with dread. As we walk down the hall and out the doors, I can hear the voices of everyone inside the rec room. Tension grips me, and when we pass, I shamefully duck my head. I hear their whispers. Dr. Amberg does too, and he places his hand on my shoulder before leading me through another set of doors.

My palms sweat as we get closer to his office, and when he opens the door and I see my mother standing in the center of the room, I let go of all my resistance, walk straight into her arms, and cry. Despite all the resentment I harbor toward her, I cling to her because I have nothing else to cling to.

She's my mother; and she's here.

Holding me in her arms, she weeps with me as her hand smooths my ratty hair. I'm so defeated in my anguish that I feel like a small, needy child, desperate for someone—anyone to swoop in and save me. To gather all my mangled pieces and fix me because I'm broken—I'm so broken, and I don't know why.

She takes my head in her hands and looks at me.

Tears stream down my face, and I give her a painful, "I'm sorry." I'm not apologizing for what I did, but for what I am.

"Oh, honey," she murmurs before pulling me back into a tight hug.

We stand like this for a moment longer before our arms fall away from each other and we dry our tears. When she runs her hand along my cheek, she tells me through thick emotions, "I love you so much."

But how could she when I'm so unlovable?

"I was so scared I was going to lose you."

I buckle beneath her words, unsure of how to respond. Being pitied, judged, and scrutinized is a hard mix of feelings to wade though. For them to know this about me, something that's so intrinsically personal is something exponentially harder to navigate.

I often wonder if my mother is disappointed that she didn't get the daughter she wanted and if she sees me as nothing but a letdown.

Not like she would ever admit the truth to those things.

"Why don't we take a seat?" Dr. Amberg suggests before Mom and I settle ourselves on the couch.

She takes my hand in hers and her eyes drop to the large bandage wrapped around my wrist.

She's horrified.

She doesn't understand.

No one can.

"First, I want to start by letting you know," he says, addressing my mom, "that both Dr. Benson and I have evaluated Harlow, and we feel that she's ready to return to the group and that she's no longer a danger to herself. So, today, she will be making that transition."

"Oh, okay." Her tone is hesitant and uncertain. "Don't you think it's too soon? I mean, what if . . . is she . . . is she safe?"

"Mom, I'm fine."

"You're fine?" She shakes her head and squeezes my hand as her eyes well with fresh tears. "Honey, you could've died."

I'm motionless when she states the obvious. Of course, I could've died. That was the whole point. I wanted to end all this misery and be free. In that very moment, I wanted it so badly.

"You're my daughter. I can't imagine life without you." She takes the tissue Dr. Amberg hands her and dabs it along the crest of her cheeks. "You're my world."

Why can't I feel her words? I hear them, and they should bring me so much joy, but I can't *feel* them. It's as if I'm being punished for some sin I don't remember committing and am being held hostage from any semblance of happiness.

"But you sent me here when I begged you not to."

"I was scared," she stresses. "The things in that notebook terrified me. You can't imagine the fear a mother feels when her child is in danger."

"But I *wasn't* in danger."

She looks down at my wrist as if to punctuate her point, and I pull my hand out of hers "This is different."

"I can't risk losing you, but I'm not equipped to help you."

"You didn't even try talking to me. You just threw me away."

"No, honey. That wasn't it at all."

"But it was. Everyone made this decision behind my back. You blindsided me."

"If I could interject," Dr. Amberg says and then waits until we turn our attention to him. "Both of you have suffered a lot of trauma. Harlow, your mother and I have talked about the effects your first attempt has had on her. That event was frightening and, as a result, she's easily triggered and errs on the side of caution."

"It's my job to protect you."

"Then why does it feel like you're just protecting yourself?"

"Protecting *myself?*"

"From Dad. From him finding out about your affair."

Nervously, she glances at Dr. Amberg before coming back to

me. "Harlow, do you really think that I would commit you to a psychiatric treatment center to keep you quiet?" She enunciates every syllable of every word, shocked that I could make such an accusation, but that's exactly how it felt. "You are—" She chokes up and takes my hand back in hers before continuing. "You are the love of my life. Everything else in this world comes second to my children."

I bite the inside of my cheek to keep my chin from quivering, but I can't hold on when I blurt, "Then why are you cheating on Dad, knowing that it's going to rip us all apart?"

Dropping her head, she begins crying again.

"Why would you do that to us?"

"I'm not perfect." She looks at me with streams running down her face. "I messed up."

"Does he know? Have you told him?"

"Yes. He knows."

I suck in a fearful breath, wondering how all of this has played out at home. "Is he gone?"

Shaking her head, she tells me, "No. He's still home."

"Are you getting a divorce?"

"It isn't what either of us want, so we are doing what we can to repair the damage I've done to us—to all of us."

A huge sense of relief sweeps through me.

"But right now, you are our main priority. Getting you healthy enough to come home."

She washes away in a swirl of colors as my eyes flood and spill over.

"That's everyone's goal here," Dr. Amberg says. "Our hands are being held out, Harlow, but it's up to you to grab them and allow us to help you."

"What if I'm beyond help?"

My mother wraps her arms around me and pulls me against her. "You are not beyond help. And I will fight for you every day if I have to."

I want to catch her words in my palm and hold them forever, but more than that, I want to believe them. Because what they want from me . . . I don't think it exists. There is something incredibly wrong with me. I feel it every single day, even on the good ones.

It's exhausting and defeating and there have been so many times I've just wanted to throw in the towel and give up. I often question why I'm still hanging on, and it must be because somewhere, in some unknown place, there's a seed of hope that keeps me going.

But where is it?

Why can't I find it?

Will I ever?

Chapter Seventeen

HARLOW

"Can I just eat lunch in here?" I ask Dr. Amberg after he calls a nurse to come take me to the cafeteria. "I let you stay in here all morning. You can't hide out in my office forever."

Leaning against the wall, I stare out the window as he gets back to whatever paperwork he's been messing with since my mother left a couple of hours ago. When our session was over, I was supposed to join everyone in the rec room, but when I asked for a little more alone time, Dr. Amberg agreed to let me hang out in here with him. We wound up spending over an hour having a one-on-one because, somehow, it's been easier for me to talk today. Since then, I've been quietly meandering around, trying not to disturb him and hoping that I could stay in here longer if I wasn't a nuisance.

Dread fills my stomach when there's a knock on the door.

"Come in."

Marcus steps in, sees me, and smiles.

"You're going to be with Harlow for the next few days while she transitions back into the group," Dr. Amberg instructs.

"No problem."

Looking over to Dr. Amberg, I try one more time with a needy, "Please."

He shakes his head. "We've talked about this. You're stronger than you give yourself credit for. Plus, why would you want to eat your lunch in here with me? This office is boring; you said so yourself."

"This whole place is boring," I murmur as I sulk over to the door.

"Oh, come on," Marcus says, "it isn't that bad."

"Yeah, not for you; you get to go home every night."

"Let's go."

"Oh, Harlow," Dr. Amberg calls when I'm halfway out the door. I turn over my shoulder, and he tells me, "I'm proud of you."

His words touch a tender space in my heart, and I give him a subtle grin before leaving.

"We've missed you," Marcus says as we make our way to the cafeteria.

"I was only gone for a day."

"Still."

"And if there's any truth to that, which I seriously doubt there is, the fact that anyone would miss me proves my point about this place being beyond boring."

"It isn't the same without your snarky glares and your constant *go bother someone elses* when someone attempts to talk to you," he teases with a smirk.

"I don't say that to *everyone*."

He shakes his head because it's pretty much true. I do say that to a lot of people in here.

As we get closer, the noise grows louder, and my fingers twist anxiously.

"Don't be so tense. I'm right here." His voice is soothing yet utterly ineffective.

My palms are already tingling, and when I enter the cafeteria, I become hyper-aware of myself. I tuck my chin to avoid looking at anyone, but when voices hush, I know they all see me. I discretely tug the sleeve of my sweatshirt down over my hand to conceal the bandage on my wrist as I walk over to the trays.

Max almost knocks me over when she runs up and hugs me. I flick my eyes to Marcus in a silent plea for help. It's too much: the hug, the attention, the humiliation of them all knowing.

"Whoa, whoa, whoa, Max. Give her some space."

I avoid her eyes when she drops her arms.

"I didn't know you were coming back today," she says excitedly "How are you?"

Here we go with the dumb questions.

"Fantastic." My tone mocks her assumption that there could possibly be any other answer besides sucky.

"Why don't you go sit and let Harlow get her lunch?"

After she scurries off, I grab my tray of food. "Will you sit with me?" I quietly ask Marcus, hating how weak I sound.

"Yeah, no problem," Marcus responds, picking up a tray for himself before following me to one of the empty tables in the corner. I make sure to take the seat that faces the wall so I don't have to see anyone behind me.

Staring down at the chicken nuggets I desperately want since I'm starving, I hesitate to pick one up. I'm too self-conscience.

Marcus pops one into his mouth; it makes me slightly jealous. "Man, these aren't half-bad."

I quirk a brow at him.

"I mean . . . it's no Chick-Fil-A."

"Wes would be mad if he heard you say that."

"Why?"

"Because you shouldn't eat hate chicken." I get up the courage to pick up a nugget. "Like, ever."

I appreciate Dr. Amberg selecting Marcus to be the one to stick by my side. He's the perfect distraction as we eat our lunch. In a strange way, I feel a little lighter than I did this morning. After all the crying and talking with my mom . . . I don't know, I guess I was able to release some of the tension that's been building inside me—a cleansing of sorts.

When lunch ends, I take my time throwing my tray into the trash so I can be the last one in the med line. I stand behind Kevin, who shoots me an uncomfortable glower and then gives me his back. One by one, each person gets their pills and then heads to rec. Stepping up to the window, the nurse sets the cup of pills in front of me, but they aren't the same ones I normally get and there's more than what there should be.

"These aren't mine."

"They are," she drones without looking up from her checklist.

"I think there might have been a mix-up."

She finally acknowledges me before returning to her clipboard. Flipping up a few pages, she stops and reads, "Fluoxitine, clonazepam, and cephalexin." She drops the pages. "Dr. Amberg signed off on your medication changes this morning."

Great. New meds.

I dump the pills into my mouth and take a gulp of water.

"Check."

I open, stick out my tongue, and then lift it.

"Cough."

When I prove I haven't cheeked anything, I'm clear to go.

"No art today, so we're going to rec," Marcus tells me when I come to a stop at his side.

"Why?"

"Something about car trouble. I don't know."

Per usual, most everyone is congregated around the television.

"USA took gold last night in the men's swimming relay," he tells me as if I care.

"How exciting."

My lack of enthusiasm gets a soft chuckle out of him.

"If you see Max coming my way, can you tell her that I just want to be alone today?"

"No problem."

I veer off to the bookcases and scan through the titles. I'm not the least bit interested in actually reading, but I figure people will be less likely to bug me if they see my nose stuck in a book. After picking out a copy of some random sci-fi novel, I head to the far corner of the room, take a seat on the floor, and lean against the wall. I doubt anyone will even notice me tucked back here.

Opening the book, I begin reading the first page, and I'm not even a paragraph in before boredom strikes. It's hard to imagine anyone actually enjoying this. It takes too long to get to the point. I'd much rather spend my time watching a movie. Television is even better—thirty minutes to an hour and you're done.

"Hey."

I peer up from the book to find Sebastian standing over me. My neck heats when I think about how he saw me yesterday.

"Go bother someone else."

Sebastian, however, sits on the floor next to me.

I refuse to look at him because I'm too uncomfortable, so I fake read in hopes that he'll go away. God, what is he doing? Why is he just sitting here and not saying anything? This is a new version of torture for me, and when I glance up to seek out Marcus, he's distracted by Jeremy, who's gesturing to the floor and talking about Gus.

"Are you okay?" His voice is soft and filled with uncertainty.

I flip an unread page and nod.

"Harlow?"

"Why are you talking to me?" I'm annoyed, dropping the book to my lap before finally looking at him.

"I just want—"

"You just want what? All the ugly details so you can go back to school and tell everyone?"

"Fuck no. God." He sighs. "I wouldn't do that."

"Right." I go back to my book.

From my peripheral, I see him rest his head against the wall. He isn't his usual assholey self—I almost wish he were because the way he's acting now is more bothersome. Predictable is better, at least then I know what to expect.

"I've been a dick."

"You're just now realizing that?"

His hand touches mine, and I tense as he pushes the book away from my face. "I'm sorry," he says with a seriousness I've never seen in him before.

It makes me uncomfortable as I stare at him, dumbfounded.

"I'm really sorry . . . I had no idea."

His apology makes me feel entirely too exposed, so I go into myself. Clamming up, I drop my eyes and do my best to hide behind my invisible walls, but he makes it impossible when his fingertips lightly touch the gauze wrapped around my wrist. Abruptly, I jerk my arm out of his reach and hide my hand inside my sleeve.

Quietness expands, giving me time to notice that he no longer has his cast on. It doesn't take long for me to grow annoyed with the stalemate, and I shift, ready to stand and walk away, but then he murmurs, "My dad died two years ago."

The force of his words jostles me. I had no clue that Mr. West died. I still remember the time in sixth grade when a group of us snuck into an R-rated movie and got busted. Sebastian's dad came to the theater to pick us up from the manager's office. He was so cool about it and never told any of our parents what had happened.

"Since then, everything's gone to shit," he continues as I listen. "My mom's an alcoholic."

I face him in disbelief. His mom, the woman who chaperoned field trips and was at every classroom party, is . . . an alcoholic?

His eyes rim in shame. "Her scumbag boyfriend lives with us." His jaw flexes before he confesses, "He gets a kick out of knocking me around."

I don't even know what to do with everything he just dumped on me or why he's even telling me this at all. In a million years, I never would've guessed *that* was his reality. He's too popular, too perfect.

"You can tell whoever. Spread it around school and destroy my reputation if you want."

My head shakes ever so slightly as I ask, "Why would I do that?"

"Because I deserve it for how badly I've treated you." He pulls his knees up to his chest and drapes his arms over them. "Now you have my biggest secret," he says. "I know that I don't know much about you anymore, but I'm assuming that what happened a couple of nights ago is your biggest secret. I guess . . . I guess I just want you to trust me when I say that I'll never tell anyone, but I won't care if you tell people about me."

"I won't." My response comes honestly.

If I had known any of this a few months ago, I might have blabbed about it, but there's a sincerity in him right now that I've never seen. It makes him more human to know he's more than the shallow, egotistical jock he presents at school. It's weird to connect with him—if that's what is even happening—to discover that we both share pain. Although it's a very different pain, it's still pain.

Chapter Eighteen

HARLOW

GAZING OUT THE WINDOW IN A TRANCE, I MINDLESSLY tap the eraser of my pencil against my workbook. Thin sheets of gray clouds glide slowly across the sky, allowing the sun to peek out every once in a while.

When I was a little girl, my family would take trips on airplanes. As we flew above the clouds, I would look down on them, thinking that was where Heaven was, but only the dead could see it. I believed souls lived on the billowy puffs of vapor, in their little houses that had little flower gardens, and if they wished for anything, it would instantly appear because God was magical like that. I would spend almost the whole flight thinking of things I would wish for like candy and toys. Looking back, I can see just how frivolous those wishes were.

Now, I'm not sure what I would wish for because all the things I want are too abstract.

"Knock it off."

Snapping my eyes from the window, I look to the other table to find Kevin glaring at my hand.

I stop tapping my pencil, and he gives an exasperated, "Finally," before turning back to his work.

"Do you understand any of this?" Sebastian asks. He's sitting next to me and keeps glancing at my workbook. "You haven't even started."

I look at the page of unsolved quadratic equations.

"Do you know how to do this stuff?"

"Voices," Mr. Garrison, the fake teacher who comes in every

day, warns. He's a glorified babysitter who makes sure we do our remedial schoolwork.

Even though it's summer, we are forced to have three hours of curriculum each day, except on the weekends. It's a crime in and of itself if you ask me.

"So, do you?" he whispers.

"We learned this freshman year."

"And your point?"

"How did you pass if you don't know how to do this stuff?"

"I cheated," he responds flippantly, as if *duh*.

"Here," I say, sliding the workbook between us and then explain how to factor the equation by moving everything to one side of the equal sign.

He follows along, but after I solve for x, his eyes are glazed over in confusion.

"You seriously don't remember any of this?"

"Don't you go to college after next year?" Wes asks him from across the table.

"Yeah, so?"

"You're going to get stuck in zero-level courses."

"Are you serious?"

Wes nods at the same time as I say, "Yeah."

He tosses his pencil and slouches in his chair.

"Maybe you should cut back on all the partying," Wes teases.

"Not a chance, man."

"Shut up," Kevin barks at me as he spins around in his seat again, scraping the legs of his chair against the floor loudly.

"I wasn't even talking just now."

"Your lips are moving, aren't they?

"Hey!" Mr. Garrison scolds, but no one pays attention to him when Kevin comes back with, "Why don't you use your mouth for something besides talking?"

"What the hell is your problem?" Sebastian bites back in my defense.

Kevin sneers, "I hope she's better at giving blow jobs than she is at killing herself."

Before I can react, Sebastian erupts from his chair, launches toward Kevin, and punches him in the jaw. Everyone is on their feet and the room breaks into chaos. I watch in disbelief as the two of them scuffle on the floor, each one taking jabs at the other. Everything happens so fast. Mr. Garrison calls for help, and seconds later, a few nurses burst through the door.

Sebastian and Kevin are restrained, but they keep throwing insults back and forth at each other. I'm in too much shock to speak, but my wide eyes find the small trickle of blood coming from Sebastian's nose as he's dragged out of the room.

Chatter grows despite Mr. Garrison's attempt to bring order back to the room.

"Seats! Now!" he demands in a harsh tone that gets everyone's attention.

I sit as a wave of guilt rolls in. I can't believe that Sebastian, of all people, stuck up for me the way he just did. They should be thanking him instead of punishing him.

The other kids keep looking my way. Some of them snicker while others stare with curiosity—or is it condemnation? It's humiliating enough that they all know what I did, but to think that some of them view me as more pathetic because I failed is . . . my god, there isn't any way to describe how that makes me feel.

"Everyone needs to stop talking and get busy!"

As they all turn to their work, I keep my chin tucked. I don't dare reach for my pencil, too fearful that any movement will draw attention back my way.

"I can't believe he did that," Wes whispers from across the table.

Max then switches her seat for the one next to mine that Sebastian was just sitting in. "Are you okay?"

I shrug and then pull my sleeve into the palm of my hand. She sees me covering my bandage.

"Kevin's a punk. Everyone knows that."

"Yeah, that guy's an asshole," Wes adds, but it doesn't change the fact that he called me out in front of everyone. "He deserved to get punched in the face."

It's nothing new for fights to break out around here. Although not a daily occurrence, it does happen from time to time, but never has one involved me or been about me.

"Is something going on between you two?"

My eyes dart to Max, and I stare at her as if she's lost her mind. "What? No," I respond on a heightened whisper. "Are you crazy?"

"No, but the guy just threw a punch for you."

"So?"

"So . . . maybe he likes you."

My eyes roll because she has no idea how far off base her comment is. Sure, we've been getting along better these past couple of days, but that's it.

"He has a girlfriend," I tell her as I grab my pencil and start on my work.

She leans across the table and grabs her own workbook, murmuring, "Has he ever beaten up someone for *her?*"

Not that I know of, but I'm not the most informed person at my school. Max wouldn't understand that, had someone made that comment to me at school, Sebastian wouldn't have lifted a finger. Heck, he would have *been* the person making the comment.

I'm starting to see that there are two sides to him—the one in Edmonds and the one here at Hopewell. There is no way for me to know which one is the real him, and then I wonder if it even matters, if I should even care.

No, I shouldn't.

"Okay, wrap it up for elective time," Mr. Garrison announces before everyone starts checking their pencils back in.

"You coming to the game room?" Wes asks as I stand. "Marcus said they got the foosball table fixed."

"I wanna go!" Max chirps.

"I think I'm going to go outside."

"Oh, well then, I'll go outside with you."

"That's okay, Max. Go play foosball."

"Are you sure?"

I paste an unconvincing smile on my face. "Yeah. I need some time alone."

"Catch you later," Wes says before they dip out of the room.

After dropping my workbook into the tub and waiting for Mr. Garrison to sign off that I returned my pencil, I turn to find Marcus standing by the door. I get that I'm on suicide watch and it's his job, but we're on day three and his presence is starting to irritate me.

"Aren't you sick of me yet?" I mutter as I walk out of the room.

"You're going to miss me tomorrow."

"What's tomorrow?"

"You're coming off watch."

"Yippee."

Outside, a few boys are on the basketball court, so I head across the grass toward the fence with Marcus in tow. "You think I could get some breathing room?" I hold up my hands, mocking, "I'm safe, I swear."

Beneath a light chuckle, he agrees, "Okay. I'll be right over here," he says motioning to the picnic table.

"Don't have too much fun."

He splits off, and I slowly graze my shoes along the blades of grass before eventually settling down against the fence. With my knees tucked against my chest, I lift my chin and wait for the sun to reappear through an opening in the clouds. I close my eyes, and seconds later, my skin warms for a moment, illuminating the darkness behind my lids to a murky red. When the color vanishes, I open my eyes to find Sebastian standing over me, blocking the sun.

"Hey," he says, and I notice a light bruise staining the crest of his cheek.

"Hey."

"Are you okay?"

Slightly confused as to how he got out of trouble so swiftly, I nod and don't protest when he sits next to me. He looks toward the court where the guys are playing. I stare at him, at his bruise, and ponder why he's asking if I'm okay when I should be asking him.

I should ask him.

Ask him, Harlow.

"Are *you* okay?"

"Yeah, I'm fine. That guy's an asshole."

"He's that way with everyone," I say. "You didn't have to stick up for me."

He turns and looks at me as if I'm crazy. "No one should be talking shit like that to you."

I shrug. "I'm used to people teasing me."

The anger quickly drops from his expression.

"I'm sorry. I didn't mean that against you."

"You don't have to lie to me." He drapes his arms over his knees. "I deserve to feel like shit."

He does and he doesn't, and I don't fully trust that the version of him sitting next to me is the genuine one. Still, there's a tug pulling me away from wanting to be a jerk to him. The thing is, he didn't have to go after Kevin today, but he did. Why he did it is a mystery. It could have been because he felt guilty for treating me like a whipping post for the last few years, in which case his actions were to make himself feel better, and ultimately selfish. Or it could have been because he didn't think I would stand up for myself since I've never stood up to him. Or he did it because defending people when they are being attacked is the right thing to do.

Whatever his reason was, I'm grateful he did it.

"Thank you."

He shakes his head as if he's undeserving of the gratitude.

"I know this is going to sound really weird, but"—my eyes meet his—"I'm glad you're here."

He squints slightly at my bizarre comment, and it gets a grin out of me.

"You know what I mean."

"Yeah, in a weird way, I do. I'm not going to lie, I was nervous as shit when I first got here. Seeing you made some of that go away."

"Why?"

"I kind of felt like, if you could do it, how frightening could it be?"

"It isn't as if I have a choice, you know?"

He nods. "Yeah, I know."

We go quiet for a moment, but when curiosity rears its head, I break the silence. "Can I ask you something?"

"You're giving me a choice?" He grins, and I match it.

"Why *are* you here?"

"After my mom bailed me out of the detention center, my lawyer suggested that if I get treatment, the judge might reduce my charge."

"Treatment just for your drinking?" I ask, already knowing that, on top of our daily group, he goes to another for substance abuse.

"They classified me with alcohol dependency and then Dr. Amberg diagnosed me with anxiety." He drops his arms and picks at the grass. "He says I use alcohol to medicate the anxiety. He has me popping pills now."

"You're lucky you didn't die when you got behind the wheel."

He turns to me, seizing my pulse with his intensity. "You're lucky you didn't die too."

I swallow, and my heart double-beats back into rhythm when I drop my head to my knees.

"I'm serious. You scared me." He pauses, and I pray that it lasts forever, but I should already know that my prayers fall on deaf ears. "Can I ask *you* something now?"

"You giving me a choice?" I respond, throwing his words back at him before peeking up.

The serious look in his eyes has me dreading the question before he asks it. "Why do you want to die?"

The answer comes easily, so I give it to him. "Because I don't know what it feels like to live."

Chapter Nineteen

"I haven't seen my dad since I got here," Wes says as we play Uno. He slaps down a draw four card and changes the color to red.

"Is he coming today?"

"Nope." He watches me for a second, laughing when a few cards slip out of my hands.

I scoff. "I have, like, the whole deck. I should just give up now because I'm never going to get rid of all these."

"No way. I want the thrill of finally beating you."

I take my time, reorganizing my cards before choosing one to play. "Has he come for any of your private sessions?"

Wes shakes his head.

"So, what's his deal?"

"I disgust him."

"Because you're gay?"

He nods as I lay down a skip, which brings it back to me. I have four more in my hand so I start dumping cards.

"Damn, girl."

"Relax. You're going to win, so let me enjoy this moment." When my turn ends, I ask, "What about your mom? How does she feel about it?"

"She supports me. But my dad isn't understanding at all. To him, I'm nothing but a fag."

"He actually said that?"

"Yeah."

"That's so messed up."

He shrugs. "It is what it is, right?"

"I can't believe he called you that. I mean, it's so wrong."

"He thinks my being gay is a worse diagnosis than my actual diagnosis."

"People are dense."

"Tell me about it."

"Why is everyone acting so weird today?" Sebastian asks when he joins us in the rec room.

"It's family day," Wes tells him. "Everyone is always on edge."

He pulls out a chair and flops down next to me. "Who's winning?"

I quirk a brow at him and nod to the deck of cards I'm holding.

He smirks. "Damn, you suck at this game."

"Thanks."

Wes plays a draw two, and I groan at the same time he asks Sebastian, "How was your one-on-one?"

"Fine," he responds, blowing it off.

Sebastian's going on his second week here, and he still doesn't say much in group. Although he's opened up to me a little, it's clear that he isn't into everyone knowing his business. Not that I can say much considering I still don't participate. Truth is, thanks to Kevin, I'm more scared now than what I was before my incident. I was hoping they would've moved him to another unit after they found out what he'd said, but they didn't. He walks around, thinking he's better than the rest of us because he's here strictly for substance abuse.

From the corner of my eye, I see one of the nurses escorting Max into the room.

"Here, play for me," I say, handing all my cards to Sebastian as I get out of my seat and go over to her.

She smiles, and it makes me smile. "How do I look?"

"Beautiful," I say and then give her a hug.

She got her feeding tube taken out today. When they told her this morning, she was bouncing off the walls. It was driving me nuts, but there was no way I was going to crush her joy. These past two weeks have been hell on her, but she finally started eating on her own, so she no longer has to be fed against her will.

"All right, everyone," Marcus announces. "We're going to go ahead and bring in the families. Remember what we discussed in group this morning and your coping plans of action. We want this time to be enjoyable, but if you feel like you need a break, just come to one of us," he says, motioning to the extra nurses who are on hand today.

As families start filtering in, the room grows noisy, and soon Max is off with her mom, leaving me standing alone while I wait. Some parents seem calm, some seem nervous, and some quickly become emotional. The same can be said for us as well.

For me, I'm pretty calm, and when my mom and dad walk in, I'm actually happy to see them.

"Sweetheart," my father says when he scoops me into a big hug.

In the month and a half that I've been here, he's only come two other times. The first didn't end so well and the second was for a family session. So, I was excited when my mom told me the other day that he would be returning from his business trip early and would be coming today.

"How are you?"

"Good." I throw him a smile. Does he even know how stupid his question was? "Hey, Mom."

She hugs me, and I don't push her away like I normally would. After our session a few days ago, I feel like we were able to take a step forward.

"Let's go outside," I suggest so we can get some space from everyone.

The staff monitors us closely as we make our way down the hall and through the doors. Out in the courtyard, they've set up several tables and chairs along with a buffet line with burgers, hotdogs, and snacks.

"So, have you been making friends?" my dad asks after we settle at a table.

"Not many. I kind of stick to a couple of people."

He looks around and smiles when he sees the large basketball court. "Do you get to come out here often?"

"Every morning and then we have the option to come out during free time," I tell him.

"Oh, I forgot to tell you," Mom says. "You had a friend stop by the other day. Well, he actually came to the house earlier this summer, but everything was so chaotic that I forgot all about it."

"Who?"

"Noah."

"What did he want?"

"He was wondering where you were." When she sees my eyes widen, she rushes to tell me, "I didn't say anything. I just told him you were away at camp."

"Who's Noah?"

"A friend from school," I tell my dad.

I wonder if he believed my mother's lie. I'm far from the type of girl who would go to a summer camp, and he knows it. Now I'm forced into a situation where I have to go along with this dumb lie and it sucks. Noah will surely see right through it.

Sebastian catches my attention when he comes outside and claims a seat at a nearby table. He's all alone with dejection in his eyes. My curiosity lingers on him as I think about what he told me about his mother the other day.

"Guess what I got us," my mom says, pulling my attention back.

"What?"

She smiles. "Subscription passes to Broadway in Seattle at the Paramount."

"Why?"

She covers my hand with hers. "I thought it would be something special you and I could do together."

I don't want to hurt her feelings because she's clearly excited, but I'm not into musicals and I'm not into the idea of forcing quality time. Just because we finally had one honest talk doesn't mean our relationship has changed. We've never done something like this before, so it feels very unnatural to be doing it now.

"It sounds fun, right?"

"Yeah," I lie and then look to my dad, who's being really quiet.

He seems uncomfortable as he wrings his hands, and I quickly pick up on the tension between the two of them. Neither is looking at the other, and I get the feeling it's deliberate.

"How long are you going to be home, Dad?"

"I fly to Heathrow tonight."

"Didn't you just get back?"

He nods, and my mom purses her lips in annoyance. She's been leading me to believe that they're staying together and working through whatever is going on between them, but what she claims isn't supported by what I see in front of me.

They're so annoying.

"Why don't I get us something to eat," my dad offers. "What would you like?"

"I guess a hamburger," I tell him.

He walks over to the food table as I sit back and drift my focus to Sebastian, who's still sitting by himself with his head resting on his fists.

"I spoke with Tyler yesterday," Mom says, but I don't acknowledge her because this visit is starting to sour my mood. "He'll be home for Thanksgiving this year."

Her voice fades into the background. She's trying too hard to pretend as if everything is fine, as if we're fine, as if I'm fine, as she blathers on and on about Broadway shows and Thanksgiving.

I give her random nods and *uh-huhs* until Dad returns with a plate of food for him and me . . . and nothing for Mom.

My mood sinks even further.

Honestly, I kind of wish my mother didn't come. Not only is she getting on my nerves but she's clearly getting on my dad's as well. He's hardly said anything, while she won't stop talking.

After I take a bite of my flavorless burger, I look at my dad and tell him, "I miss Dick's Drive-In."

As he chews, he lifts his brows as if he's about to say something, but my mother speaks first. "You want me to bring you a burger from there? I can do that next week."

God, she's trying way too hard.

I don't give her a response, and when I take another bite, my dad says, "As soon as you come home, you and I will go together."

I give him a small smile, which I can tell irks my mom.

"Anyway," she starts again, "I was thinking we could do something different for Thanksgiving this year and go to a nice restaurant."

I tune her out as I continue to eat. While I'm busy trying to avoid eye contact with her, I look over to Sebastian who's slung back in his chair with his arms crossed over his chest. He's the only one out here with no family. As much as mine annoys me, they at least showed up. A part of me wants to invite him to sit with us, but I know better than to subject him to that.

"Harlow? Are you listening to me?" my mom nags, and when I look at her, her lips are pinched into a tight line. "What are you staring at?"

"Nothing," I snap defensively.

"Why are you taking that tone with me?"

"What tone?" My influx of irritation is noticeable.

My focus is pulled away again when I see Sebastian stand and walk over to a couple of the staff. He looks angry, with his fists balled at his sides before Marcus leads him back inside.

"Do you know that boy?" my mom asks when she notices where my attention has gone.

Rolling my eyes, I remind her, "I live here. Of course, I know him."

She drops her hand onto the table with an exasperated, "What is with the attitude? I was hoping to spend a nice afternoon together."

Is she out of her mind?

"A nice afternoon?" I mock. "Look around, Mom."

"Calm down," my father reprimands.

"Are you seriously going to take her side again?"

"I'm not taking anyone's side," he says. "I'm just asking you to calm down."

I shove my plate to the center of the table before crossing my arms and sitting back in a huff.

"Harlow, please," she says as if I'm the problem.

With a snide tilt of my head, I give her the bitchiest plastic smile I can conjure, which chafes her.

"What has gotten into you?"

"What do you mean? Isn't this what you want, a nice pleasant afternoon where we all sit around as if this whole situation isn't the shit show that it is?"

"That's enough, young lady," my father berates. "You are not going to sit here and talk to you mother like that. Show some respect."

"Why should I respect her? Huh? Tell me. I really want to know."

"I'm trying," she says, emotion coating her words. "I don't know what you want from me."

"You aren't trying."

"I am."

"You don't even know me."

"How can you say that? You're my daughter."

"So why did you get us tickets for the Paramount? When have I ever shown an interest in that stuff?"

"I thought it would be something nice we could do together."

"Well, it's a crappy idea."

"Your mother's heart is in the right place."

"Just like it's in the right place when she's with her boyfriend?"

My dad turns red, and even though my entire body flames in fear for how I just spoke, I force myself to keep my composure. My façade is covered in splinters, and I feel myself splitting more and more as the silence stretches. It's a spiraling of emotions that has me on the verge of tears, but my mother's are already falling.

"Do you need a break?" Shanice asks when she comes over.

Before I crumble completely, I give her a cowardly nod. If I try to speak, I'll only cry.

"Harlow, wait," my mom pleads, but my dad remains silent and pissed as Shanice takes me inside.

Chapter Twenty

I PUSH MY HANDS AGAINST THE DOOR, CAUSING IT TO OPEN with so much force it slams into the wall. Blood boils, rising through my core and burning up my neck. Marcus keeps a hand on my shoulder as he leads me past the rec room and down the stretch of hallway toward the private counseling rooms.

My nails bite into the flesh of my palms because I have my fists clenched so tightly, and the moment I walk into the small room, I throw one into the doorjamb.

"Whoa." Marcus grabs my arm. "Take a deep breath for me."

Searing pain slices through my hand, and I shake it out as I pace around the room, breathing heavily in and out of my nose. I'm the only piece of shit here who doesn't have a single visitor. No one came to see me, not that anyone would because only my mother knows I'm here. I'm her only son who she hasn't seen in a couple of weeks, and she can't even bother to come. It's fucking humiliating and a reminder of where I stand in her life.

She's thrown me away as if I mean nothing.

"Do you need to let it out and scream?"

Lacing my fingers tightly behind my head, I keep pacing. The pressure inside me is unreal.

"I fucking hate this shit," I grit.

My heart pounds so hard that it awakens the emotions I used to silence with alcohol.

I feel it, the life flooding back into them.

It stirs until it explodes and crashes down on me—the jagged edges of my once perfect life carving their wicked truths all over me. I can no longer hold it in because I've been stripped of my weapon against it.

When my lungs deflate, I drop to my knees right into the dusty shambles of the walls I've been living behind for the past two years. The walls alcohol allowed me to build, but it's been taken away, leaving me entirely unprotected.

Crumpled on the floor, I heave in ragged breaths, and for everything I've been robbed of, I cry. Like a pansy loser, I hang my head and just cry because at the end of the day, I'm just a kid who wants his mom, who wants to feel safe and loved and protected. I never knew how badly I needed that until it was gone. Now I'm terrified I'll never get that back. I'm too young to go at this life alone; I don't want to.

"You're okay," Marcus assures when he kneels by my side and rubs my back, but it's all bullshit.

I'm not okay.

Nothing is okay.

I hate my life—I hate so much about it. I hate my dad for dying and leaving me alone. I hate my mom for not being stronger. I hate that I have to constantly hide from everyone. And right now, I hate myself for crying like a little bitch.

"Is everything okay?" Greg, a staff member, asks when he opens the door.

I lift my head just in time to see Shanice walking by with her arm wrapped around Harlow, who's also crying. She glances my way, her teary eyes meeting mine for a split second before she steps into the room across the hall from me.

"Could you get us an icepack?" Marcus asks Greg, but I can't tear my attention away from Harlow, who begins sobbing into her hands right before Shanice closes the door.

"You need anything? Some water maybe?"

"No." I kick my legs out from under me before scooting over and leaning against the couch. Wiping my face with the sleeve of my shirt, I ask, "Did she even call?"

"Who? Your mother?"

"Forget it. I don't want to know."

The door opens again, and Greg tosses Marcus the icepack. "Do you need anything else?"

"No."

He steps out of the room, and Marcus passes me the icepack for my knuckles.

"We'll get the doctor to come look at your hand, okay?"

I try moving my fingers and end up wincing in pain. They are probably fractured again.

"How do you feel?"

"Pissed," I respond.

"What do you normally do when you feel this way?"

Keeping my eyes on my hand, I tell him the truth because I'm too drained to put up a front. "I drink."

"Do you want to drink now?"

I nod, too scared to talk because I don't want to cry again. This place has me unarmed and defenseless, and I hate it.

"How do you feel about that?"

From under my brows, I glower at him and scoff, "How do you think I feel?"

"Probably the exact same way I used to feel after I got sober."

I lift my head and look at him.

"You seem surprised."

He's right. I am. I guess I figured everyone who worked here would have a squeaky-clean past.

"I have five years of sobriety," he reveals. "I can still remember what it felt like to be where you are right now. You're in the thick of it, and I know how much it sucks, but I also know that you can pull through this and get yourself to the other side." I don't realize I'm shaking my head until he calls me out. "You think I'm talking out of my ass?"

"Yeah, I do."

"That's what our addiction does. It manipulates us into believing it holds more power than we do."

He speaks as if it's the enemy, but he's wrong. Alcohol consoles in a way nothing or no one else can. It isn't my enemy; it's my savior. So, if I have to spend the rest of my life on my knees in front of it, I will, because it's the only thing that makes this life tolerable.

There's a knock on the door, and when Marcus opens it, Shanice asks, "Hey, Unit C needs me really quick. Can you keep an eye on Harlow? She's calmed down, so . . ."

"Yeah, no problem. I got it."

"Thanks."

After she disappears down the hall, Marcus moves to stand in the doorway and asks across the way, "Do you need anything?"

"No," Harlow responds, so I know her door is open even if I can't see it from where I'm sitting.

Pulling my knees up, I rest my forehead on them as embarrassment over her seeing me cry swells. If only there were a place for me to run and hide, but there isn't. I'm stuck, but so is she. This must be how she felt when I saw her restrained to a bed, how mortified she must've been to be seen at her weakest. I try to use that to help curb my own mortification, but it doesn't do a whole lot. Not being alone at rock bottom doesn't make being at rock bottom any easier.

"Is it cool?" Marcus asks, pulling me out of my thoughts, and when I look up, Harlow is standing next to him.

"What?"

"Is it cool if she comes in and talks to you?"

I nod, and when she walks in, Marcus steps out and stands next to the door because, heaven forbid they leave us unattended. My eyes track her as she makes her way over and sits on the floor next to me.

"What happened to your hand?"

"I hit the doorjamb," I tell her before stretching my legs out in front of me. Lifting the ice pack, I show her my knuckles, which are already bruising.

"You just got your cast off."

"Yeah, I know."

Her attention is making me uncomfortable. For the first time, someone knows my truth.

She and I used to be friends when we were younger, but somewhere along the line, everything changed. During these past two weeks, I've come to realize that I have no reason to dislike her. I only picked on her because everyone else was and it seemed like the cool thing to do.

It was all bullshit.

"What happened?" she asks after a span of silence.

The urge to lie is instinctual at this point, but she already knows so much, so why bother? "My mother didn't even bother showing up today." There's a pain in her eyes when I tell her this, but I go on and reveal, "She doesn't even call me or show up to therapy sessions."

"Have you tried calling her?"

I chuckle beneath my breath, but there's nothing funny about it. "What's the point?" She goes quiet, and in a strange way, telling her this stuff makes breathing easier. "I hate her," I admit, feeling safe enough to unload that.

"Why?"

"Because I needed her after my dad died, and when I turned to her, she had already turned to alcohol." Memories of how she used to be when my father was alive hit heavily, forcing me to fight back the rising sadness. "It's horrible that I feel like that. I mean . . . she's my mom." A tear slips out, and I quickly wipe it as if I can hide it from her.

"I hate my mom too."

"Why?"

And this time, it's her eyes that flood. "She doesn't know how to love someone like me."

"What do you mean *someone like you?*"

"I'm not normal." Her voice cracks, and when she blinks, tears spill down her cheeks.

My chest pulls toward her like a magnetic force, and when I drop the icepack and slip my arm around her shoulders, she leans into me. Even with her crying, there's something soothing about holding her in my arms. Maybe it's the fact that I can relate to her in a way I haven't found with anyone else, that we get each other on a level no one else can understand.

Our pieces are broken in different ways, but to know that I don't have to pretend to be perfect around her alleviates so much of the pressure I'm constantly under.

Marcus peeks in, and I tense because it's against the rules for us to be touching like this, but he doesn't say a word. He simply turns away, and when he does, I wrap my other arm around her and hug her. It feels selfish on my part, but if she wasn't getting any comfort out of it, she'd push me away, but she isn't.

"Do you ever get tired of faking it all the time?" she whimpers.

Resting my cheek on top of her head, I nod. "Yeah."

"I don't want to do it anymore. I don't want to be this way."

"Can I ask you something?"

She lifts her head, and I let my arms fall away from her.

"What?"

"The first day I was in group, when Dr. Benson mentioned you being a fighter before . . . what did he mean by that?"

She lets go of a deep sigh and hangs her head.

"This isn't your first time here, is it?"

"No." Her voice is soft and another tear falls. She runs the cuff of her sweatshirt across her cheeks to dry her face as she sniffs and struggles to compose herself. It takes a moment before she finally looks at me. "When you said that we had each other's biggest secret, you were wrong."

"What do you mean?"

"What happened last week wasn't the worst."

I'm scared to ask because her digging a screw into her arm is pretty damn disturbing. I can't imagine what it is that she hasn't told me.

She turns and pulls the sleeve of her shirt up to just above the bandage. My eyes lock on her wrist, and when she peels back the gauze, my heart screeches to a halt as shock loops around it.

Beneath the superficial cut of the screw is a brutal scar that runs double the length.

I stare at it in horror, and when my eyes reach hers, I ask, "You've done that before?"

She covers her wrist back up and nods. "I was never pregnant," she whispers. "I was here."

With a deep sigh, I tuck my knees to my chest and drop my head into my hands. The gravity of what this girl is dealing with is beyond anything I can wholly comprehend. Whatever it was she drove into her skin, she did it with only one intention because that scar is the marker of a merciless attempt at death, and that shit scares me.

"I'm sorry," she says thickly. "I shouldn't have—"

"No, don't do that." I turn to face her straight on, taking her hand in mine and wrapping my other hand around the bandage hidden under her sleeve.

"I've never shown anyone."

"I'm glad you showed me." I blink slowly, hating myself for helping spread that stupid rumor about her. "I'm so fucking sorry."

"For what?"

"I knew you weren't pregnant. I should've never said that dumb shit."

"It's better than the truth."

Shaking my head, I tell her, "I don't want this for you. I want to help."

Her shoulders sag. "You can't. I'm unfixable."

"That's bullshit." The thought of her trying a third time and succeeding terrifies me. Just knowing that I'll never understand the depth of her misery twists my gut into painful knots. "I need you to try."

"Why?"

"Because . . ." I let my words fall when they catch me by surprise. It makes me uneasy to say them, especially to her. I've said them to Kassi, but they were a lie. I gave them to her in vain because I'm weak. But Harlow deserves the truth, so I swallow my hesitation and tell her, "Because I don't want to lose you." Her fingers wrap around my hand that's still holding hers. "And because I don't want *you* to lose you."

"It doesn't feel good to be me."

"I want to show you that it can." I take my hand off her wrist and slip it behind her neck, pulling her back to me. "You said it yourself; you don't want to be this way anymore. So, if you're so tired of it all, then try to do something about it."

Her hand grips mine tighter, and I strengthen my hold as well.

"Promise me, Harlow. Promise me you'll try."

Chapter Twenty-One

HARLOW

"YOU MEMORIZED MY NUMBER, RIGHT?" Wes asks Max because we aren't allowed to share that stuff with each other. She gives him a tearful nod, and he tells her, "Call me when you get out of here."

"I will."

He gives her a hug as she continues to cry, and when she steps aside, Wes turns to me, and I smile. He's going home, and I'm happy for him, but I'm jealous as well.

His eyes are coated in pity as he tilts his head and holds out his arms for me to step into.

Sadness is a very real thing, and it expands painfully in my chest as I hug my friend. His leaving only reminds me how far away I am from where I need to be to get out of here.

"I'm going to miss you," I tell him as I pull back. "But I'm not going to miss your ugly blue hair."

"Hey now!" He laughs. "It isn't that bad."

"It's pretty damn bad, man," Sebastian says before the two of them clap hands and go in for a quick hug. "You take care."

"Yeah, you too," he responds, eyeing Sebastian's new cast. "Be good to that damn hand."

"Wes, you ready?" Greg calls from the doorway of the rec room.

"Yeah." He turns back to the three of us and smiles. "Hurry and get out of here so we can hang out in the real world."

We all nod and say one last goodbye, but truth is, we won't see him again. That isn't how this works. We become tight while locked away, but once free, we're nothing more than a memory for each other.

"Good luck," Max calls out before Greg takes Wes through the secured doors that lead to freedom.

When Max looks at me, her face is covered in tears, and I slip my arm around her. Wes was her best friend in here, but no matter how happy you are to see someone get better, when you see them leave, it causes an upheaval of emotions. In a way, it makes the ones being left behind feel more trapped.

"Let's go watch," she blubbers before drawing back and rushing to the windows that look over the front parking lot. She motions me to join. "Come on."

I shake my head, and she turns to wait for Wes to leave the grounds as I drag myself over to the wall and lean against it.

Sebastian follows me. "You okay?"

"I bet you'll be next," I murmur.

When he first got here, I couldn't wait for him to be gone, but now, the thought of him leaving makes me sad.

"You anxious to get rid of me?"

I slide down the wall until I'm sitting on the floor.

He sits next to me. "What's wrong?"

"I don't want to be all alone in here."

The corners of his lips lift into a sly grin.

"Why are you looking at me like that?"

"I don't think you despise me anymore, Cricket," he teases.

My eyes narrow. "Don't be so sure about that, and stop calling me Cricket. It's annoying."

He chuckles under his breath. "I still remember that day in science class."

"Please, for the love of all that is holy, don't."

"All those damn crickets in your hair." He laughs.

"I was traumatized! Like, *seriously* traumatized." The memory causes my whole body to shudder, which makes him laugh harder. "I'm glad you find this so amusing."

"I'm sorry; I'll stop," he says, wrestling to get rid of his smile. It takes a few seconds, but he finally manages it. "There, all better."

"You sure about that?"

He's forced to bite his lip when another grin threatens to break free.

Max knocking on the window draws our attention. I watch as she waves and hollers, "Take care," loud enough for Wes to hear down below. It sends another wretched pang through my stomach, and all the levity Sebastian just gave vanishes.

He must feel the shift because his face drops and he whispers, "You're going to be okay."

"Am I?"

"Group!" Shanice announces, and when Sebastian stands he holds his hand out for me and helps me up.

As we all file out of the room, his hand is still holding mine, but no one notices aside from Max, who's right next to me. She looks down at our entwined fingers, and I let go of him. When her eyes catch mine, she ducks her head and drops back in the crowd as we make our way down the hall.

Dr. Benson is already sitting in his chair when we walk in and find our usual seats, but one remains empty—Wes's.

To my left, Sebastian leans in, murmuring, "Try," right before Dr. Benson calls our attention, but mine remains on Sebastian. He wanted me to promise I would try harder. I couldn't give him my word because it would've been a lie.

Noticing Wes's empty chair, I think about what I would be doing if I were out of here.

I'd be at the beach, smelling the salt and feeling the mist on my face as the wind kicks through my hair. Closing my eyes, I imagine myself sitting on the driftwood. I can almost hear the waves as they break along the shore, but I'm thrust back into my reality when I hear Sebastian's voice.

"My dad died two years ago."

Turning my head, I look at him in shock, surprised to hear him talking when he's normally so quiet in group.

"He was coming off a long shift at the hospital and crashed into a tree. His car caught on fire; he had to be identified by his dental records."

My heart stammers at how horrifying that would be, and I don't realize I'm holding my breath until he looks at me and gives the slightest hint of an encouraging nod before turning back to Dr. Benson.

"Life was never the same after that."

He doesn't stop talking, and I can't believe how honest he's being in front of everyone, but I know why—it's for me. He's proving a point, that if he can try, so can I. The thing is, if he continues to participate, and I don't follow suit, I'll be here by myself because he'll be released and I'll be left behind.

Shifting my attention to Max, I wonder how much longer she has. Her feeding tube is gone and she's been eating more, so it's only a matter of time before she's goes home as well.

"How did you cope?" Dr. Benson asks him.

"I was numb for a while. It didn't seem real," he says. "The phone would ring, and I would honestly think it was my dad calling. That somehow it was all a huge mistake because there was no way he could be dead." He clears his throat, and it flexes as he swallows hard. "After a few weeks, the numbness faded. I'd been so disconnected that I hadn't realized that my mother had started drinking pretty heavily. I figured if it dulled her pain, it would dull mine too." Turning his head, he looks into my eyes when he admits, "I use alcohol to cope."

"This is a good first step, Sebastian."

He shifts back to Dr. Benson, who's giving him a proud nod.

"Acknowledging truths isn't easy. Life can turn on us in an instant, and it's a shock to our systems. If we're unprepared and ill-equipped to deal with the aftermath, we can find ourselves turning to unhealthy behaviors as a way to cope and self-medicate."

Sebastian's voice is full of pain as he talks about losing his dad, and it makes me think about my own dad and how it would feel to lose him. As angry as I am with my parents, the lost girl inside me begs to cling to them still.

My heart tremors in muddled agony that comes from so many different angles. It overwhelms, sending a tear down my cheek. I'm scared to bring attention to myself by brushing it away, so it lingers until it dries on my skin.

"Harlow?"

My eyes fall shut, and I sigh in dread. They're all looking at me now; I know it.

"Would you like to share what you're thinking?"

Clenching my hands together, my strength collapses. So much of me wants to surrender and beg for help, beg for someone to save me and take away this never-ending hopelessness that clouds every inch of my existence.

But I'm scared, and I'm not entirely sure of what or why.

Sadness swims in my eyes, blurring my hands as sorrow detonates within, ricocheting off bones and tendons. It shakes me to the core, and I hold my breath and plead for the strength not to let it consume me, but the walls are closing in. Pressure mounts, sending a brilliant ache up my throat, strangling me. My chest heaves, and when I can't hold it in any more, I cover my face with my hands as tears break free.

There's a hand on my back, and then another one—Max and Sebastian. I want to shrug them off because that's what I'm good at—pushing people away.

It isn't until I feel a hand on my knee that I timidly look up to find Dr. Benson kneeling in front of me.

He cares, I know he does, but I can't understand why when I'm so useless—shot full of holes.

Inhaling and exhaling pain through these gaping wounds of mine is insufferable, but these wounds no longer bleed because they've already drained the life out of me, yet they still remain—festering while they spread their decay throughout my soul.

I can't live like this anymore.

I just can't.

Whimpers grow as I begin crying, all the while staring desperately into Dr. Benson's eyes as he watches me crumble into pieces.

Sebastian takes my hand in his as I succumb to resignation, and I grip him back as if he's my life source.

Dr. Benson squeezes my knee and says, "Tell me what you're feeling right now."

"Lost."

"How can I help you?"

Staring into his eyes as tears pour down my face, I surrender. "Fix me."

As soon as the words are out, I fold over and rest my head on his shoulder as he holds me, rubbing my back and assuring, "You aren't broken, Harlow, but I will do everything I can to help you, okay?"

I nod against him, knowing it's an impossible feat.

Chapter Twenty-Two

"**H**OW DO YOU FEEL ABOUT TODAY'S SESSION?" Wadding up the tear-soaked tissue in my hand, I look at Dr. Benson and release a cathartic breath before saying, "Good, actually."

He's satisfied by my response and how well our one-on-one session went. After breaking down in group the other day, I've found myself clinging to the hope that, perhaps, I might be able to dig myself out of this misery. So, when he suggested that we increase my individual therapy sessions, I agreed without any pushback.

I don't want to go on living like this.

Dr. Benson looks down at his watch. "We ran over a bit today. Study hall has already begun," he tells me.

"Great," I complain as we stand. "Whoever thought school during the summer was a good idea should be fired."

He chuckles when he pushes the door open. "It can't be *that* bad."

"Seriously?" Throwing him a cynical look, I shake my head as he walks me to the classroom. "It borders on inhumane treatment."

He laughs. "I always liked school."

"That's because you're a nerd."

"Ouch." He feigns being insulted, pressing his hand to his chest as if my comment truly hurt him before he opens the door and teases, "Have fun learning."

Everyone is already situated and busy working when I walk in and check out a pencil. I then take my seat next to Sebastian. Jeremy sits in Wes's old seat next to Max, who looks annoyed by his presence.

I actually find the unusual way his brain operates to be fascinating.

"Hey," Sebastian whispers as I flip open my workbook. "How did it go?"

"Good," I give him simply and he smiles for a split second before he goes back to whatever it is in his lap that's capturing his attention.

Leaning back, I look at what he's doing under the table. "What is that?" I ask when I see something folded in his hands.

"A turtle."

"A turtle?"

"Yeah, look," he says, showing me the creation made from a page out of his math book. "Jeremy's been teaching me origami."

Looking over at his roommate, I find him working on his own piece. "Is this how you two bond?" I joke.

Sebastian shakes his head while Jeremy keeps his down, saying, "Origami's cool." But before I can respond, he tilts his head to the floor and snaps, "Yes, it is." Max huffs in irritation as he argues with the rats. "It is not dumb."

"Gus came back this morning," Sebastian informs me. "He's been giving him shit all day."

"So, you're into origami? Don't you think that's kind of lame?"

Jeremy shushes Gus as Sebastian scoots his chair in closer to me. "No way. Check it out," he says after making the last fold and holding his creation out to me.

I take it and admire the turtle. Flipping it over, I inspect the intricate work. "How did you even do this?"

He snatches it away. "I thought you said it was lame?"

I quickly take it back. "I meant *you* were lame," I tease, trying to keep my voice down.

"Please," he dismisses as if someone insinuating him being anything less than cool is asinine.

"Do you know how to make anything else?"

He shakes his head. "No, this is all Jeremy's taught me."

"It looks hard."

"It isn't too hard. I can show you if you want." He then tears out another page from the back of his book and lays it on the table between us. I watch as he folds the corner down diagonally and rips off the excess paper to make a square sheet, and when he slides it over to me, he instructs on a hushed voice, "Just fold it in half and then in half again."

Step by step, he guides me along, taking over when I get confused. After what feels like a hundred folds, the paper starts to resemble a turtle, and I smile.

"Lame, huh?"

I nudge him. "Whatever."

He helps me with the last part, tucking the corners of the shell beneath the underbody, and then it's done.

"See, it wasn't too hard."

"That's because you did most of it."

"You guys are going to get in trouble," Max warns.

I look over at Mr. Garrison, whose glasses are about to slip off the tip of his nose while he nods off.

I point to him, and when Max peers over her shoulder, he lets out a honk of snore that jostles him awake. She covers her mouth to muffle her laugh as she turns back around.

"Here," I say, sliding my turtle across the table to her. "Happy birthday."

Today she turns seventeen, and it sucks that she has to spend her birthday in this place.

She smiles. "Thanks."

"I heard they're bringing in cake," Jeremy says. "Chocolate."

As they start whispering back and forth, Sebastian passes me his turtle. "You can have it."

"You know I can't keep this. They'll make me throw it away," I tell him. It goes against the rules because people in here will use the edges to cut themselves.

"Then hide it."

I glance around, making sure no one is watching before slipping it under my shirt and tucking it into the side of my bra under my arm.

Sebastian laughs, and when I have it securely hidden, I swat his arm.

"Lucky turtle," he quips.

"You're gross."

With the rec room decorated in purple and green streamers and music playing from a rickety old stereo, we all stand around the cake table and sing a dreadful version of the "Happy Birthday" song to Max as she stands uncomfortably in front of the large sheet cake with a single lit candle.

Jeremy was right; it is chocolate, and I'm dying to get a taste of something that didn't come out of the cafeteria.

Max closes her eyes and makes a wish before blowing out the flame. Like a bunch of sugar fiends, we wait impatiently for Shanice to cut and serve the cake. As soon as I get my piece, I grab a spoon and head over to the wall to sit on the floor away from all the commotion.

Digging in, I take a bite and close my eyes, savoring the store-bought cake that reminds me of when I was a little girl, celebrating my special day at the ice-skating rink with all my friends.

"Check it out."

My eyes open to Sebastian standing in front of me with a plate in each of his hands.

"How'd you score two pieces?"

"Max gave me hers," he says as he sits next to me. "If you're nice, I'll share."

I roll my eyes and take another bite, remembering him being at the rink for my twelfth birthday. It was only a few years later that we would become mortal enemies.

"Finally," he says and then takes a bite, adding with his mouth full, "real food."

I catch Max watching me from across the room and give her a smile before she ducks her head and turns away.

"I feel bad for her," I mutter before shoving another spoonful of frosting into my mouth.

"Who?"

"Max." When he gives me a perplexed look, I tell him, "I mean, it's her birthday, and they bought her a cake."

"So?"

Dropping my spoon, I look at him straight on when I state the obvious, "She has an eating disorder."

"Oh," he responds, realizing the absurdity.

"Seems cruel."

The two of us fall into a comfortable silence as we eat our cake and watch everyone around us. It's a madhouse of weirdness that you'd have to see to believe, and the noise combined with the dreadful music becomes too much.

"God, I'm so ready to go home," I complain, but Sebastian just shrugs. "What's that all about?"

"I don't know. It could be worse."

"Worse? Take a look around. How could it be worse?"

"You should come to my house for a day." He takes another bite and keeps his eyes down. "I kind of like being here. It's safe."

Things at home must be pretty bad for him to feel this way, and seeing the wave of sadness that just washed over him strikes me hard. I can't peel myself away from looking at him, and when he notices me staring, I give a faint, "Is it really that bad?"

He nods, handing me his plate in avoidance of my question. "You can have the rest."

I take it and set it next to me.

His eyes meet mine again, and there's an unspoken connection, an honesty that can't be defined, and somehow, we just get each other.

"Is it hard?" I ask. "Hiding the truth from all your friends?"

Again, he nods, and I find myself nodding with him because I get it—the need to lie and to pretend you fit in. And then I wonder if he will hide our friendship once we're out of here.

A flit of movement from over his shoulder catches my attention just in time for me to see Max sneak out of the room unescorted.

"Where is she going?" I mumble as I track the room to locate all the staff, only to find that no one has noticed she left. Being right next to the door, I push to my feet but don't straighten to my full height.

"What are you doing?"

"I'll be right back."

Then I duck out and rush down the hall, not entirely sure where she ran off to. When I reach the girls' hall, I hear retching and charge toward our room, making it just in time to see her vomiting into her laundry basket.

"Max, no!"

I go to where she's kneeling on the floor, and when she lifts her head, she has tears streaming down her face. "It's okay," I try to assure her but it comes out frantically, knowing we could get caught in here at any moment.

Darting over to my laundry basket, I pull out one of my dirty sweatshirts and bring it over to her so she can wipe her mouth. She scoots back on her bottom until she's against the wall and then kicks her basket across the room while she buries her head in the shirt and cries.

"It's okay," I keep repeating as I sit next to her and wrap my arms around her shoulders. "You're okay."

She shakes her head as she sobs helplessly. All I can do is hold her. She's made so much progress over the last couple of weeks, and having a setback like this has to be devastating.

"It isn't okay," she blubbers and then drops the sweatshirt away from her face. "I'm so disgusting and ugly."

"What are you talking about? You aren't ugly at all."

"You're just saying that to be nice. It's what everyone does."

"Look at me," I tell her, and then I wait for her to do it before asserting, "You are *not* ugly."

She drops her head away from me as she softly weeps. Silence fills the gaps between us until she murmurs, "He doesn't even notice me."

"Who?"

"Sebastian."

That was not the name I expected to hear.

"Sebastian?"

She nods, wiping another tear. "He likes you."

"He doesn't like me," I tell her. "Not the way you're thinking."

"Yes, he does," she says, turning back to me. "You two are constantly together."

"We've known each other since we were kids, that's all."

"Then why was he holding your hand the other day?"

I sigh, hanging my shoulders because she has it all wrong. "He has a girlfriend. And when we get out of here, I seriously doubt we'll be friends."

"Why?"

"Because I'm a loser."

She shakes her head.

"It's true. Everyone at school picks on me, including Sebastian."

She blinks slowly and casts her focus down to her feet as I consider how this is all going to play out. It hurts to think that everything would go back to the way it had always been. Truth is that I like Sebastian, but only the one in here, not the one at school—that guy is a jerk. But I've found myself relying on him lately, and the friendship we're building in here feels genuine, but is it really? Or am I just so desperate for a connection that I'm misreading things—misreading him?

"I've never held a boy's hand," she confesses under her breath.

"Neither have I. At least not a boy's hand that actually likes me." She lifts her attention to me.

"I've never had a boyfriend," I say, blushing a little before admitting, "I've never even kissed a boy before."

"Really?"

"Like I said, I'm a loser."

"I don't think you're a loser."

Cracking a weak smile, I tell her, "You might be the only one who thinks that."

Another tear slips down her cheek, and she rests her head on my shoulder. As I lean into her, we sit in the dark room that's witness to all of our insecurities. But within the past few minutes, mine have doubled.

"Sebastian isn't worth your energy," I say. "You don't know him like I do—he's a prick."

But is he?

I don't know.

I don't want him to be because he's the closest friend I have in here, and I'm scared to lose that. It worries me to think that these feelings might not be reciprocated on his end, that, in his eyes, I'm still just a freak.

When the light turns on, we jump and then see Shanice standing in the doorway.

"What's going on?"

Max starts crying again, and when Shanice sees the vomit in her laundry basket, she calls for another nurse to come before walking over to where we're sitting and laying a hand on Max's back.

"Are you okay?"

Switching my arms for Shanice's, she whimpers a pitiful, "I'm sorry."

"What's going on?" Marcus says when he steps in.

"Take Harlow back to the party," she tells him, and when I stand, I look down to Max as she cries, and my heart breaks for her.

"You aren't going to punish her, are you?" I ask. "It's her birthday."

"Go back to the party, Harlow."

"Come on," Marcus says before we head to the rec room. "I know you don't need me to reiterate the rules, but—"

"She just needed a friend."

Without another word, he leads me into the rec room, and I spot Sebastian over by the television with most of the others. He and Jeremy are laughing about something, and I can't help but wonder what's inside his head and why he's even wasting his time with me—the worthless.

He looks up and locks eyes with me. A second passes, maybe even two or three before I turn and go back to Marcus.

"Everything okay?"

"You think I can go to the breathing room until it's time for bed?" I ask, needing space from the group.

"Yeah, let's go."

Chapter Twenty-Three

HARLOW

After picking up my breakfast tray, I veer away from my normal table because everyone is laughing at something Sebastian said. After talking to Max last night, I've been thinking too much, and now I'm leery of him. It isn't what I want, but the feeling is there nonetheless.

I end up at an empty table next to the windows and pick at my blueberry muffin while I sink into my mind. As the mist collects on the glass, I wonder if the sky ever grows frustrated. Washington is constantly on the brink of a full-blown storm. The gloom and rain are incessant, yet it rarely ever erupts.

Clouds are tangled in pent-up devastation, much like myself.

I feel too much, but it's trapped inside of me just as the thunder and lightning.

The weather doesn't rage very often . . . neither do I.

"What's going on?" Sebastian asks when he sets his tray next to mine and takes a seat. "Why aren't you sitting with us?"

"It's never bothered you in the past." My defensiveness comes automatically.

"What do you mean?"

"Nothing."

"Have I done something?"

I pluck out a blueberry and slip it into my mouth, avoiding eye contact because this whole situation has me extremely insecure.

"Harlow."

"Why are you even talking to me?" I finally look at him as he stares at me in confusion. "Forget it."

"I don't want to forget it," he says. "What's going on?"

Nervously, I continue to mutilate the defenseless muffin with my fingers.

"You know I'm not going to leave you alone until you talk to me."

Dropping my hand down to my lap with a heavy sigh, I ask, "Are we even friends?"

He appears dumbfounded as he shakes his head. "I thought we were, but if I've misunderstood something . . ." His words dissolve as timidity forms in his expression. "What is this all about?"

Leaning forward, my shoulders sink. "I don't know. I guess I'm just unsure of what to expect when we . . ."

I feel stupid talking to him like this, as if he owes me anything when we leave here. But the truth is, he's become a source of comfort for me—someone I can talk to and be open with, someone from my past who knew me before I fell into the depths of this depression that's taken over my life. In a weird way, he feels like a safety blanket.

"When we what?"

"When we go back to school," I finish. "I mean . . . everyone you hang out with hates me. The whole school—"

"Screw them," he says. "I'm not going to stop being your friend." Shifting in his seat, he faces me. "You're the only real one I have."

"You have a ton."

"But it's all lies. You're the only person I don't have to pretend with, and I don't want to lose that," he says, smoothing the frayed edges of my uncertainty. Placing his casted hand over my wrist, which has finally healed, he asks, "What about you?"

"What do you mean?"

"Where do I stand with you when we get out of here?"

Turning my hand over, my palm meets his, but I don't hold it. It isn't until he tightens his fingers around mine that I tell him, "I don't want to stop being friends either."

We stay locked on each other for a moment before his lips crack a subtle smile.

"What?"

"You still got that turtle in your bra?" he jokes.

Snatching my hand away, I slug him in the arm, and he busts out laughing. "You know I'll lose privileges if I get caught with it, right?"

"You don't use any of the privileges here anyway."

He's right. I never watch television nor go to the workout room. They'd be hard-pressed to find something of importance to take away from me, unlike Max. She's restricted from television for the next few days. It seems like a light punishment, but with her OCD, her not being able to watch her nightly shows wreaks havoc on her need for routine.

After we finish breakfast, Sebastian and I join Jeremy and Max in line to get our meds, but I don't tag along with them for art class afterward because Dr. Amberg has me scheduled for a family therapy session.

"Good luck," Sebastian says when Marcus comes to get me.

My parents are already in Amberg's office when I enter. It's been a couple of weeks since we've had a session all together, but I'm hopeful this one will be better than the last.

"Hi, sweetheart," my father says before giving me a hug that lasts longer than the one I give my mother.

When we take our seats, I'm next to my dad on the couch while my mother sits adjacent in one of the chairs next to Dr. Amberg.

"I know it's been a while since you were able to join us," Dr. Amberg says, addressing my dad. "I wanted to let you know that there has been much progress with Harlow and her participation here." My father smiles at me. "She's been more motivated in group with Dr. Benson and has been very open during her one-on-ones with me."

"That's so good to hear," he responds, taking my hand in his. "I'm really proud of you."

I nod, feeling a sense of pride, but it isn't for anything I've done. It's more focused on the hopes that they might just let me out of here soon.

"With that being said, Harlow, your parents wanted to talk to you about something and felt it best that it be done in this setting because your progress is what's most important to us."

Unsettling anxiety twists in my gut when I look over to my

mother. She's tense, wringing her hands and keeping her focus on Dr. Amberg. Turning to my father, his head hangs as he looks down at his feet.

"What's going on?"

My dad's palm is hot and damp against mine, and I slip my hand out of his.

Dr. Amberg acknowledges my mother. "Jamie?" he says, encouraging her to talk as he motions in my direction.

She reaches over to the small table next to her chair and pulls a tissue from the box before dabbing her eyes.

"Your father and I . . ." She begins before stalling.

"Dad?" I turn to him with apprehension as my stomach twists.

He finally looks at me with pitiful eyes as he takes my hand again, but mine remains limp as I feel my family ripping at the seams. My gut is telling me that their marriage is over, but I don't want to believe it, and neither one of them are saying anything, which is only making this worse.

"Just tell me."

He grips my hand a little tighter before crushing me. "Your mother and I have decided to get a divorce."

A dagger spears through the center of my world, inflicting more than just pain, but a torrential avalanche of anger. My body burns with it, and the sounds of my mother weeping only dumps more gasoline onto the flames as I turn to her.

"I hate you," I seethe. "This is all your fault."

"I'm so sorry."

"Harlow, please. This was both of us."

I snap my head at my dad when he says this and rip my hand away. "Are you kidding me?"

"Marriage can be really tough."

"Especially when you have a wife who's screwing around on you."

"Harlow!" he scolds.

"If we could all just take a moment," Dr. Amberg interjects. "This is never an easy thing, and it is completely understandable that you're upset, Harlow."

Crossing my arms over my chest, I sit back with a jaw locked so tightly that my teeth just might crack as I breathe heavily in and out of my nose.

Dr. Amberg continues talking to me, yet every word is drowned out by my mom's crying. It's all I can hear, but her soulless tears mean nothing to me because this is all her fault, and when I can't stand it any longer, I snap, "Shut up! Just stop crying because it means nothing! No one feels bad for you."

"I'm not asking for you to feel bad for me. I feel enough of it for myself."

"Good."

My dad shifts toward me. "This was my choice, honey."

"A choice you made because of what she did," I tell him. "Why are trying to defend her? She cheated on you."

"I'm not defending her, but she is still your mother, and we are still a family."

"Yeah right." Pressing my lips together, I stare down at the floor.

"I never meant for any of this to happen."

"Stop talking, Mom."

My throat thickens with sadness, and it's taking everything in me to keep my tears back. I'm mad—I don't want to cry on top of that, but my heart is breaking. Like, literally, breaking into razor-sharp pieces that slice me open as they crack off.

"Your mother and I love you very much."

I shake my head, not because I don't believe in his love but because I don't believe in hers.

"And we are always going to be here for you. Nothing changes."

"Everything changes." I'm forced to grasp on to courage just to look at him, and when I do, I see his tears, which actually mean something to me. "Are you moving out?"

Slowly, he nods. "Eventually, yes."

Another shard snaps off, and my voice exposes my agony when I whimper, "I want to come with you."

My father hangs his head. "I wish you could."

Tears flood my eyes before spilling over and he gathers me in his arms. "This isn't fair."

"I know."

"Just for one year until I graduate," I beg while clinging my arms around him. He squeezes me, and I cry harder, "Please, Dad."

"I'm not home enough to take care of you."

"I'm almost eighteen; I can take care of myself."

He doesn't respond, no one does as my father continues to hold me. I want to do so much more than cry, though. I want to ball my fists and scream so loudly that it shatters the windows and causes my mother's heart to bleed worse than mine is.

I want to be thunder and lightning, but more than that, I want to be free. Free from this place, free from my mother, free from everything. I want the clouds to part so I can feel what it's like to run through the heat of the sun, to fly without anyone throwing stones at me.

Can't I just breathe? For once, just for a moment, actually breathe?

When I begin to quiet, and my father loosens his arms from around me, Dr. Amberg hands me a tissue, explaining, "Because of your father's travel schedule, your parents feel it's best that you stay with your mother as you continue moving forward in your treatment."

"Harlow?" Her voice is weak, but I don't care.

I don't even acknowledge her when I ask my father, "What about Tyler? Does he know?"

"Yes, we told him."

"When?"

"Before he flew back to North Carolina."

My mouth gapes. "So, you knew when you were here for family day and you lied to me."

"We wanted to wait for the right time. And with . . ." He drops his eyes to my wrist, and I hate that he does. "We wanted you to focus on getting better instead of worrying about us."

"I'm not some broken doll," I defend, even though I know it's a lie.

"No one said that you were."

"Then why do you treat me like I am?"

Letting go of a deep breath, his shoulders slacken. "This is tough, and we're trying to make the best decisions, but there's no instruction manual for how to handle all this." He takes my face in his hands and looks me in the eyes. "You are my daughter, and I love you. God, I love you so much. Just because things didn't work out with your mother, nothing will ever come between you and me, do you hear me?"

I nod, but I can't do this. I swear, the emotions piling onto my shoulders have me teetering on a cliff's edge.

Turning my head out of his hold, I look over to Dr. Amberg with a defeated, "I don't want to do this anymore."

As soon as he nods, I walk over to the door and wait as he calls for someone to come get me. My skin grows itchy, and I can't stand still. I need space.

"Harlow, I'm so sorry," my mother says, but I don't want to hear it.

Ducking my head, I shift my feet as I wait impatiently. An eternity passes before Marcus opens the door and takes me out of the room.

"Everything okay?"

No. Everything is all wrong.

I nod, but it's a little too frantic, and he sees it—the anxiety rattling me.

"Do you need a breather?"

I nod again, and he takes me to one of the small therapy rooms. As I pace the floor, my breathing grows shallow and frantic. No matter how many steps I take, it doesn't stop the utter devastation from boiling beneath my fragile surface.

My hands turn cold and jittery as Marcus calls for someone to come, and when I hear Sebastian's voice, I turn to see him step into the room right before Marcus closes the door, leaving Sebastian and me alone.

Our eyes lock, he walks straight over to me, and the moment he has me in his arms, I cry.

Thunder and lightning—I cry.

Chapter Twenty-Four

HARLOW

"Y ou have to do it like this," Max snaps while she sorts the puzzle pieces by color. Her fingers skitter anxiously through the pile as she organizes them meticulously into piles.

Sitting back, I let her do her thing because testing her OCD is something I refuse to do. I did it once and she turned into a rabid beast. So while Max continues to sort, my eyes drift around the room as I watch the other groups.

Coping skills class has been replaced with this stupid activity: learning to work and problem solve with our peers. Instead of giving us something that relates to the real world, they gave us puzzles. I mean, puzzles? Really? What teenager is sitting around doing puzzles? Old people in nursing homes do this crap because their lives have wasted away and they have nothing better to do than to spend hours putting together tiny pieces of cardboard only to break them apart and shove them back into the box.

It's a pointless activity.

"Max, are you letting Harlow help you?" Shanice asks as she strolls past our table. Max twitches a few times, not liking the idea. "Maybe let her sort some as well."

To appease Shanice, I pick up a piece before she walks away.

"What pile do you put the ones with multiple colors in?"

She plucks it out of my fingers and huffs. "In the multiple color pile," she says as if I'm an idiot.

"Why the hell is everyone doing puzzles?" Sebastian asks when he joins us at our table.

"Cooperative learning, I guess."

"Cool." He scoops up a bunch of pieces, and Max loses it, swatting his hand and sending the pieces to the floor. "Dude, chill."

"Max, count to ten," Shanice says when she walks back over.

After Sebastian gathers the pieces and Max is able to calm down, we sit back while Max returns to the puzzle.

"So, how was your session with Dr. Amberg?" I ask.

It should be an easy response, but he hesitates as caution softens his eyes.

"What happened?"

"I'm going home," he says, and my body stills.

Common sense tells me to smile and congratulate him, to be happy that he's getting out of here and going home, but I do none of those things. Instead, I'm sad and jealous. More than anything, I'm consumed by loneliness even though he's still here.

My smile is pathetic and doesn't reach my eyes when I nod. "When do you leave?"

"In three days."

Reaching under the table, he rests his hand on my knee. "You're going to be fine. Just keep working hard and you'll be out of here soon."

"What are you two whispering about?" Max questions.

"I don't know if I want to tell you. Are you going to hit me again?"

She cocks her head. "I barely tapped your hand."

"He's going home on Monday."

Her face lights up the way mine should have. "Wow, you're so lucky."

"Thanks," he mutters before turning to me and lowering his voice again. "You okay?"

So many people have come and gone since I've been here that I don't bother getting to know them or being their friend because, what's the point? Friendships made here only live within these walls. And although Sebastian has assured me that ours will survive beyond this place, I still have my doubts.

He squeezes my knee, and I tell him, "I don't want to be here alone."

"If I could take you with me, I would."

From the corner of my eye, I see Max watching us, puzzle forgotten.

"I want you to call me as soon as you get out," he says.

"I don't even have your number."

"I'll write it down for you and you can hide it in your bra next to the turtle."

On a breath of a laugh, I shake my head. "You think I've kept that turtle in my bra this whole time?"

"You haven't?"

I shake my head.

"Well, where are you hiding it then?"

"Inside the cushion on the couch by the games in the rec room."

"Inside of it?"

"In the back of the far-left cushion, there's a small rip."

He chuckles at how ludicrous it is, and I do too. I swear this place is more locked down than jail.

"I'll try to get a pencil today and write my cell number down."

I nod, and when I turn back to Max, she already has all the edge pieces connected.

"Can I get a pile to work on?"

She hands over one of the sorting trays without looking up at me. I know my friendship with Sebastian makes her uncomfortable, and I feel bad about that, but I won't ignore him.

"So, what are you going to do for the rest of the summer?" Max asks him while keeping her head down.

"Heck if I know. I have to figure out what I'm going to tell people when they ask where I've been for the past month."

As I secure a piece in place, I murmur, "Too bad you can't tell them you were pregnant." When I peek over at him and see the frown on his face, I smirk to let him know I was kidding.

"Why would he tell people he was pregnant? That makes no sense."

"Don't worry about it," I dismiss and then ask her, "Have you thought about what you're going to tell people when you go back home?"

Max sets down the tray of blue pieces and starts working on the green ones. "I doubt anyone has even noticed I'm gone."

"Why?"

She lifts her eyes to Sebastian. "Because I don't have any friends."

And now he's the one who's uncomfortable.

"Harlow," Greg calls from the doorway, "you have a phone call."

"Your brother?" Sebastian asks.

"Probably."

They normally don't allow us to take calls whenever, but I've been trying to get ahold of Tyler since my parents told me about the divorce, and the staff agreed to let me talk to him when he called me back.

Greg leads me to the desk and then hands me the phone.

"Hello?"

"Hey, Low." Hearing my brother's voice is a comfort. "How's it going?"

"Still locked up."

"How much longer until you get to go home?"

"Hopefully not too much longer." I situate myself in one of the chairs against the wall. "So, Mom and Dad told me they're splitting up."

"They did?" His voice pitches in surprise.

"How come you didn't tell me?"

"They told me not to."

"Since when do you listen to them?"

He avoids my question by asking, "When did you find out?"

"Earlier this week."

He sighs heavily. "It sucks. I know Dad travels a lot, but I didn't think they were having any real problems."

"What did they tell you?"

"Nothing too much," he says. "Just that they'd grown apart."

"That's what they said?"

"Yeah, why? What did they say to you?"

Switching the phone to my other ear, I tell him the truth. "Mom's been having an affair."

"What?"

"The day before she sent me here, I caught her kissing some guy."

He goes quiet, and we sit in silence as he digests what I just told him. "Why would she lie to me if you already knew?"

"Why does she do half the crap she does?"

"That's so messed up," he mumbles. "I can't believe she did that to Dad."

"She did it to all of us, Tyler, not just him."

Another long pause stretches before he asks, "Who's the guy?"

"I don't know, but I wonder if she's still seeing him."

"You want me to ask?"

"Does it even matter?"

Honestly, I'm so over it all. I only have one year left until I graduate, and then I'm out of here. It's bad enough that I still have to live with her, but the last thing I want is to be a part of her drama. The less I know, the better.

Growing annoyed from just talking about it, I shift the subject, telling him, "I miss you."

"Yeah, I miss you too, Sis."

"Did you get all moved in?"

"Uh-huh. The house is cool. We threw our first party last weekend," he says before continuing on about some mishap with the keg or something.

It's almost otherworldly to hear him talk about his life at college, and I can't help but wonder if I'll be lucky enough to have the same experiences. There's really no need to wonder, though. I know that I won't, and that sinks my mood as I listen to him until he cuts the call. "Hey, it was good talking to you, but I have to run."

We say our goodbyes, and he promises to keep in touch better than he has been before I hand the phone back, but there's no one at the desk.

"You done?" Greg asks as he comes over to me, and when I hand him the receiver, he leans over the desk and hangs it up.

He walks me back to the group, which is now in an uproar. The staff is yelling at everyone to calm down, and Greg pulls me away from the door as Kevin and another kid, Derek, are escorted out.

Peeking in at the aftermath of the commotion, I find several chairs knocked over and puzzle pieces scattered on the floor.

"What did I miss?" I ask when I'm finally let into the room once everyone is settled down.

"Just another fight," someone tells me as I walk over to Sebastian and Max.

Tears coat her cheeks as they scoop puzzle pieces onto trays. They don't notice me until I crouch down and start to help them out.

"What happened?"

"Derek and Kevin got into a fight," Sebastian says before standing and dumping a bunch of the pieces onto the table.

"Why?"

"Who knows?" he says, and when Max sits down in her chair, he takes a seat next to her, asking, "You good?"

She nods and starts her sorting all over again.

"How did your call go?"

"He didn't have a clue my mom cheated."

Max looks up. "They didn't tell him?"

I shake my head.

"What did he say?" Sebastian asks, drawing my attention back to him.

"I mean, what could he say?"

He lets out a slow breath. "That whole situation is messed up."

"I'm dreading having to spend the next year with her."

"I feel you. I'm happy to be getting released, but home is the last place I want to go."

"Is that guy still living with your mom?"

He nods, and his leg starts to bounce anxiously up and down.

"Can't you avoid him?"

"No. Kurt gets off on making my life hell."

"I can't believe your mom doesn't say anything."

He doesn't respond, so I drop it. Here I am whining about my parents getting divorced when one of his is dead and the other . . . I don't even have any words for his mom.

"Clean up and then groups," Shanice announces.

Max is agitated and refuses to break the pieces apart after starting to fit them back together again.

"I'll get it put away," I tell her.

After she leaves, Sebastian stays behind to help me put everything up.

"I'll catch you later," he says before going off to his substance group while I head to social skills group.

For the next hour, I do the bare minimum to get by while my thoughts are still with Sebastian. I'm worried that, when he goes home, he's going to go right back to drinking. I think about the few times I saw him drunk and how mean he was.

I can't really blame him for wanting to drink; it's how he copes, not that it's right, but it is what it is.

I want to ask him about it, but it's too invasive. It would be the same as him asking if I'm going to hurt myself again or if Max is going to make herself throw up again. We're all aware that these are the things we do and are very careful to tread lightly around the topics.

Sebastian drinking again would upset me, but I have no right to tell him not to.

With so many questions surrounding what our friendship is going to look like on the outside, it makes me uneasy. In a very strange way, I kind of wish we could stay here forever so that nothing has to change.

When group is over, Max and I head into the cafeteria to grab our afternoon snacks before taking them into the rec room. The kids from substance run late, but soon enough, Sebastian makes his way over to me.

"How did you score cookies?" I ask, eyeing the package in his hand.

"They were sitting out."

"They weren't when I was in there."

He flops down next to me on the couch as I dig into my bag of greasy potato chips.

"Can I have one?"

He looks at me as if I'm crazy to even ask. "Dude, they're chocolate chip."

"So?"

"So, they're my favorite."

"Rude." I sneer as I pop a chip into my mouth.

"Is this where the hole is?" he asks, and when I nod, he wedges his hand down behind the cushion. "Where?"

"On the left corner."

When his lips turn up in a grin, I know he's found it. "There it is," he murmurs before pulling his hand out and opening his package of cookies.

I look across the room where Max is sitting alone and nibbling an apple. "I think she misses Wes."

"Who?"

"Max."

"He was kind of cool," he mutters before taking a bite.

After I finish my snack, I get up and toss my bag in the garbage, and when I return, Jeremy comes walking over to us. I watch as he leans down to whisper something into Sebastian's ear. They fist bump, and after he walks away, Sebastian smiles at me.

"What was that all about?"

"He put my number on your call list."

"What?"

With a devious smirk, he nods. "I wanted to make sure we could still talk after I leave. So, if you want to call me, tell them to dial your cousin, Ryan."

My mouth drops open, and I would give him the biggest hug ever if I thought I could get away with it.

"How did Jeremy do that?"

"No one really pays attention to him pacing around all over the place. I figured he'd be the perfect one to sneak behind the desk."

I smile at him, a real, genuine smile that causes his to grow too. It's the kindest thing he could've ever done for me, and the fact that he did it all on his own soothes my worry about him still being around for me when we're both out of here.

"Thank you."

"I'm going to miss you."

My smile fades as the sense of loneliness begins to settle over me like a led blanket. "I'm going to miss you too."

Chapter Twenty-Five

SEBASTIAN

FREEDOM GRANTS NO FREEDOM AT ALL.

At least not in my world.

Last Monday I got discharged from the Hopewell Recovery Center. I had a pit in my stomach the whole day as I waited for my mother to come pick me up. A part of me hoped she wouldn't, but, eventually, she did. Harlow cried when she hugged me goodbye, and hell if it didn't make me consider doing something stupid just to extend my stay. But I'm confident that it won't be long until she's out of there too.

Still, it hurt to leave her behind.

My mother seemed happy to see me when she picked me up, but as we drove home, her mood slowly soured. Kurt's car was parked out front, and when I stepped inside, I was greeted with a drunken, "Welcome back, you little fuck-up."

I would've left right then, but my license is suspended, and I need to stay on the straight and narrow until my next court date. The hope is to show the judge that I've gone through treatment and am taking my recovery seriously so that I won't have to do a stint in juvie.

This week has been rough. It was one thing to be sober when I was locked up, but to stay dry when I live with two alcoholics is a whole new battle, and I'm not convinced it's worth it.

"Dude, if you aren't going to talk to her, just turn your phone off," Brent complains when my cell chimes, yet again, while we play video games. "Shit's annoying."

"It's your fault. I told you not to tell her I was back, but then you go and gab it to Emily like a little bitch."

"I told her not to tell Kassi."

"That's weak, man. You knew she would be the first person Emily would tell."

"I don't know why you coming back to town is such a secret." He pops a round of bullets into my avatar and kills me, jumping up and throwing his fist into the air when he does. "Hell, yeah!"

I shake my head before he flops back into his chair as we start another round.

As soon as I got my cell phone back, I called Brent to come pick me up. I didn't want to risk him seeing the monstrosity inside, but I had to get out of there, so I just waited for him at the end of our long, wooded drive. I've spent every day with him this week, but have managed to avoid Emily. The fact that I've been ghosting her best friend all week is surely going to get me an ass-beating.

"Seriously, though," he continues, "what gives with you and Kassi?"

"Just not into her anymore."

"You ever going to tell her or do you get a kick out of having a chick blow up your phone non-stop?"

I shrug as I reload and duck out of the enemy's way before another text alert dings my phone. Any sane person would turn it off, but I never know when Harlow is going to call and I don't want to miss it when she does.

"You know you're going to see her tomorrow at school. There's no way you can avoid it," he says, and he's right.

Everyone has to go up for prep day to get their class schedules, parking tags, and everything else. We will most likely run into each other, so I should just call and end things, but damn, I'm not up for dealing with her reaction. As much crap as she put up with from me, I'm shocked she hasn't been the one to end things.

"You picking me up tomorrow?"

"I'm supposed to be going with Emily."

I tap the button on my controller that makes my avatar pull the pin before he tosses the grenade. It lands right in front of Brent's avatar and blows it into mangled pieces.

"Dude!" He's pissed, and I laugh to myself before he asks, "How long am I going to have to carpool your ass around town?"

"I have a court date in two weeks and then I'll know for sure."

"You think you'll go to juvie?"

"I hope not." My phone starts ringing, and when I check the screen, it reads: Hopewell Recovery. "I gotta take this," I tell him as I get up and head out of the room. "Hey," I answer, closing the door behind me when I step into the hall.

"Hi," she says, but I can barely hear her with all the commotion on her end.

"What the hell is going on?"

"Jeremy is freaking out."

"Why?"

"After you left, they discovered he'd been cheeking his pills and giving them to Kevin."

"I thought he hated Kevin."

"He does. Kevin bullied him into it, so Jeremy hasn't been taking his meds, and his delusions are off-the-rails bad right now."

Jeremy creeped me out when I first met him, but being his roommate was a trip, and I actually wound up liking the guy. "That sucks."

"Yeah, I feel bad for him," she says as things quiet down enough for me to hear her.

"So, how are you?"

"Ehh. I have a session with Dr. Benson and my parents later today."

Leaning against the wall, I release a deep breath as I think about how upset she tends to get after family sessions. She almost always has to go to one of the small rooms with a nurse to calm down, and it sucks to think that the only real support she has left in there is Max.

"You want to call me afterward?"

"I feel like I call you too much as it is."

"You can call me as much as you want, you know that, right?"

There's a long pause on her end, and when I'm just about to say something to break the silence, she gives a somber, "I miss you."

My chest thumps, and I drop my head. "I miss you too."

"At least you can go and do things."

"I can't do shit. No license, remember? So, I need you to get out soon because Brent is over having to drive me around everywhere." Again, she goes quiet. Even though she's never said it outright, I know it annoys her that the person she despises the most is one of my best friends. I don't blame her. We made her life hell. "It's my birthday today," I tell her, shifting her focus.

"What? Why didn't you say anything?"

"I just did."

She huffs. "You know what I mean."

"It's no big deal."

"Um, you're eighteen; it's a huge deal," she tells me before giving me a sincere, "Happy birthday."

I smile, but it doesn't last long. Not that I don't appreciate her saying it, I do, but it's knowing that no one else will that has me bummed.

"Thanks."

"What else is going on?"

"Not much. Prep day is tomorrow."

"I wish they'd let you get my schedule and parking tag. As if people don't have enough to tease me about, I'll be the only one whose mother is there."

Growing up in this town, we pretty much know everyone's parents, so there's no way people aren't going to notice. "She can't go another time?"

"Nope."

"It'll be fine," I try to assure her. "I wouldn't worry about it."

"I just hope I'm out before school starts."

I still feel horrible for helping spread the rumor about her being pregnant when she missed half of her junior year. "I won't let people talk shit if you aren't."

"People talk no matter what, you know that," she says, and it's the truth. "Anyway, how are things at home?"

"Mom and Kurt were still sleeping when I left this morning, so I didn't have to deal with anything."

"Do you think your mom would be as bad as she is if Kurt left?"

"At this point, yeah. She's in it pretty deep," I tell her. "As much as I hate the guy, I'm scared to think of what would happen to her if they broke up."

"What do you mean?"

"I feel like she needs a constant babysitter, and even though he's always blasted, at least she isn't alone in case she drinks too much and gets alcohol poisoning or whatever."

"You think he'd call for help?"

"God, I would hope so."

"That's scary to think about," she responds softly, and it is.

I hate thinking about what could happen to her, to possibly lose her. It terrifies me because she's all I have.

"Oh, guess what," she says before continuing, "I finally made a turtle on my own without Jeremy's help."

"Yeah?"

"It's a little janky, but it's decent."

"Dude, are you going to leave me hanging all damn day?" Brent gripes when he busts out into the hall.

"Chill, man. Just give me a second."

He walks past me and heads downstairs.

"I should probably go," I tell her. "Call me later, okay?"

"All right. Bye."

"Bye."

After heading into the kitchen, I find Brent rummaging through the fridge. "Toss me a soda."

He launches a can over his shoulder, and when I catch it, he turns with a cocky smirk, asking, "Now I know why you're over Kassi."

"What are you talking about?"

"Cause you're under some new chick."

"Not even close."

"She's going to be pissed." He pops the tab on his can and takes a swig. "You know this is going to make my life hell, right? Emily is going to *hate* you."

"So? How does that make your life hell?"

"Because you and I are friends."

I shake my head and take a gulp. "Well, there's no new girl, so you don't have to worry."

～

"You're seriously being a jerk," Emily says from the front seat as Brent drives up to the school. "First you leave for the summer and don't bother telling anyone, and now you won't even call or text Kassi. Why are you being such a douche?"

"God, you act like I'm married to the girl. So, my mom sent me away after I got arrested, who cares? I didn't know I had to check in with everyone."

She huffs and faces forward while Brent remains way too quiet. It's for his own good to stay out of Emily's line of fire.

"Unbelievable," she garbles under her breath, and I wish she would just lay off.

When we pull into the parking lot, Emily is out of the car before Brent can kill the engine.

"Like I said," he exhausts when he turns around and looks at me, "this shit is making my life hell."

I shrug.

"You really have to break up with Kassi?"

"Seriously? You want me to keep going out with her because you're scared of your girlfriend?"

He holds up his hands in defense. "Whoa. I never said I was scared of her."

I laugh and get out of the car.

"Emily's right, you know?" he says as we walk toward the school that's already crowded with tons of students. "You totally bailed on all of us this summer."

"It wasn't personal."

To them, I've been MIA and was an asshole for never calling. I get it, but at the same time, I'm not about to admit that I've been living in a mental facility. Life is hard enough without having to lose my reputation. It's the one thing that grants me normalcy in my screwed-up life.

When we push through the doors and walk into the school, everything feels different.

"Yo, Sebastian," a buddy of mine hollers, and I acknowledge him with a flick of my head before I clap hands with Justin, who plays lacrosse with me.

I'm casual with my grin as I make my way through the crowd of people, saying hi to all my friends like a total fraud.

"Dude, where have you been? You missed out on some major parties," another one says before grabbing my hand and pulling me in for a bro hug.

"Busy, man."

"You've got some making up to do."

After chatting with a few guys on the team, I find myself standing in a long line to pick up my senior schedule. Why they can't email these out, I have no clue. It would be so much easier than herding us all back here when summer isn't over yet just to waste a day standing in lines. Not that I should be complaining. It isn't as if I have anything better to do.

"Welcome back, Mr. West," Mrs. Alvarez greets when I step up to the table.

"Hey," I mutter as she flips through the stack of student cards.

"Here we go."

She hands over my schedule, and I scan through my classes as I walk away, cringing when I see I have Mrs. Fritz for Government. That woman is known to be a crusty old shrew.

"Did you get your schedule?" Brent hollers across the crowded hallway.

Squeezing through a couple of girls, I hold out my card to him, and he swipes it out of my hand. "Mrs. Fritz, dude." He starts laughing. "That sucks."

"Tell me about it."

I glance over his shoulder, and my gut twists when I see Kassi talking to Emily, who points in my direction. Kassi's eyes meet mine, and I can't tell if she's sad or pissed or a mixture of both.

"Shit," I groan under my breath, and when Brent turns and sees them, he pats my back.

"Just get it over with."

I nod, snatch my card back, and start walking. Emily, with her hands perched on her hips, shoots me a bitchy glare before whispering something into Kassi's ear and stalking off.

Girls, man.

"What's up?"

"*What's up?*" Kassi sneers. "That's all you have to say after ditching me? What the hell?"

She's loud, drawing attention to us, and it's annoying.

"Can we go outside and talk?"

Crossing her arms over her chest, she turns on her heel and heads toward the exit. I follow, and when we get outside, she stops, keeping her back to me. A few seconds pass before I step in front of her. She looks at me with tears in her eyes, making me feel like a shit person for treating her so badly. There's no winning in this situation, and I hate that I have to hurt her when she's done nothing wrong aside from falling for me.

I should come with a warning sign.

"Hey." My voice is gentle, but I refrain from touching her.

"Where have you been?"

"After I got arrested, my mom sent me to stay with my aunt for a while in San Diego."

"And what? You couldn't call to tell me?" Her eyes narrow, forcing a tear down her cheek.

"She took my phone."

Before I can dodge her, she reaches behind me, shoves her hands down my back pockets, and pulls out my cell.

"She gave it back when I came home," I tell her before grabbing it. The last thing I need is for her to snoop and find countless incoming calls from Hopewell Recovery.

"So, why haven't you been answering my calls or texts?"

"Because I didn't know what to say to you," I respond honestly, pushing my phone back into my pocket. I wait for her to say something, but she doesn't, giving me no choice but to continue. "Look, I don't think we—"

"You're breaking up with me, aren't you?"

Like a coward, I nod and watch as her face crumples and more tears fall.

"What did I do?"

"Nothing," I stress.

"Then why?"

The fact that she isn't throwing swings at me is shocking.

"Because I can tell you aren't feeling it anymore," I respond and instantly kick myself for putting this crap on her, so I add, "And I'm not feeling it either."

"I thought we loved each other."

"Kassi . . ." I reach for her arm, but she steps away. "I'm not trying to be a dick."

"Yeah, I know," she lashes. "You don't have to try, you just are one."

"Kass, come on," I call out as she storms off, but all I get is her middle finger from over her shoulder before she slams her hands against the door and walks back inside.

Not a minute later, Brent comes out with a snide look on his face. "Damn, that chick is *pissed*. What did you say to her?"

"Nothing, man. Only that I didn't think we should see each other anymore."

"Come on," he says. "I gotta take you home."

"I thought we were chilling at your place."

"Emily threatened to cut my balls off if I hung out with you tonight."

"Man, these girls are tripping," I complain as we walk to his car. I'm more irritated that I'll be stuck at home all night than I am about Brent taking Emily's side.

When Brent slows down before pulling into my drive, I stop him.

"You can let me out here."

"Cool," he says. "I'll give you a call tomorrow."

"Later."

When I walk in, I'm hit with the stench of weed. All the shades are drawn and the television blares from the living room. I aim straight for the stairs, but stop when I see a handful of people I've never seen before hanging out on the couches.

"Want some?" one of the guys asks me, holding up a joint, which garners Kurt's attention.

"Nah, he's a fucking loser," he says and when I look over at my mother, she's laughing.

I should pull myself away and go to my room, but I can't.

I'm stuck, missing the comfort of being locked up. At least there, nobody stomped on my heart like these two do. How can I even call this woman my mother as she snickers at me as if I'm a fucking joke instead of her son?

I hate this place, and I hate her.

"Oh, are you sad?" Kurt says in a pitiful puppy voice before he busts out laughing. "Look," he says to anyone who will listen, "I think he's gonna cry."

"Fuck off." I break myself away and go upstairs, passing an old family portrait that hangs on the wall. I can't look at it, at us, at my father, at what used to be. To remember hurts too much, so I'd rather forget.

A current of heat begins streaming through my body and when I shut myself in my room, anger begins to boil. Somehow, I've managed to keep myself together for this past week since being home, but for what?

Why?

Is it even worth it?

A voice inside whispers to my remedy, and I can't think of a single reason not to give in. Swallowing thickly, I punch my cast into the wall when tears swell. Emotions strangle me, reminding me of all my pain and how I'm too weak to manage it.

Pathetic heartbreak slips down a cheek, and I'm shoving clothes into a backpack so fast, tossing in a few more items before grabbing an armful of blankets.

I clamor down the stairs angrily, go over to the foyer, and grab my car keys that are sitting on a small table.

To hell with my suspended license.

No one even notices me above the loud television as I make my way out to the garage where my car is. After tossing everything inside, I head into the kitchen and grab a couple of bottles from the liquor cabinet because I have nothing left to lose.

It's all been taken from me already.

As soon as the garage is open, I hammer down on the gas, and speed off.

Chapter Twenty-Six

HARLOW

"School starts in less than two weeks, correct?" Dr. Amberg asks as he scribbles something in my file.

"Yeah, why?"

Lifting his head, he pushes his glasses up the bridge of his nose and crosses his leg over the other. "I'd like to see you at school on the first day this year."

A glimmer of hope illuminates within me. I didn't get this opportunity junior year, which only fed peoples' curiosity and led them to the conclusion that I'm a teen mom.

High school is so dumb.

"So, what are you saying?" my mother asks.

Dr. Amberg smiles. "I think it's time for you to go home, Harlow."

"Are you serious?"

"You've been making great strides over the past month, and after visiting with Dr. Benson and some of the nurses, I feel it's time for you to get yourself back out there."

A sigh of relief falls out of me, and my mother takes my hand in hers. When I look at her, she's smiling softly, and I return my own before addressing Dr. Amberg. "When can I go?"

"I'll have you set up for discharge on Friday." He pencils a note in my chart and closes the file. "How does that sound to you?"

"It sounds great."

"What will her treatment look like moving forward?" my mom asks.

"Same as last time. Outpatient sessions with me at my private office once a week." He then turns to me. "Since we adjusted your meds again a few days ago, I want to touch base with you over the course of the next couple of weeks, but if you start experiencing any side effects, you need to call, understood?"

"Yeah, okay."

"A new school year can be triggering to some, so during the time you have left with us, I'm going to schedule you for some extra one-on-ones to get a plan in place as you transition."

I nod, antsy with anticipation. I've spent my entire summer locked away, and I want nothing more than to eat real food, sleep in my own bed, and spend time at my favorite spot on the Sound. In addition to all that, I'm excited to see Sebastian. I never thought in a million years I'd feel this way, but I do. The best thing that came out of this whole tragedy of a summer was our friendship.

He's been gone for a week, and even though I talk to him every day, it isn't the same—it'll never be the same as it was while we were in this place together. No one could ever imagine what life is like here as a patient, but we do.

We lived it every day.

Now I'm ready to leave it behind.

"I can't wait to have you back home," my mother says. "It's been lonely without you."

I could say something snarky, but I won't. It isn't worth it, so instead, I ask, "Were you able to get my schedule yesterday?"

"I did. I didn't even think to bring it, but I got your parking tag and a new spirit shirt as well."

"Mom, nobody wears those. They're lame."

"Well, maybe you could wear it to sleep in." She grins, and I know she's trying, I just wish she would do it in a different way. Which way? I have no clue.

"Are there any questions you might have, Jamie?"

My mother shakes her head.

"If you think of any, feel free to call me. But we've done this once before, so we'll just stay on course," he says. "I think Harlow's going to do great." His attention shifts to me. "I'm really proud of you."

"Thanks."

He schedules my mother to return in three days for our exit

session, and when Marcus comes to get me, my mother stands and gives me a hug.

"I love you so much."

"I love you too, Mom." I walk out to leave, but stop short of the door and turn back. "Oh, could you get ahold of Dad and see if he can call me?" He left for another work trip last night, and I can't make international calls from here.

"I'll call him today."

"Thanks."

"Must've been a good session," Marcus says as he leads me back to the group. "You're never this happy after family sessions."

"What makes you think I'm happy?"

Slowing his pace, we nearly come to a stop when he squints and leans in close to me. "Right there." He points to the corner of my mouth. "A speck of a grin. You can hardly see it, but it's there."

I roll my eyes, and we start walking again. "So, because I have a speck of a grin, I'm happy?"

"Coming from you, it's probably more like ecstatic," he jokes.

"I'm not always a grump, you know?"

He chuckles, saying, "I know. I'm just giving you a hard time."

Marcus is my favorite person on staff here, and I don't know how I would've survived some days if he weren't here to help make them more tolerable.

"I get to go home," I tell him.

"Free at last," he responds theatrically, smiling big as I nudge him with my elbow. "This place isn't going to be the same without you."

"Please, there're far more entertaining people here than me."

When we reach the door that leads outside to where everyone is doing yoga, he says, "True, but you're special. I hope you know that."

I know better than to believe him because I'm far from special. They probably train the staff to say crap like that to build us up, but I go ahead and give him a meek, "Thank you," before going outside.

I make my way over to the group just as Jeremy tips over, unable to hold his tree position. I jump out of the way to avoid him taking me down too.

"You okay, Jeremy?"

Some new kid shushes me, and I shoot him a scowl before reaching down to help Jeremy to his feet.

"Thanks," he whispers before I step over to where Max is balancing on one leg with her hands pressed together.

I hate yoga, but we're forced to do it every week. It's a less than calming exercise for those of us who are coordinately challenged.

Kicking off my shoes, I stand next to her as the instructor leads us into the downward dog position.

It's one I can actually do successfully.

"How was your session?" Max asks on a hushed voice.

"For once, it went well." I look over at her from under my arm. "I get to go home at the end of the week."

"You're leaving?"

I nod, expecting her to be as happy as she is for everyone else when they get released, but her eyes slip from mine and her lips tug into a frown.

"Max?"

"I'm happy for you." Her tone is sullen and far from happy.

"What's wrong?"

When we swoop into the upward facing dog pose, she stays quiet, avoiding my question.

I drop down to my knees and tap her arm. "Hey, I thought you'd be happy."

"I am."

"You're not."

Lowering to her knees as well, she sags her shoulders.

"Talk to me, Max."

"I don't want you to go."

"You'll be out of here soon enough." My words are meant to be encouraging, but they fail.

"You're the only friend I have left in here." Her eyes finally lift to mine. "We aren't going to talk when you leave, are we?"

"Max . . ."

"It's cool," she resigns as she hangs her head.

I could lie and get her hopes up that we'll hang out and go to the movies together, but I don't want to fill her head with false hope, so I gently lead her to the truth. "I live in Edmonds and you live in Everett."

She nods but keeps her head down.

I feel bad, so I toss her a bone. "You're on social media, right?"

"Yeah."

"You can friend request me and we can keep in touch that way."

Her lips pull into a smile as she looks at me, and I already feel guilty because I haven't accessed my online accounts since freshman year. I never get on them because, just like her, I don't have any friends. There are probably fewer than twenty people who follow me, and one of those is my mother. She made it a rule that if I created an account, she would follow me to make sure I didn't post anything inappropriate.

Before we get into trouble for not participating, we go back to our poses and finish out the class. After we get back inside, I find Marcus.

"Hey, can I make a call?"

He eyes me suspiciously, suspecting I'm up to something since I've gone all summer without using the phone to constantly asking to use it.

"Come on."

"All right," he responds wearily, and while everyone goes to grab a snack from the cafeteria, I go to call Sebastian.

"Can you call Ryan?" I ask Greg, who's sitting behind the desk, and after he verifies my fake cousin in the authorized number notebook, he dials and then hands me the phone.

"Thanks." I pull the cord over to my usual spot against the wall and sit in the chair.

"Hey, you," he says groggily when he answers, and I smile like I do every time we get to talk.

"Hey, yourself. Were you sleeping?"

"Uh, no, just . . . just lying low." He sounds *off.* "You never called me back yesterday."

"I tried but everyone wanted to use the phones, and when it was my turn, it was time to go to group."

"That sucks. How did your session go with your mom?"

"It went well," I tell him. "She was even here a little while ago for another one."

"Two days in a row? That's weird."

"It's good news though." I smile. "I'm getting out of here."

"No shit? Are you serious?" There's excitement in his scratchy voice.

"Yeah. Dr. Amberg wants me to start the school year with everyone else."

"When's your last day?"

"Friday," I answer before asking, "Are you feeling okay? You sound tired."

"I didn't get much sleep last night."

"Is everything all right?"

He breathes heavily, stalling for a beat before saying, "It's just my mom."

"What happened?"

"I really don't feel like talking about it."

Something is definitely off, but I don't pry. Shifting the conversation, I ask, "How did yesterday go at school? Did you get your schedule?"

"Yeah. What about you? I didn't see your mom."

"She was there."

"Do you know what classes you have?"

"No, not yet."

"Dude, you'll never believe my luck," he groans. "I got stuck with Mrs. Fritz."

"That blows," I say, trying to mask my laughter. "The gods are clearly against you."

"Tell me about it."

"So, what are you doing today?"

"I have to go to the doctor."

"Why?"

"To get my cast off."

"Maybe you can keep it off this time," I tease.

He chuckles under his breath. "Yeah, maybe . . ." He sighs. "I might go down to the docks. Justin, texted right before you called and a few guys from the team are hanging out there later, so I'll probably meet up with them."

It's weird to hear him talk about his friends that I have nothing to do with. It's as if he's living in a completely different world, and although he and I have a lot in common, there's also so much that we don't.

"That sounds . . . *fun*, I guess."

He laughs. "You suck at faking it, you know that?"

A line begins to form for the phone, and when I get a snide eye from the new kid, I tell Sebastian, "I should probably get going. People are waiting to use the phone."

"I won't make any plans for Friday," he says, putting another smile on my face. "Call me later?"

"Yeah. It's movie night, so the phone should be free."

"Miss you, Low."

"Miss you too."

Chapter Twenty-Seven

HARLOW

ALONE FOR THE FIRST TIME SINCE SUMMER BEGAN, I stand in the doorway of my bedroom. There's no one looking over my shoulder or telling me where to be, and it's a strange feeling, like a bird being released into the wild. I want the freedom, but I'm not sure if I can handle it. Not that I would ever admit that to anyone because to do so would come with consequences.

Everything in my room is organized and clean, unlike how it was left.

I wonder how much my mother snooped through my stuff while I was away. Not that she would find anything, but still, it's an invasion. My whole world has been invaded, and I want it back—my privacy. I want to go to the bathroom without being monitored, change my clothes without having to have someone unlock my closet, or sleep at night without a flashlight being shone in my face every fifteen minutes.

I want to scream into the open space of this world because I'm bitter about the time that was stolen from me. But what's time when it means nothing, when it holds no value?

Still, I resent that it was taken without my consent.

I'm tired of feeling powerless. Staring at my bed, I go back to the first day of summer and see my mother throwing my belongings into the duffle bag that's now slung over my shoulder.

She blindsided me and took away any choice I thought I held and had me locked away.

Two and a half months—gone.

And for what?

It isn't as if I'm cured. The weight of desolation still presses down on me. It's there no matter how many pills I shove down my throat, no matter how many therapy sessions I do, art projects I create, or yoga classes I breathe through—the bleakness remains.

"Harlow, could you bring down your clothes after you unpack so I can throw them into the wash?"

"Yeah," I call down to my mother before stepping fully into my room.

Slipping the bag from my shoulder, I let it fall to the floor as I walk over to my desk. My fingers glide over my laptop before I turn and look out the rain-covered window. I stare off into the gray sky as silence hums in my ears. It's an abrupt contrast to where I just came from. Chaos and noise are constants at Hopewell. It's rare that you ever get a moment of peace, and now that I have it, it makes me anxious.

It's too still.

"Is everything okay?"

My mom steps slowly into my room, and when I push away from the window, I nod.

"I thought you might want this back," she says, holding out my cell phone.

I bet she meddled through it as well.

"Thanks." I take the phone, and we fall into an awkward silence that stirs sadness.

I'm home, and yet, I'm so far away.

Why?

I know it shouldn't be like this, but it is.

It's the one place I should belong, so why do I feel misplaced?

"Would you like me to fix you some lunch?"

I shake my head as I try not to cry.

Her smile is weak when she says, "Well, I'll let you settle in," before she goes back downstairs.

I sit on my bed and power up my phone. When the screen finally comes to life, countless missed calls and texts from Noah appear in my notifications. The last time he reached out to me was nearly a month ago. Scrolling back to the beginning of summer, I start reading through some of the messages.

> Noah: You owe me from bailing on me after school yesterday. Maybe we could catch a movie this week. Cool?
> Noah: Why aren't you answering your phone?
> Noah: There's an indie band I'd like to check out that's performing in a couple of weeks at Spines, that bookstore you told me about. Wanna go?
> Noah: What the heck is going on? Are you pissed at me?

I keep flipping through the texts.

> Noah: Stopped by your house today. Your mom said you're away at a photography camp or something like that. Why do I feel like that's a lie?

I scan through a few more until I hit the last one.

> Noah: It was cool knowing you. I'll leave you alone now.

Falling onto my back, I stare up at the ceiling. Great, the only friend I've managed to make at school thinks I ditched him for camp. I know I should call him, but the lie my mother fed him was beyond lame and there is no way he bought it. And right now, I don't have the energy to try to explain my way out of it.

If only there were some guidebook on how to reenter and adjust back into your old life, it would make this easier. But, then again, if there were, it would probably just say to be honest because mental illness isn't something that should be kept in the dark. *Reduce the stigma and talk.*

Whatever.

I watch the blades of the fan as they spin around and around, moving but never really getting anywhere. Just like myself, no matter where I go or what I do or how far I run, life dumps me right back where I started.

But Noah isn't my only friend anymore. Sitting up, I reach into my back pocket and pull out the three things I've been keeping hidden. My two turtles and Sebastian's cell phone number he stashed in the sofa cushion before he left. I unfold the tiny piece of paper and punch in his contact info, save it, and then call him.

It takes four rings for him to answer. "Hello?"

"Hey, it's me."

"You out?"

"Yeah," I tell him. "I'm calling from my cell."

"Where are you?"

"Home, but I don't want to be." I thought hearing his voice would make me happy, but it doesn't. And even though I don't feel quite right, I don't want to be alone. "Can I come see you?"

"Yeah," he responds. "Where do you want to go?"

His place is out of the question, and he can't come here either because I don't want my mother prying. Although, it wouldn't be the first time he's been at my house. When we were younger, he came over a few times with some of our other friends. I'm surprised she didn't recognize him when she saw him at family day at the facility, but then again, the last time she saw him he was no older than thirteen.

"Marina Beach? Down by the driftwood?" I suggest. "I can come pick you up."

"I'll meet you there."

"How?" I ask since he can't drive because of his suspended license.

"Don't worry about it," he says before asking. "Meet you in an hour?"

"An hour?" I question because the beach is only ten minutes away.

"Yeah, I need to hop in the shower and take care of something first. I'll see you in a bit."

"Okay, bye."

Shoving the turtles back into my pocket, I forego the unpacking and head downstairs to find my mom in the kitchen. "Hey, do you have my car keys?"

She looks up from the piece of mail she's reading. "What do you need your keys for?"

"To go on a drive," I say slowly as if it isn't obvious.

"Oh, I . . . I thought we could spend the day together." She does a bad job hiding how uncomfortable she is with the idea of me leaving.

"I've been cooped up all summer; I don't want to be cooped up in the house on my first day out."

"Where are you going?"

"To the beach."

She opens her mouth to say something, but then she hesitates.

"Mom, come on. What's the problem?"

She sighs and sets the mail down.

"You don't trust me."

"It isn't that I don't trust you."

"Then why are you acting this way?"

"I'm just worried."

"Because you don't trust me," I reiterate.

"Because I love you."

Trying to control my frustration, I take a deep breath and hold it for a few seconds before telling her, "I'm not a criminal. I haven't done anything wrong."

"I never said you were." She rounds the island, opens one of the drawers, and pulls out my keys. "I don't want you gone long."

"What's long?"

"Be home in two hours." When she hands over the keys, I concede, "Fine. Two hours."

"And I want you to call me."

Already walking toward the door, I roll my eyes and then grab my hoodie from the entryway closet. "Fine."

"Call me when you're headed back too."

God, she's already getting on my nerves, and I haven't even been home a solid hour.

"Harlow?" she nags when I don't answer.

"I hear you."

I head out to the driveway and hop into my car. As I'm backing out of the drive, I turn up the music and flip on the windshield wipers. Driving after not being behind the wheel for months feels weird, and when I come to a red light, I tilt my head back and look up at the puddles of rain accumulating on the sunroof. The car behind me honks, and I startle, noticing the light is now green.

A handful of minutes later, I pull into the lot, which is empty. I figured it would be with the weather today. Since I have about a half hour to kill before Sebastian gets here, I make my way down to the water to wait.

I've missed this place too much to linger in my car.

Settling myself on one of the many large pieces of driftwood, I pop my hood over my head, close my eyes, and take a deep inhale, filling my lungs with salty air.

Rain pelts softly against my face, and I grow heavy with happiness.

Or is it sadness?

I have no idea which, but it overwhelms and thickens within my chest, consuming every inch of space. Before I know it, hot tears mix with the cold rain on my cheeks.

I'm not actually crying, yet I am.

Everything I've been through this summer comes crashing down on me, and somehow it doesn't seem real, but rather a dream I just woke from.

Time passes as I sit here, listening to the waves as they break along the shore. This is the one place I used to run to and collect my thoughts, but now, I'm more confused than ever. I'm not sure where to plant my feet after toppling back out into the real world.

"Hey."

Looking over my shoulder, I see Sebastian. I stand, but then I freeze, suddenly unsure of how to act around him. Seeing him for the first time outside of the facility, I don't know, he almost feels like a stranger walking toward me.

The closer he gets, the wider his smile stretches, and it grants me a sliver of comfort, but it isn't until he steps right in front of me and pulls me in for a hug that I'm able to exhale. He's only hugged me twice before and both were stolen in moments of distress.

We don't need to steal anymore, and that thought alone has me gripping him even tighter.

This summer has changed so much—it took me to an extremely dark point but sent me out with a new friend I don't have to hide anything from. He's seen me at my worst, and because of that, I can just be myself—I don't have to pretend to be okay because he knows I'm not.

When his arms slacken and he pulls back, I notice his bloodshot eyes and wonder if he's been crying. "Are you okay?"

"Yeah, I'm good," he says close enough for me to smell the truth. He isn't upset, he's been drinking.

Attaching a fake smile to my lips, I take a seat on the driftwood next to him and fumble with what to say. As he zips up his jacket and tugs the hood over his head, I look behind him to the expensive sports car parked next to my car. "That's yours, right?"

"Yeah, why?"

Our eyes lock, and there's no way he can't see my concern.

"Don't look at me like that," he says dejectedly.

"I don't want you to get in trouble. If you got caught driving on a suspended license . . ."

"I can't stay in that house with them." His words come out dripping with pain, reminding me of the old Sebastian, the one who was always sloppy. Dropping his head, he confesses, "I don't know what to do," as he kicks the heels of his shoes against the densely-packed sand.

"It's that bad?"

He nods. "It's only gotten worse."

"Have you been going to your meetings?" I ask, aware that, as part of his outpatient treatment, he has to attend weekly AA meetings.

"Yeah. I have my hearing in front of the judge next week."

"Are you nervous?"

He stares out over the water. "It is what it is."

I wish I could do something to help him, but I don't know what that would be. I used to see him around and think that he was nothing but a spoiled, egotistical jerk, breaking the rules because he thought it made him cool. Now, I see the truth—that his life is a collision course of devastation.

As stupid as it is, I go ahead and pull the turtle I made out from my back pocket and hand it to him.

"What the hell is this?"

"It's my turtle."

When he cracks a smile and laughs under his breath, I lean in and nudge him with my shoulder.

"This is *not* a turtle."

"What do you mean?" I point out all the parts to prove him wrong, saying, "See, there's the tail. Flip it over. Look, there are the legs."

"It's completely deformed."

I snatch it back. "You are so mean."

"Low, look at it."

I examine it for a second before pulling out the other turtle— the one he made—from my pocket. "Well, it isn't as good as yours, but I'm getting better."

He then swipes it out of my hand.

"What are you doing?" I ask when he tucks it into the pocket of his jacket.

"Keeping it."

"Why? You made fun of it."

"Because I want to keep it," he says with a smirk on his lips, and it's nice to know I helped put it there.

We wind up spending every minute of my remaining time hanging out together, and when time is up, my mother is already calling.

"At least she cares enough to check in on you," he says after I hang up with her and groan in annoyance.

"She makes me feel trapped."

We stand and walk to our cars, but I'm not ready to go just yet.

"What are you doing for the rest of the day?" I ask.

"I don't know." His eyes drop for a beat, and he shoves his hands into his pockets. "What about you?"

"I'll be at home."

His expression falls, and it has me thinking all sorts of new thoughts about what his days and nights look like, roaming around this town on his own. I can't imagine how it must feel not to be welcome in your own home and to have to fend for yourself. Pity is the last thing he needs from me, so I try to smile for him.

"Call me later?"

He nods. "Yeah," he says before pulling me in for another hug, and I suspect it's more for his sake than mine.

Either way, I need the comfort too, so I accept it without comment.

Chapter Twenty-Eight

HARLOW

"WHAT ABOUT THIS?" MY MOTHER ASKS AS SHE shows me a cropped sweatshirt with leopard print trim.

"Eww."

She shakes her head, but before she hangs it back on the rack, she holds it up as if she's actually considering buying it for herself.

"Mom, no."

"Why not? It's cute?"

"Trust me, it isn't."

I stroll around the clothing store she dragged me into, but there isn't a single thing in here that I would be caught dead wearing. The pop music playing overhead is enough to give me cramps.

When my mom suggested we go shopping for back-to-school clothes, I didn't put up a fight, which she was more than thrilled about. The thing is, for months, every minute of every hour has been consumed with activities. Even though I didn't enjoy most of them, they still served to occupy space in my head. The constant schedules kept me from myself.

Now that I'm home, all I have is empty time.

Yanked from continual happenings, I'm no longer distracted.

Seconds diminish into mile-long minutes, allowing me to become reacquainted with the true depths of my despair.

So, I took her offer today with the hope that moving amongst the living would help fill some of the vacancy.

To say this past week hasn't been extremely low would be a lie.

I force myself to get out of bed every morning, to brush my

teeth, and put on fresh clothes. Food is poison to my body, yet I eat to fool my mom into thinking everything's fine.

It isn't fine.

I'm not fine.

During my last appointment with Dr. Amberg, he asked how the new meds were working. I should've been honest, instead, I lied as if everything's okay. Truth is, I wonder if it's the meds that are making me worse. It would be an easy thing to fix, but I'm terrified to let him know that I'm *not* okay, terrified of what the consequence might be if he were to become aware of the truth.

It'll fade though. This mood will shift—it always does.

I'm on the low end of low right now, but hopefully after school starts and I find my new routine, the hopelessness that's drowning me should subside a little.

"Have you found anything worth trying on?" Mom asks as she weaves her way through the racks.

"They're having a sale on socks," I respond in lackluster humor. "The ones with tiny avocados all over them are dope."

Unamused, she tilts her head. "Okay, fine. You aren't into this store," she says. "You can pick the next one, but at least let me buy you one thing today that isn't an earthtone color."

I pinch my face at the thought.

"What? You used to love yellow."

I can't even deal.

Turning to head out into the mall, I tell her, "Yeah, when I was eight."

The next store we visit has their fall clothes out, offering me a big selection of long-sleeved tops that I start pulling off the racks.

I already have several items in my arms when my mother holds up a green sweater and smiles. "What about this?"

"It's an earthtone."

"I know, I know, but it's so pretty, don't you think?"

She gives me a smile and lifts her brows as she waits for my opinion, which actually surprises me.

Because she's right; it's really pretty.

"I like it."

"So," she says, stretching out the word, "is that a yes?"

When I nod in approval, her face lights up, but she holds in her excitement for my sake when she simply smiles before turning back to the racks. My eyes stay on her as she continues to shop and a sense of love washes over me, but it's quickly eclipsed with guilt for how I treat her. I know she wants a good relationship with me, and I see her trying all of the time. If only it were enough to make me feel the love she's trying to give me, but it mostly irritates me. I wish I knew exactly what I needed so that I could simply tell her, instead, all I do is blame her.

"Ohh! Look at this!" she says excitedly when she shows me a yellow top. "Can we add it to your yes pile?"

It's hideous and totally not me, but in this moment, I don't have the heart to let her down.

"Sure."

After I find a few pairs of jeans and a new coat, the cashier bags everything up while my mother pays.

"Are you hungry? I think we've earned some lunch," she says as she eyes our shopping bags.

"Yeah, sure."

The food court is packed, and while we stand in line to get a couple of slices of pizza, I hear a familiar laugh. I don't want to look, but I do anyway as I peer over to my left. Sure enough, it's Brent and half the lacrosse team. Quickly, I scan to see if Sebastian is with them, and before I turn away, I see him standing on the other side of the group.

Tension strangles me, and when they burst out in a ruckus of laughter, the urge to dip out of this line and escape is astounding. As the line creeps along slowly, I keep my head down while my mother rambles on about wanting to try their veggie pizza and how she's going to start eating better.

I nod along with random *uh-huhs* to keep her appeased.

After we finally make it up to the counter, get our food, and pay, we go in search of a place to sit. When my mom starts walking toward the kids from my school, I tell her, "I think I saw an empty table back over there," nodding behind us.

"There's one this way, dear."

She keeps moving ahead, and I try my best to dodge behind a lady who's pushing a stroller, but it's a failed attempt.

Eyes fall on me as their snickering grows, and soon enough, Brent calls out, "What the fuck is Cricket doing here?"

My mom is too far ahead to hear them, and I panic as I try to move through the swarm of people going in every which direction while someone in the group laughs. "She's such a loser."

But it isn't until I hear, "Yo, where's your baby?" that I look over at them, but my eyes only catch Sebastian's. He hangs on to me for only a second before he turns to Justin with a harsh, "Shut the fuck up, man."

Justin slings another insult, but I don't stick around to hear what he says as I rush over and find my mom.

"Can we go?" I try to keep my voice calm, but it comes out too quickly.

"What?"

The alarm in her eyes has me nervous, so I whip up a lie. "I mean . . . can we find a bench to eat at outside of the food court? It's too crazy in here."

"Oh, uh . . . sure."

She stands and gathers her bags, and I wish she would hurry as my ears hone in enough to hear a faint, "Who the hell would lay, Cricket?" followed by more laughing.

When she takes too long, I grab her drink for her and rush out.

"Is everything okay?" she asks when she catches up with me.

"Yeah, it's a zoo back there. How can anyone enjoy their food?"

I find a bench outside of a department store and far away from Sebastian's friends.

"This is a much better idea," my mother says as we situate ourselves.

I feign chill, but inside, I'm a mess, rattled from what just happened. It isn't that I'm not used to being teased, but to now be friends with Sebastian . . . I don't know what to think or how to feel.

It isn't as if he slung insults my way, but the fact that he hangs out with them irritates me. I get that it's important to him to fit in, that he needs it to compensate for all the crap he has to deal with that none of them know about. We talked about it this summer, and I get it, but still, I don't like it.

At the same time, I hate that he tried sticking up for me. I wish he had kept his mouth shut, but he didn't, and it probably raised a few red flags with them. I mean, why would someone like Sebastian defend a loser like me?

I don't know how we're going to manage being friends in the real world, and that thought alone makes me so sad. But how on Earth is this supposed to work?

"How's the pizza?"

"Good," I say automatically. When she looks at my untouched slice, I pick it up and take a bite, repeating, "Good," as I chew.

She smiles. "This was fun. I've missed spending time with you."

Yeah. Loads of fun.

If she only knew.

"Are there any other stores you want to go in?"

"Not really. I'm kind of ready to leave, if that's okay?"

She gives a nod and we finish our lunch. Somehow, I manage to force down half my slice before tossing the other half into the garbage before we grab our bags and drive home.

Dumping all my new clothes out onto the bed, I go to my desk to get my scissors, but they're gone.

"Mom," I yell from my room, "where are my scissors?"

"What do you need scissors for?"

"To cut the tags off."

"Just use nail clippers."

I press my lips together in a heap of frustration for the mere fact that she treats me like a baby. Seriously, I can't have scissors?

Picking up a top, I use my hands to pop off the tags before moving to the next item. When they're all off and I'm digging in my closet for some empty hangers, the doorbell rings. Curiously, I peek out of my room as my mom opens the door, but I can't see who's on the porch.

"Is Harlow home?" My neck flames, and I duck back into my room.

What the hell is he doing here?

"Harlow, someone's here to see you."

"One sec."

My mother invites him in, but before she starts prying, I head downstairs.

"Hey," Sebastian says when he sees me.

"What are you doing here?"

My mother looks between us, and when I hit the bottom step, he responds, "My phone's dead or else I would've called."

"I'm sorry," she says to him, "you look really familiar."

"Mom, it's Sebastian."

It takes a moment for the light bulb to go off, and when it does, her brows lift. "Sebastian West?"

He nods.

"Oh, my gosh. I haven't seen you since you were in . . . what? Sixth or seventh grade?"

"Something like that."

"Look at you, all grown up."

"Mom, please."

She catches my hint and takes a step back. "Well, I'll let you two talk," she says before disappearing back into the kitchen.

"What are you doing here?" I ask again. "How did you even remember where I live?"

"I knew this was your neighborhood, so I drove around until I saw your car in the driveway."

Taking this conversation out of earshot from my mom, who's most likely eavesdropping, I lead him upstairs to my room.

As soon as he walks in, he breathes a heavy, "I'm sorry about what happened."

I go right back over to my closet and pull out the hangers because I'm not sure what he wants me to say.

"At the mall," he clarifies as if I need reminding.

"It's fine," I mutter as I drop the hangers onto the bed and start slipping a sweater onto one of them.

"It isn't fine."

"Just drop it."

"I don't want to." He takes the top out of my hand and sets it down. "They're dicks."

"Trust me, I know."

He sighs and sits on the edge of the bed. "This is complicated."

"It doesn't have to be." I walk over and take a seat next to him.

"What do you mean?"

"Just . . . go back to how it used to be."

His brows furrow. "I don't want to."

"What if I do?"

He drops his head, and we fall into silence as I think about what next week is going to look like when we're back in school. The thing is that, although we've changed, nothing else around us has. There's no way we can be friends at school and not catch heat for it.

"I don't want to be the center of attention," I admit, and when he looks at me, I explain, "If people saw us hanging out at school . . . if they heard you sticking up for me, everyone would start talking and wondering why."

"So?"

"They talk about me enough, but for the most part, I go unnoticed. But they all notice you."

"You don't want to be seen with me?" He's hurt by this, I can tell in his voice, so I shrug.

"I don't want to be seen at all."

As we stare at each other, I urge him to understand where I'm coming from, but when he starts to slowly shake his head, I beg softly, "Please."

"You really expect me to just keep my mouth shut when they start saying shit about you?"

"You act like this is something new for me . . . that I haven't been dealing with it for years."

"That doesn't make me feel any better."

"I just think we should stay in our own corners while we're at school."

It really is for the best. I can only imagine the gossip that would start spreading if people found out we were friends and the attention it would bring my way. It makes me anxious to even think about and causes my left palm to itch. When he notices me rubbing it, he takes my tingling hand in his.

"Okay," he agrees reluctantly, earning him a feeble grin in return.

In the quietness of my room, we sit, holding hands, and I don't know about him, but my mind drifts back to this summer and how everything felt easier between us when we were hidden away. Memories cause my fingers to strengthen around his, and when they do, he rocks into me.

"It feels weird, huh?" he asks.

"What does?"

"These secrets we have. It sort of puts us on an island."

It's exactly how I've felt since returning from my first stint at Hopewell.

Leaning my head onto his shoulder, we sit a while longer before he heads out.

"What was that all about?" my mom asks when I shut the front door.

"Nothing. We were just comparing our class schedules," I lie as I walk into the kitchen to get a soda from the fridge.

She follows me and takes a seat at the island, saying, "He looks awfully familiar."

"Because it's Sebastian."

"No, I mean, like I've seen him recently."

I pop the tab and tell her, "You probably saw him at family day."

Her eyes drop as she searches her memory, and when they lift to mine, they're a little wider. "He was at Hopewell," she states, and I nod. "Why was he there?" she asks, catching me by surprise.

"Mom!"

"What?"

"I'm not going to tell you that."

"Why not?"

"For the same reason I wouldn't want him telling people why I was there. It isn't anyone's business."

She opens her mouth and then closes it before leaning forward. Clearly, she wants to say something but is doing a horrible job at hiding it.

"What?"

Clasping her hands together on top of the counter, she looks over at me. "I want to make sure you're hanging out with the right people."

Slowly, I set the can down. "Are you serious?"

She looks so dumbfounded that my anger spikes.

"So, because he was at Hopewell, that makes him questionable in your eyes?"

"No, I mean—"

Shaking my head in disbelief, I snap, "News flash, I was there too—*twice*! So, what are you saying? That everyone's parents should question if I'm *suitable* enough to be friends with their kid?"

"No, that isn't what I'm saying."

"That's *exactly* what you're saying." I can't control my frustration as it pours out of me. "You are the wrong woman to be judging when it was *you* who sent me there."

"Harlow," she scolds harshly, standing from her seat, but I'm already halfway to the stairs. "Harlow, get back here."

"Just leave me alone."

As soon as I hit my room, I slam the door, pick up my phone, and call Sebastian, only to be reminded that his cell is dead when his voicemail picks up. I toss it without leaving a message as my other hand starts aggravating me. Clenching my teeth, I swallow against the storm of emotion that threatens to erupt and begin banging my palms together as I try to diminish the rampant needling.

Chapter Twenty-Nine

IT'S UTTER MAYHEM WHEN I WALK INTO THE SCHOOL. Excitement surrounds as everyone reunites with friends they haven't seen since the last school year ended. Girls squeal, guys high-five, and lockers slam. The noises bleed together to ignite my anxiety as I keep my head down and make my way to class.

"Hurry it along," a teacher calls out, but no one pays her any attention.

Pushing my way up the stairs, I almost get knocked into a couple who's making out. I have no clue who they are since they're practically eating each other's faces, but they are oblivious to the chaos around them.

When I walk into my first class, I find an inconspicuous seat in the back row. Since it's the first day and there really isn't anything to busy myself with, I pull out a notebook and pretend to be preoccupied as all the desks start filling up.

After the morning announcement and attendance call, the teacher actually goes around the room and has us stand up one by one to introduce ourselves and tell the class something fun that we did over the summer.

"So, I'll start. Hi, my name is Mrs. Caldwell," she says enthusiastically. "I just graduated from U-Dub last year, and the most fun thing I did this summer was getting married." She flashes her sparkly ring as I try to hide my ick face.

She smiles as she goes around the room and listens to everyone. The closer it gets to my turn, the more stressed I become. My palms are actually sweating, and the back of my neck is burning with anxiety. Needles prick along my skin, and when she points to me, I cringe before I push out of my seat, keeping my eyes glued to the teacher to avoid having to see the entire class staring at me. My heart pounds, rattling my voice when I speak.

"I'm Harlow, and I spent part of my summer in Miami." I lie to fit everyone else's comments about their vacations.

"What about you," Mrs. Caldwell says, pointing to the next kid as I take a seat and try to calm my rampant heart rate.

I sit through the rest of the hour, listening to the teacher talk about what projects we will be doing, how she grades, and blah, blah, blah.

I already know that Sebastian will be in my next class, which is senior English—it's the only class we share this year. A part of me is nervous to see him when the bell rings, but another part of me is comforted. It's a weird combination that has me on pins as I walk and find him already sitting a few rows from the front. My heart double-beats when he looks up at me as I make my way down one of the aisles, eventually selecting a seat a few back from his.

In a twisted way, I kind of miss Hopewell. We didn't have to hide there because I was safe from ridicule, unlike here. The only person I had to worry about was Kevin, but after he and Sebastian got into that fight, Kevin never really messed with me again.

A couple of guys walk in, clap hands with Sebastian, and claim the desks around him, but when Emily files in, she glares in his direction, strides past him, and takes the empty seat next to me, which was the last thing I expected.

"Dude," one of his friends says while laughing and then slugs him in the arm.

Class is called to order and another hour drags along. The day continues uneventfully, and I'm thankful for fourth period to come around because it's our allotted time for the newspaper staff and I can finally relax. But it ends much too soon, dumping us into our lunch hour.

I hate lunch, and since it's the first day of school and we have nothing to work on, our teacher, Mr. Duncan, says we can't hang out in the class like we typically do later in the year.

After stopping by my locker, I take my time getting to the cafeteria. I'm not hungry, but I grab myself a soda and a bag of chips before scanning the room for an empty table because the one I used to sit at last year is completely full. As I track the room, I spot Noah, and not a second later, he catches me looking at him.

Crap.

"Move out of the way," Justin barks as he purposely bumps into me before going over to where Brent and Sebastian are sitting.

Defeated, I drag myself over to where Noah is because I only have two options: ignore him and lose the only friend I have in this school other than Sebastian or face him and try to salvage what might be left of our friendship.

He sits alone in the back of the cafeteria, and when I take a seat across the table from him, he seems irritated.

"Hey."

"Hey?" he responds. "Really?"

My head scrambles as I try to think of what to say because I didn't bother making a plan for this conversation even though I knew I would most likely be having it.

He stabs his fork into the lumpy mashed potatoes on his tray and takes a bite.

"I can't believe you're actually eating that?"

"My mom doesn't put money on my snack bar account, so . . ."

Pushing my hands down in my lap, I sit for a moment before giving a meek, "I'm sorry."

He sets the fork aside, and I force myself not to look away from him because this is extremely uncomfortable.

"Why have you been avoiding me?"

"I haven't—" I catch myself because I have been for the past couple of weeks. "I mean . . . it wasn't intentional."

He quirks a brow. "If it wasn't intentional, then what was it? An accident?"

"No, it wasn't that either."

"So, what gives?"

I hang my head, grappling with what I should tell him as my hands fidget restlessly.

"Look, if you don't want to be friends, I get it."

I look up. "I want to be friends."

He shrugs as if he doesn't care either way, and I lean forward and fold my arms on top of the table as I sigh. "I would've called, but I didn't have my phone."

"Why not?"

I stall before saying, "Because I had to . . ." My knees bounce crazily from beneath the table. "I had to go take care of myself for a while."

His face morphs in confusion, and I don't realize I'm tugging my left sleeve over my hand until he's looking. I pull my hands under the table and tuck them in my lap again.

Clarity strikes him and his expression straightens. "Are you okay?"

"I'm fine." My response is too fast, too forced. "Just . . . don't ask any questions, okay?"

He nods. "Okay."

We stare at each other in extreme awkwardness, but there's no easy way to segue the conversation, so I throw out the first thing that comes to mind, saying, "Seriously, though, you should talk to your mom about your lunch account because those potatoes look disgusting."

"They aren't *that* bad."

"At least pack your lunch."

His attention shifts over my shoulder, and when I turn around to see what's distracting him, he teasingly mumbles, "We've got a domestic disturbance at the jock table."

Kassi is livid over something Sebastian did or said and is on the verge of tears. I can't hear what they're arguing about but whatever he says next has her storming off with Emily trailing right behind. Sebastian's ticked until Justin says something that causes them all to laugh.

"They're so annoying," I mutter when I turn around.

"So, what are you doing after school? You wanna hang out?"

Although I have plans to meet up with Sebastian later, I know that I can't push off Noah if I want to get our friendship back on track, which I do. "Yeah. I have some things I have to do, but I can call you when I'm free."

"Cool."

We finish our lunch, and by the time last period rolls around, I'm more than ready to get out of here. My phone vibrates from inside my backpack, and while everyone is coming in and finding their seats, I slip it out and read the text Sebastian just sent.

Sebastian: We still on for Marina after school?

Before I can type anything, Noah walks in. When he sees me, he smiles and takes the seat to my left.

"Finally, we have a class together." He drops his backpack to the floor and digs out a notebook.

"Has today been dragging for you, or is it just me?"

"It isn't just you," I start while concealing my cell under the desk to sneak a quick response. "I'm ready to get out of here."

Me: Yeah.

"Who're you texting?"

"No one." After I drop the phone down into my bag, Kassi enters the class with one of her friends. They take the desks diagonal from me, which is close enough to overhear her say, "I still really love him."

"You shouldn't," Cara tells her. "He was a total ass to you at lunch."

I sink down into my seat, wondering what the heck happened, but their conversation is cut short when the bell rings and class begins. Distraction has me glancing Kassi's way while the class syllabus is being handed out. The two of them have been going out for over a year. They're pretty much *the* couple that has all the girls staring at them in envy. Not once over the summer did Sebastian mention her, but I never asked about her either. Not that I care. It's his business, but after what happened at lunch, I'm curious as to what's going on.

The moment the final bell rings, I gather all my things, hit my locker, and head toward my car. As I'm pulling out of the lot, my phone buzzes from the passenger seat, and when I lean over, I see his text.

Sebastian: Got hung up with Brent. On my way soon.

Battling afterschool traffic is a headache, but once I'm on the main road, it thins out, and I make the short drive over to the beach where we often meet. It's a nice day, no jacket needed, and the sun is actually shining. So when I arrive and settle on one of the logs, I kick off my shoes and socks and dig my toes into the cold, wet sand.

While I wait, I follow through on the promise I made my mom this morning and shoot her a quick text to check in.

Me: Survived the first day.
Mom: How did it go?
Me: Fine. But I found out that we have to dissect a pig in my anatomy class.
Mom: That's horrible.

I hear a car pulling in, and I look behind me to see it's Sebastian, so I send her one last text.

Me: I have to go. Meeting a friend at the beach for a little while.

"Dude, I can't believe the sun is out," he says before grabbing my hand and pulling me to my feet. "Come on, let's take a walk."

I follow him down to the shore, but when I get too close to the waterline, a wave breaks and rushes up and over my feet. "Oh my god, that's cold."

Sebastian laughs. "Why the hell are your shoes off?"

"I wasn't planning on walking."

As we fall into a comfortable stride, he asks, "Who's that kid you sit with at lunch?"

"Noah?"

He nods.

"Just a friend I met last year."

"I've never seen him before."

"That isn't surprising."

He narrows his eyes in jest, and I smile.

"How did your day go?"

He shoves his hands into his pockets. "Fine, I guess. What about you?"

"Same." Still wondering about what was going on between him and Kassi in the cafeteria, I aim the conversation in that direction when I complain, "Your girlfriend sits next to me in last period."

He smirks. "Don't sound so excited."

"She's annoying."

"Yeah," he agrees, staring at his feet while we stroll along. "She isn't my girlfriend though."

He glances my way and shrugs.

"Is that what was going on at lunch today?"

"Nah, that was her being pissed because I never called her to tell her what happened at court."

He called me though. I was relieved when the judge reduced his sentence from a DUI to a wet reckless and minor consumption, which probably had a lot to do with Sebastian going to Hopewell on his own instead of being sentenced to go. On top of his license still being suspended, he has to continue with his AA meetings every week and check in with his probation officer once a month until he graduates.

He goes on to tell me, "I broke up with her the week I came home."

"Why?" The question slips out carelessly, and I instantly regret asking.

I expect a reaction out of him, but he gives none when he

freely answers, "Because it was bullshit." When I don't comment, he fills the space, adding, "Don't get me wrong, I liked her and all, I just didn't love her."

"She loves *you*." He eyes me curiously, and I shrug. "I overheard her telling Cara in class."

"She shouldn't. She doesn't even know me."

"Does anyone?"

Keeping his head forward, he reveals, "You know me."

I keep my eyes on him as he continues to look straight ahead before telling him in return, "You know me."

When he finally looks my way, he smiles and hooks his arm around my neck as we continue our lazy walk along the beach.

Chapter Thirty

"DO LIZARDS LIVE IN FORESTS?" ANNA, NOAH'S LITTLE sister, asks when she barges into the small den where we're studying.

"I don't know. I think so."

"How do you not know? You're almost done with high school."

"Go ask Mom," he says, and she scurries off.

Noah swivels the desk chair around and opens a new webpage. "Okay, the process of aging," he mumbles as he types it into the search bar.

We're two weeks into school, and we've already been assigned our first research paper for anatomy. Luckily, we share the class and will be partners all year, which means we'll also be dissecting things together.

The door opens and Anna pokes her head in again. "What about monkeys?"

"Why are you bothering us with this?"

"I have to build a forest habitat inside a shoebox," she says. "I really wanted the ocean, but Payton picked it before I could, and I got stuck with the forest."

Noah huffs as she babbles on. "Go annoy Mom."

"Second grade is just as hard as twelfth, you know?"

"Yes," I say, and when she looks at me, I tell her, "Monkeys live in forests."

She smiles before turning back to her brother. "See, even your friend is smarter than you."

"Out!" Going back to the computer, he grumbles, "She is so irritating."

"She isn't that bad."

He deadpans on me.

"She's only a kid."

"You don't have to live with her."

My phone chimes from deep within my bag, and he gets back to work as I dig it out.

Sebastian: Just got out of my AA meeting. Now I'm ready for a drink.

Me: Aren't they supposed to make you not want to drink?"

Sebastian: Not after listening to everyone's sob stories for an hour. You wouldn't believe some of the shit these people have done.

I hate that he still drinks. At first, I wasn't comfortable saying anything to him about it, but I know I need to. We've gotten so much closer, and it doesn't feel right to keep my feelings about this to myself. I just have to find the right time.

Me: I'm sorry. If it makes you feel any better, I have to go see Dr. Amberg tomorrow after school.

Sebastian: Can I see you after?

Me: Yeah, I'll call you when I'm leaving.

"Who are you texting?" Noah questions.

"No one."

"Why are you being secretive?"

"I'm not. I'm just talking to my brother."

He shoots me an unconvinced look before saying, "Well, I found some stuff for our paper, and I need you to take notes.

Me: I have to go. Talk later?

Sebastian: Yeah.

I tuck my phone back into my bag, and not two seconds later, Noah's mom walks in.

"Were you being rude to your sister?"

"Mom, she's coming in here every ten seconds and asking stupid questions while Harlow and I are trying to work on a paper."

She glances over and gives me a soft smile before telling Noah, "Try to be a little nicer to her, will you?"

"Fine."

"Harlow, are you staying for dinner?"

"No, not tonight," I tell her. "My dad's coming home."

When she steps out, I look over at the clock on the desk and sigh. "I should probably get going."

"Already? We haven't even gotten anything done."

"I know, but I haven't seen my dad in forever." Honestly, I haven't seen him in five weeks, and last time I did, I was still at Hopewell.

"We really need to work on this," he says when I start packing up my books. "What about tomorrow after school?"

"I can't. I'm busy."

"With what?"

I zip up my backpack and sling it over my shoulder. "With stuff."

"Why are you so busy all of a sudden? You never have any free time to hang out."

"We hung out last week."

He cocks his head in irritation. I get what he's saying. Thing is that I give most of my time to Sebastian, but lacrosse season doesn't start until February and he hasn't been hanging out with his friends that much, so he has tons of free time.

"I'm sorry," I tell him, feeling a twinge of guilt. And even though I don't really want to do much of anything these days, I offer, "How about we get together this weekend. You want to go down to Seattle?"

"Yeah, we can do that," he says as he stands and walks me out.

As I drive home the urge to cry takes over. There's no reason for it, but it's there, completely out of the blue. Lately, it seems that if I stop moving for a second, I'm fighting back tears. The sadness is overwhelming at times. I thought about telling Dr. Amberg when I see him tomorrow, but I don't want to raise any concerns.

I'm doing everything I should be: attending weekly therapy, taking my meds, and journaling. Unlike before, I'm extremely cautious with what I put into my notebook, which makes the exercise pointless. I don't find myself turning to it often, but I do talk a lot with Sebastian. Yet still, I'm depressed. Like *really* depressed right now.

I've forgotten what it feels like to take a breath—a real, solid breath—because there's an incessant tightness around my throat. Emotions lodge there, and no matter what I do, they won't go away.

It was only a few hours ago that I was sitting in class and it all became too much. I had to run out before anyone saw the tears in my eyes. I wound up locking myself in a bathroom stall where I buried my head in my hands and silently cried for a while over nothing.

Existing is painful for a person like me.

It hurts all the time.

Some days are more manageable than others, but the pain is always present.

Like a shadow, it follows. Even when I can't see it, it's still there, filling me with its torment.

When I pull up to the house, I'm anxious to see my dad, but when I hop out and rush inside, he's nowhere to be found. It isn't until I walk back to their bedroom that I'm reminded of our family's devastation.

They're in there, fighting and slinging vile words back and forth that I'd never expect to hear from my parents.

"You did this to yourself," my father screams. "What did you expect when you started sleeping with another man? That I would be okay? That I would forgive you?"

"No, of course not." She's crying. "But we have a family. You can't give up on us."

"Don't you put this on me. You're the one who gave up on us. You!"

"I'm so sorry. I don't know what I can do to make you believe me."

"Nothing," he seethes. "It disgusts me to even look at you."

The empty hole in my soul expands, allowing a frigid gust to blow through it, chilling me to the core. I've never heard him so angry before, but I can't blame him. My mother deserves it.

She's ruined our family.

"Jonathan, please—"

"It isn't even worth you begging. I hate you." His words are razor sharp, and when the door swings open, his face is fuming red.

He startles when he sees me.

"Harl—"

Before he can get my whole name out, I'm running out the door, and straight toward my car. I turn the key, throw it into reverse, and look up in time to see him standing in the doorway of our house that's no longer a home.

Tears rise, he blurs, and I drive away.

Their voices echo in my head as I get as far away as I can. My hands tremble against the steering wheel. How is this my life? We're a family—ever-lasting and strong, but we're falling apart.

Rolling up to a red light, I wipe my face and grab my phone.

Me: Are you busy?
Sebastian: Just hanging with friends. Everything okay?

No. Nothing is okay.

Me: Yeah.

It's the first lie I've told him, and when the light turns green, I head over to Marina Beach. A shiver jostles me as I sit on a piece of driftwood. It's especially cold for it being the end of September, and with the sun setting, it only feels colder. Droplets of rain trickle over the hood of my raincoat, and I pull it around me tighter while I cry.

The broken heart I've been walking around with for years is damn near pulverized at this point.

I don't want this life. I don't want my family to be torn to pieces.

Before I know it, my mind takes me places I don't want to go to. Thoughts of my dad remarrying and starting a whole new family feed the fear that I'll one day be forgotten. My mother finding someone new and that person moving in and claiming my father's place is incomprehensible.

When he moves out, then what? I barely see him as it is.

Will that be it?

Will he even have time for me?

The sky darkens as the sun sets behind a thick veil of gray, and I rock back and forth in an attempt to warm myself. Only, I don't want to be warm. The cold numbs me on the outside and distracts me from feeling too much on the inside.

I sense movement behind me, and when I turn, Sebastian is there.

"What are you doing here?"

"You aren't okay, are you?"

My eyes fall from his.

"Come on," he says, holding his hand out for me, "it's freezing out here."

Slipping my palm against his, we walk over to his car and get in. He turns on the heater, and when he reaches into the back seat and grabs a couple of blankets, I slip off my wet coat and wrap myself up.

"What's going on?"

As I grip the edges of the blanket, my emotions begin to thaw.

"You didn't have to leave your friends for me," I tell him.

"I wanted to."

He stares at me from across the dark car, the lights from the dash illuminating his face.

"So, what happened?"

"My parents were fighting."

"Your dad's already home?"

I nod. "He said he hated her."

The warmth of his car melts my frozen tears, but I can't swallow them because the strain in my throat hurts too much when I try.

I turn away from him and look out the side window, saying, "I don't want my family to split up."

"Maybe it'll be better once they're apart."

I shrug. "Maybe."

He reaches over and takes my hand, and when I look at him,

he tugs me closer, hugging me from over the small console that separates us. Tucked against his neck, I cry and mumble, "I hate this."

"I hate it for you."

"It isn't fair."

His hand slips behind my head, and he strengthens his hold. "Nothing about this life is fair."

And then I think about him and how his father was stolen from him in an instant. I can't even imagine my dad dying. It seems stupid for me to be crying over my parents when he's going through something so much worse.

"I'm sorry."

"For what?"

I pull back and wipe my face. "Because my problems are stupid compared to . . ."

"Compared to what?" he says, and when I look at him, he asks, "Compared to mine?"

Bashfully, I nod, and he shakes his head.

"Your problems aren't stupid, Harlow."

I lean my head back against the seat and look up through the sunroof. "Why can't things just be simple?"

"I don't know," he breathes.

I go to school every day and look at everyone, wondering why they get to be so free and happy while I'm sentenced to a life of suffering. Their lives are so easy. I'm jealous. I wish I could live in the shallow like they do instead of drowning in the depths of despair for no reason at all.

None.

Sometimes I wonder if it's this place, that if I run far enough, I could leave it behind.

Whatever *it* is.

Maybe freedom is the cure.

What if there's nothing wrong with me at all?

What if it's everyone else?

"You ever feel like getting out of here?"

"You mean Edmonds?"

I roll my head to the side and look at him. "Yeah."

"All the time."

"Where would you go?"

"I don't know," he says. "I think about moving but never seriously. What about you?"

"I do the same."

"Are you really wanting to leave and go somewhere new?" When I nod, he adds, "Maybe we should start thinking about it more seriously."

"We?"

"You aren't planning on ditching me, are you?" he asks with a mild smirk, which causes me to grin.

"Are you serious?"

"I'm serious," he tells me, and I swear it gives me a particle of hope, something I can hold on to that will get me through graduation.

The idea of the two of us running far away from this place and starting fresh somewhere new has me wanting to hug him because I doubt I would've actually found the courage to do it on my own. But to know that he's with me on this, that we could do it together, snuffs the doubt and makes me believe this might actually be possible.

When Sebastian reaches over and turns down the heat, I become aware of how hot I am and shrug off the blanket. I turn to toss it into the back seat and notice he has a bag and a pillow back there as well.

"What's all this?"

"Hmm?" He looks over his seat and then back to me.

"Are you sleeping in your car?"

He isn't quick to respond as shame washes over his expression, but eventually, he tells me the truth. "Sometimes."

"Why?"

He faces the windshield and looks out toward the Sound. "Shit gets really bad at my house."

"Why didn't you tell me?"

He shrugs. "It's embarrassing."

"Sebastian." When he looks over at me, I tell him, "Next time, call me."

"What do you mean?"

"Stay at my house."

He lets go of a humorless laugh. "Yeah right. I'm sure your mom would love that."

"I'll sneak you in."

"I'm not going to risk getting you in trouble."

"You won't," I tell him blindly, knowing that I have zero clue how to pull something like that off, but nothing about this situation sits well with me. "I'm serious. I don't want you sleeping in your car."

"It's not that bad."

Tilting my head, I silently call out his crap. This is a small sports car; obviously, it isn't comfortable.

"It isn't," he defends weakly.

"Promise you'll call me next time," I tell him, and when he hesitates to respond, I press, "Sebastian, promise me."

Reluctantly, he nods.

"Say it."

"I promise."

Chapter Thirty-One

SEBASTIAN

"WHAT ABOUT FLORIDA?"

Harlow scrunches her nose in distaste, and I laugh.

"No."

"Why not?"

With zero influx in her tone, she responds, "On what planet would you equate me to a sunny Florida girl?"

"Don't you miss the sun?"

She shrugs. "Ehh, kind of, but not really." She takes the laptop from me and starts punching the keys.

"Is your house always this quiet?" I ask as she searches for another college.

"Yeah, why?"

"It's nice." I sink back into the couch, lean my head against the side of her arm, and watch as she scrolls through the Boston University's website. "No."

"What do you mean *no?*"

"Boston? Don't you need really good grades to get in there?" After a few taps, she finds the GPA requirements, and when I look at the number, I tell her, "I'm already out."

"Now you have me curious. What's your GPA?"

I swear her grin is concealing laughter. "I'm not sure I want to tell you."

"You kind of have to. We're trying to get into the same college."

"Tell me yours first."

"Three point eight."

"I'm going to drag you down."

She giggles, nudging her elbow into me. "Shut up. No, you aren't. It can't be that bad."

"No, I'm just teasing. I think I'm pulling a three point five."

"Thank god. You had me worried."

"What? You thought I was all looks and no brains?"

"Why are you assuming I think you're good-looking?"

Tilting my head up to her, I give her the most charming smile I can, but her façade is strong, and she doesn't even crack a smile.

"I'm home," her mother announces when the front door opens. "Oh." She stops when she sees me and shifts the bouquets of flowers she's holding. "Hi, Sebastian."

"Hey."

"What are you two doing?"

"Looking at colleges," Harlow tells her.

"I remember my days as a Husky," she reminisces as she strolls into the kitchen and out of our view.

The two of us chuckle under our breath.

"We should schedule a tour," she calls out. "You would love it there. It's so beautiful when all the cherry blossoms are in bloom." She peeks her head around the corner, adding, "You know I was a Chi-O, which makes you a legacy."

I try to hold in my laughter. This woman is delusional and completely unhinged if she thinks Harlow has any interest in joining a sorority.

Harlow closes the laptop and grumbles something under her breath as she sets it on the coffee table.

"I should probably go ahead and drop the bomb on her that I'm not staying in Washington," she whispers with dread in her eyes.

"You want me to stay for moral support?"

She shakes her head. "You should probably save yourself and go."

"I was hoping you'd let me off the hook," I tease to try to make her smile, and it works, but it comes with a slug to my arm.

As Harlow walks me out and we pass the kitchen, I shout, "Later, Mrs. Stephenson"

"Goodbye."

"Call me and tell me how it goes," I say as we walk over to my car.

"I will. Have you told your mom yet?"

"There's no point in telling her. My trust fund became my own when I turned eighteen, so it isn't like I need her permission or anything."

She drops her head, and I see the tension building in her.

"What's wrong?"

"What if she says no?"

"It's your choice, Harlow. She can't tell you where to go to college."

"Unlike you, my mom will be footing the bill."

"Then take out loans," I say, unsure of the different options. "Don't worry about it. You'll have me; we'll figure it out."

She gives a weak smile and slowly starts walking backward. "Wish me luck."

"You'll be fine," I tell her before she turns and heads inside.

When I make it back to my house, my stomach sinks the way it always does. This place used to hold so many great memories, but my mother has done a good job of destroying each and every one of them. As the time passes, I find it harder and harder to remember the life we once had.

When I step inside, it's eerily quiet until I hit the stairs and my mother calls out a faint, "S-Sebastian?"

"Yeah." I walk down the hall that leads to her room and find her sitting on the edge of the bed in tears.

"I need your help."

"Where's Kurt?"

"He got arrested," she says. "Can you call to see if a bail has been set?"

"Fuck that."

She reaches out and clamps her cold hands around my forearms, begging, "Please."

"When did this even happen?"

"The other day." Her blinks are slow as she struggles to get the words out. "I don't know. What day is it?"

I would tell her, but it wouldn't mean anything. She's so lost in her drunken world.

"I'm not calling," I say. "He can sit in jail for all I care."

"He can't. I need him."

"No, you don't."

"I do."

"Mom," she starts crying, "look at yourself. He's sucking the life out of you."

She shakes her head—it's all she can do, and when I kneel in front of her, she clutches my arms tighter.

"Just let him go. Forget about him."

"I love him."

"He's a piece of shit. You can't see it because all you do is sit around and drink, but he's destroying us." I do what I can to talk some sense into her. "Can't you see the hell we're in? I can't do this anymore." Her puffy eyes lift lazily to mine, and I look her dead on when I tell her, "You're going to lose me."

"I can't."

"You will. I'm over this shit, Mom. I'm done."

She pulls me into a hug that is neither warm nor comforting. I don't know who she is, but I hug her back and pretend that some version of my mother still lives inside of this woman.

She reeks of alcohol and body odor when she used to always smell of perfume. To think about the way she used to be hurts, and I can't pretend that it doesn't.

"It was bad enough losing Dad; I don't want to lose you too."

Her arms slacken and she draws back, looking at the pain in my eyes. I don't try to hide it because I need her to see what she's doing to me.

"Kurt is only using you; you guys are burning through Dad's money. You really think he's going to stick around when it's all gone?"

"He isn't like that."

"He doesn't even have a job. All he does is sit around, drink, and smoke weed."

She shakes her head, and it pisses me off that she's so clueless.

"Do you even love me?"

"Of course. You're my son."

"Then put me first," I beg, my voice straining under all the hurt she's inflicting. "I need you. You're the only parent I have left, but Kurt has to go."

"We love each other."

"God, Mom." I sigh, shaking my head. "You're delusional if you think that."

"You don't understand—"

"I do," I say as my anger erupts. "You need help." I stand and yank my arms out of her hold. Staring down at her face, which is nearly unrecognizable, my heart pounds bitterly for how selfish she's become. "Choose, Mom. Him or me?"

She shakes her head in disbelief that I would put that on her, but I don't care.

"I'm serious. I'm over this."

She opens her mouth to speak, but nothing comes out. It's when she gives me a defeated shrug that I know her answer. It snaps my heart in two, and it takes every bit of strength I have not to lash out and hit her. Instead, I swipe the liquor bottle off her nightstand and stalk out of her room.

"Sebastian," she wails, but I'm done.

I go straight to my car, blast the stereo, and drive to the docks, which are now empty as the sun sets. Sitting on the edge of the wall with my legs dangling over, I unscrew the metal cap and take a long pull of whiskey. I swallow it and bite my teeth together as my throat burns, but soon, it fades and sends a much-needed warmth through my chest that aches so badly.

After a few more swigs, my vision blurs from behind the tears I hate. I'm so mad that I shouldn't be crying, but I am, which only pisses me off more.

Everything is so out of control, and no matter what I do or say, I'm powerless. The realization that I'm going to have to go through life alone is debilitating. I don't want to think about it, but I have no choice. Devastation sits on my shoulder as resentment brews inside.

The two don't mix, fighting ruthlessly for dominance, pushing me to my breaking point and I lose it, screaming into nothingness, wondering if anyone can hear me.

My lungs deplete, silencing me while my echoes slowly die.

The next drink scorches my sore throat, but it doesn't stop me from continuing, and by the time the sun is long gone, I've emptied the bottle.

I'm drunk, and it feels so good to finally be free. Grabbing the neck of the bottle, I sling it into the water and watch as it sinks. It's captivating as I slip into a numbing daze, but it's cut short when everything illuminates.

Turning around, I squint against the bright headlights of a few cars. I stumble to my feet because I'm not in the mood for any company.

"Sebastian!" someone calls out, and when the last car turns off their headlights, I have to blink past the dark spots in my eyes a few times before I make out Brent.

"What's up?" I slur before swaying too far and overcompensating when I try to regain my balance.

He laughs as the whole group starts to gather.

"I thought I told you not to invite him," Emily snaps.

"I didn't."

Unable to stand with much control, I shuffle to the side before someone grabs my arm.

"You're wasted."

I know that voice.

"Hey, Kass."

"Are you okay?"

I nod. "I was just leaving."

"Good," Emily says before grabbing Brent's hand and pulling him over to the rest of the group.

"You can't drive like this," Kassi murmurs

"Like what?"

"Drunk," she says. "Come on, I'll give you a ride."

With her hands wrapped around my arm to keep me steady, she leads me over to her car.

"Why are you out here all by yourself?"

"I needed to think."

She unlocks the doors, but I don't get in. Instead, I turn and lean back against the door, using it to keep myself propped up as I stare at her, bleary-eyed.

"I'm worried about you."

"Yeah?" I question as I reach out and stroke my knuckles down her cheek because I miss the attention she used to give me. "How worried?"

She reaches up, and I don't know if she wants to hold my hand or push it away, but I don't give her a choice when I take it and pull her in closer to me.

"I miss you," she says softly.

I attempt to smile, but it feels sloppy on my lips. "I miss you too," I tell her because, shit, I'd say just about anything to feel the love she used to give me. I need to feel that she—hell, anyone— cares about me. To give me any attention at all that takes away this pain inside me.

I'm in so much agony, and I hate it.

"Are your parents home?" I ask, too wasted to tiptoe around what I want.

Her lips turn up in a grin. "No. So . . . does this mean you want to get back together?"

The lie easily rolls down my tongue, but before I can give it to her, it gets stuck. I waver for a split second, but it's enough for her to catch on to.

Her smile drops, and she steps back. "You're kidding me, right?"

"What?"

"You just want to use me for sex?" When I don't move to respond, she lashes out loudly, "Why are you such an asshole?"

"Because I am!" I yell in frustration before pushing myself off of her car and walking over to mine. I should turn around and apologize for being a dick to her, but misery begins spilling into my emptiness, and suddenly, my throat tightens in emotion, preventing me from saying anything, so I don't even bother trying.

"Wait," she calls out as she follows after me. "Don't drive."

She's too nice, but it's the wrong kind of nice.

"I'm serious." She holds out her palm. "Give me your keys."

"Kassi," Emily shouts from down at the dock, "just let him leave."

"You should get back to your friends," I tell her as I slide into my car and then drive away.

Chapter Thirty-Two

HARLOW

FOR THE PAST HOUR I'VE BEEN ABLE TO SMELL THE lasagna that my father has been downstairs cooking. He makes it for me every year on my birthday, and even though he's in the process of moving into his new house, he held true to the tradition.

Yeah, that bomb was dropped on me last week.

His new place is only a five-minute drive from here, and when he took me to see it a few days ago, I cried a little.

To know he has a new home that isn't my home destroyed a piece of me. I didn't want him to know how upset I was, so I waited until I was alone later that evening to let it all out.

A tapping on my door pulls me away from my math book. "Come in."

My dad steps inside and closes the door behind him. "Dinner's ready, but I wanted to give this to you now." He holds a tiny box in his hand.

"What's that?"

"Your real birthday gift."

"You already gave me money," I say as I walk over to him.

"I thought you'd like this better."

He hands over the box, and I slip the top off, revealing a key. "Did you buy me a new car?" I tease . . . kind of.

He smirks. "It's a key to the new house." He slips his arm around my shoulders, adding, "*Our* house."

I smile as I look down at the brass key.

"I want you to know that we're still a family and that my home is always going to be yours too. So, you can come over whenever you want, okay?"

After setting the box on the bed, I give him a hug. "Thank you, Dad."

Ever since I went away to Hopewell, things have felt off between us. He's been so distant, traveling a lot more than usual. We don't talk as much as we used to, and I've been questioning if his love for me has diminished right along with the love he used to have for my mom. There have been times I've wanted to ask him if it has, but this right here is all I need to know that it hasn't.

Dropping a kiss to the top of my head, he gives me a tight squeeze and then pulls back. "I can't believe my baby girl is eighteen."

"Finally."

He smiles so wide that it crinkles the skin in the corners of his eyes.

"I love you."

"I love you too," he says and then stands. "Come on, let's go eat."

We head downstairs, and my mother already has the dining table set. I can't remember the last time the three of us ate a meal together. As we take our usual seats and start serving our plates, there's an uncomfortable silence among us. I look past my mother and notice a few more moving boxes stacked against the wall, but the key in my room offers me a tinge of comfort that I'm not completely stuck here with her.

"So, where is Sebastian taking you tonight?" Dad asks.

"We're going to the movies."

"You guys have been spending a lot of time together." His tone is suggestive.

"We're just friends."

"But you do spend a lot of time with him." My mother cuts into her lasagna.

"So?"

"What about the girls at school or the girls on the newspaper staff?"

"Mom, really? You're the one who's always harping on me to have friends, and now that I have one, it isn't the *right* kind of friend?"

"I never said that."

"It's what you're insinuating."

After taking a bite, she says, "I just want to make sure that you're surrounding yourself with good people."

"He is good."

"Well, I'd like it if you could find a girlfriend to spend time with."

"Jamie, please. Lay off."

I shoot a discreet smile to my dad for sticking up for me.

"I want you home by curfew," she says, giving up.

"I'm eighteen," I defend.

"Why does every kid think that once they turn eighteen the rules disappear," she mutters, and I roll my eyes.

"Dad, say something."

With a subtle nod, he tells her, "She has a point."

"She is *not* an adult."

"I understand, but maybe we should give her an extension since she is older."

Irritated, she begins stabbing her fork into her salad repeatedly. "He makes me nervous."

"Oh, my god, are you kidding me right now?"

She stares at me from across the table. "Don't think I'm not aware of what goes on in that house. This town is only so big, and people talk."

"That's enough," my father says, and I'm about to blow a gasket.

"You have no idea what his family has been through," I try to defend, not that it's any of her business.

"Both of you, stop!"

Leaning back in my chair, I huff, refusing to look in her direction.

The room goes quiet, and after my dad takes a sip of water, he sets down his glass and tells me, "I agree with your mom that you aren't an adult yet. Yes, you're eighteen, but while you're still in school, you'll have a curfew. Now," he adds, "the two of us will talk and come to an agreement on extending that curfew, but for tonight . . ." His words drift, and when he faces my mom, he says, "Let her have tonight."

Her mouth drops, and I smile.

"She is *not* staying out all night with that boy. Are you crazy?"

"They're just friends."

"This is the problem, Jonathan," she snaps when my phone buzzes in my pocket. "I'm the only one trying to protect her. You're her father, and yet, you set no boundaries."

Sebastian: On my way.

"Maybe the problem is that you set too many boundaries. You barely let her breathe."

She slings her napkin onto the table. "That is not true!"

They continue to argue, not noticing when I leave the table and head upstairs to grab my coat. While I slip the key to my dad's house onto the ring with my others, their voices grow louder, and suddenly, they're back to fighting about the affair. That is possibly the only good thing about my dad moving out—I won't have to listen their screaming matches any longer.

I'm over it.

As soon as the doorbell rings, I run downstairs, tossing a, "Bye," over my shoulder that I doubt they even notice, and rush out.

Their yelling spills out of the house loud enough for Sebastian to hear.

"What's going on?"

"Same fight, different day," I say, trying to brush it off as we walk over to his car, but I can't shake it. The incessant gloom that follows me never dulls.

When he pulls away from the house, I keep my focus out my window while I bite my cheek to keep myself from falling apart.

"Hey," he says gently, laying his hand on my knee.

A thousand pounds of ache splits me open, and I blink fast to keep the tears away. I'm trying so hard to be strong, to not feel this way, to not be myself, but this gaping wound is everlasting, and I don't know how much longer I can keep pretending that everything is fine.

"Do you think we can do something else tonight?" I hate that my voice trembles.

At the light, he pulls a U-turn, and I don't need to ask where he's taking me—he just knows. I keep my forehead pressed against the cold window as he drives over to Marina Beach. My chest is tight, and when I look up into the sky, I wonder if that's where the other half of me is—the better half. It has to be somewhere, right?

After he parks, I go down to the sand and sit on a piece of wood as I stare out over the water that shimmers under the light of the moon. It isn't often we get a clear night, and the reflection it casts without the clouds is brighter than usual.

Sebastian sits next to me, and I feel bad. "I'm sorry."

"For what?"

"Ruining our plans."

"Don't worry about it."

I look over at him to find he's already looking at me, and I get an overpowering need to drop the character I've been playing since I left Hopewell. The magnitude of this low I can't find my way out of has been gnawing away at me, but the fear of what will happen if someone finds out is what keeps me silent. Yet, there's a look in Sebastian's eyes that lets me know that maybe I don't have be afraid of him finding out.

"Can I tell you something without you getting all worried?"

"You can tell me anything."

Having this come so close to the surface has me splintering, and my eyes rim with tears. They're always there, eager to break free. It's utter agony trying to keep myself together, but I can't anymore. I just can't.

"I'm sad." The words come, and the proof slips down my cheeks as my throat constricts painfully, causing my voice to strain when I tell him, "Like, *really* sad."

His brows cinch in concern. "It's bad?"

"Yeah." I breathe on a desperate whimper, and he threads his fingers with mine. "I had to tell someone because all I do is hold it in and it's so painful pretending that everything's okay when nothing is." He pulls me close, and I tuck my head against his neck. "All I want to do is cry—all the time—and I have no idea why."

"Why haven't you told anyone?"

"Because there's no one I trust. If I say anything, they'll all freak out."

He draws back and takes my face in his hands, asking seriously, "Do I need to be worried?"

"No."

"I need you to be completely honest with me because this scares me."

He has every reason to be scared—he's seen what I'm capable of. "No, I promise."

He nods, but he's reluctant. "Come here."

When he holds me again, the relief of him knowing makes breathing a little easier, but it doesn't do anything to lessen my sadness as I quietly weep against his shoulder. I hate that I'm like this, but what else can I do when I'm already doing everything? Maybe some things are meant to be broken for a reason, whatever that reason may be.

He pushes back and before I can wipe my face, he stands, confusing me when he peels off his shirt.

"What are you doing?"

"Getting in," he says before unzipping his pants.

"That water's freezing. Are you crazy?"

He smiles. "Yeah, I am. Haven't you heard? We both are." The chilly air already has goose bumps exploding over his skin as he scrambles to remove his socks. He then pulls me off the driftwood to stand in front of him, and his tone is deliberate when he tells me, "But you're eighteen now. They won't ever be able to lock you up again." My chin quivers, but before my emotions get the better of me, he says, "Come on; take your clothes off."

The mood shifts instantly, and I stifle a giggle when he starts bouncing around in nothing but his boxer briefs. "No way!"

"Get in with me," he dares with a smile that melts my defenses, and when I start to shake my head and back away from him, he just grins. "Come on, Low. Take your clothes off."

God, the joy sparking in his eyes gives me a tiny twinge of jealousy, and I'm so desperate to feel what he's feeling that I pinch my eyes closed, stalling for a beat before mumbling a freeing, "What the hell?" and ripping my shirt off. The cold air bites my skin, and I move in a frenzy as I unbutton and shove my pants down, but he's already off and running.

"Wait for me!" I call out, chasing after him.

"Shit!" he shouts the moment he hits the water, and I'm squealing because *damn it's freezing.*

"Holy crap!" The water is so frigid that it takes my breath away, but I somehow manage to fill my lungs with laughter as the two of us tumble recklessly into a wave.

He's laughing too, and we're so loud that the night fills with the echoes of our mayhem. My heart pounds like a cannonball against my ribs, and when he grabs my hand and tugs me close to him, we're breathless.

"I've never seen you smile like this before," he says, completely winded.

My chest heaves heavily. "Like what?"

"Like you really mean it."

And I do. For the first time in forever, I feel free.

"God, I can't take it anymore," he bites painfully before we bail and run back to shore.

I'm a fit of giggles as we race to our piles of clothes, scoop them up, and dart to his car. He tosses me a couple of blankets from his back seat and turns the heat on high. We're nothing but shivers and chattering teeth as we huddle as close as we can to warm up. Our pulses race while we continue laughing in short bursts until our voices fade.

His forehead is ice against mine, but his breaths warm my cheeks. Slowly, we thaw, inch by inch, until my muscles start to relax, and I slacken against him. It only lasts a moment before he slips his hand behind my neck and, out of nowhere, presses his lips to mine.

My eyes are open, but his are closed, and I have no clue what he's doing, what I'm doing—what *we're* doing. A second later, he's pulling back and staring into my eyes—confused just like I am. But I've come to know him well, and I don't get the feeling that the kiss was anything more than him simply wanting to feel connected, to feel grounded, which is something neither of us has felt for a really long time.

We need it—the connection.

And even though I have no clue how to kiss a guy, I know I'm safe with him when I pull him back to me. This time, I close my eyes, and he offers me a comfort unlike anything I've ever felt before. I could stay in it forever, but he abruptly draws back with a devious smile.

"I have an idea."

"What?"

"It's a surprise," he says, grabbing our clothes. "Get dressed."

Squirming around in his small car, we manage to pull our clothes back on, bonking our heads together a few times in the tight space.

"Where are we going?" I ask as he drives across town.

"You'll see."

When he pulls into a strip mall, I assume we're going to the Chinese takeout place to grab some food until he pulls into a spot right in front of a tattoo shop.

"Uh-uh, no way."

He shakes his head and laughs. "You're such a chicken."

He gets out of the car, walks around the front, and then opens my door. "I don't know about this," I mumble, glancing toward the tattoo place.

Resting his arms on the hood of the car, he looks down at me and asks, "Are you against getting one?"

"No, I just . . . I have no idea what I would get."

"I'm gonna choose."

"What?"

"You trust me?"

Nervously, I tell him, "I should probably say no."

"But you do?"

With a heavy sigh, I close my eyes and nod before he takes my hand and helps me out of the car.

"Oh god." I cringe as he leads me into the shop.

"You'll be fine. I won't choose a skull or anything like that," he teases.

While Sebastian talks to the guy behind the counter, I sit on the bench at the front of the shop, anxious and second-guessing going through with this. They look over at me before going back to talking in hushed voices as the guy sketches something on a piece of paper. I try not to think too much, but all I can do is consider the million reasons why this is a bad idea.

"You ready?" When I don't answer, he tells me, "You're going to love it."

"How can you be so sure?"

"Because I know you."

And believing that he does is all I need to smile and stand. "This is crazy."

"So was jumping into the Sound, but you did it anyway."

"I'm Sam," the guy introduces, and I shake his hand before he asks to see my ID and has me sign some paperwork. We then follow him back to one of the booths. "Just have a seat and relax."

I sit in the chair and recline, but there is no way I can relax. My heart is racing too fast.

"You look like you're going to puke," Sam says, and Sebastian chuckles. "Is this your first tattoo?"

"Is it that obvious?"

He smirks as he shoves his hands into a pair of purple latex gloves, and then he asks Sebastian, "Which arm?"

"Her left."

"My arm?"

Sam pushes the sleeve of my sweatshirt up, and I jump, darting my eyes to him. "I'm just going to clean the area with an alcohol swab," he assures, but that isn't what has me in knots; it's the fact that he's staring right at my scar. My stomach turns in sheer mortification as I watch him. He muddles on the other side of my shameful tears that have me locked in place.

After he tosses the swab into the trash, he looks at my failed attempt. With his thumb, he traces along the memento of my darkest moment, but it's when he lifts his eyes to mine and gives me the tiniest hint of a nod—a nod that conveys understanding—that I calm a little.

"You gotta look away now," he says, and when I lay my head back and face Sebastian, a tear spills out.

I reach for his hand to hold, and he gives it to me as he sits next to me. Paper presses around my wrist, and I have no clue what's going on.

"Are we good?"

Sebastian leans over me and gives an approving, "Yeah. You're good," before looking down at me. "You ready?"

"Is it going to hurt?"

"No worse than any of the other shit we go through," Sam says. "Take a deep breath."

The buzzing of the gun is the next thing I hear, and when the needle makes contact, I close my eyes. Sebastian never lets go of my hand.

Time bends into an abstraction, and I swear this is right where I'm meant to be—in this very moment with my best friend, the only person I trust enough to see me for exactly who I am. It's strange how paths can cross, how we misjudge so easily, how nothing is as it seems. I'm not sure if that's a good thing or a bad thing, but I don't ponder it for too long before the buzzing stops. Sam continues doing something to my wrist, and when I finally open my eyes, Sebastian has a cheesy grin on his face.

"What?" I ask, but he doesn't respond.

"You ready to see?"

I face Sam when he says this and then look down to see a thin gray strand stretching around my wrist, almost like a delicate bracelet.

"Look underneath," Sebastian tells me, and when I turn my hand, I see it isn't a bracelet at all.

It's a ribbon.

Over my scar, it's tied into a tiny bow with the tail ends loosely curled. It's simple and unobtrusive, and makes the most gruesome part of me a little less ugly.

Laying my head back, I hold my wrist above me and cry as I settle in the fact that, with Sebastian, I don't have to worry about explaining the whys when there aren't any to even explain.

Chapter Thirty-Three

HARLOW

FROM OVER MY SLEEVE, I RUB MY WRIST TO SOOTHE THE itch that's been irritating me. Sam gave me some ointment to use while the tattoo heals, but I left it in my room this morning. I've managed to hide the ink from my mother, which hasn't been hard to do, but my dad knows. He caught a glimpse of it the other day when I was hanging out at his new place.

He was pretty calm about it, and I was beyond relieved when he agreed not to tell Mom.

I'm in the clear for a while because he left for Australia yesterday.

As everyone rushes to their last class of the day, I stop by my locker to grab my anatomy book and spot Sebastian and a few of his friends on the other side of the hall. Spinning the dial to my combination lock, I hear Brent's unmistakable laugh. I'm so ready for Thanksgiving break next month so I can get some time off from this place.

When I lift the latch and open my locker, something falls out. It isn't until I squat down that I see it's an origami turtle. I smile, and when I stand, I flip it over to find a note from Sebastian.

You need to make your deformed turtle some deformed friends.

I laugh under my breath as I look over my shoulder. He reaches into his pocket and slips out the top part of the turtle I made him. When Sebastian gives a pouty face, I shake my head before we both crack smiles. As I turn back to my locker, I catch Kassi glaring at me from down the hall. She then shifts her eyes over to Sebastian, and I know she saw our exchange. I grab my book, close my locker, and head to class.

Noah is already at his desk when I enter the room.

"Hey, were you able to finish the research last night?"

"Crap," I mutter.

"Harlow, it's due tomorrow and you promised you'd get it done."

"I know, I'm sorry," I tell him, but he's already aggravated.

"What is going on with you?"

"Nothing, I just . . ." I try to think of a lie, but I'm distracted when Kassi comes walking in with Cara.

Both shoot daggers at me, and my skin flames.

"I can't afford a bad grade," Noah says, but it's in the background as I pretend to write something in my notebook, hoping they will just ignore me and go to their seats.

"Hey, slut." Kassi's voice is just loud enough to get the attention of a few nearby students.

My skin radiates in mortification, and I sink down in my seat. I don't need to look up to know that people are staring at me.

"FYI, my boyfriend isn't into the whole teen-mom thing, so you can stop the flirting. You just look desperate."

A few people start snickering. I want to run, but I'm paralyzed with anxiety.

"What the hell is your problem?" Noah defends, but I wish he wouldn't, he's only drawing more attention.

"You aren't seriously sticking up for this loser, are you?"

"Why are you pretending to be Sebastian's girlfriend? The whole school knows he dumped you."

God, Noah, stop.

"Then why was he out with me the other night?"

She and Cara laugh obnoxiously, but it's cut off when Mr. Wilcox walks in. "Textbooks out, everyone."

My pulse is on fire as I steep in utter embarrassment, wishing to the gods above to vanish me into thin air.

"She's a bitch," Noah grumbles under his breath, and I drop my pencil before my death grip snaps it in two.

"I don't need you sticking up for me," I whisper, and when I finally get the courage to move, I look at him from the corner of my eye to see he's ticked off.

Well, I'm ticked off too. At Noah, at Kassi, and even at Sebastian. He shouldn't have put that turtle in my locker.

Grinding my teeth, the hour passes and I have nothing to show for it. How can I possibly pay attention when I'm too busy festering in irritation?

I'm already packed up before the bell rings, and when it finally sounds, I make a mad dash out of the class as Noah calls for me to wait. But I don't. Before anyone else can have a chance to say anything to me, I start pushing my way through the halls.

"Harlow."

"I'll talk to you later, Noah," I say, but I know he can't hear me above all the noise now that school is out.

"Hey, there you are." Jennifer, the new editor jumps in front me, forcing me to stop. "I know you're photographing the homecoming game this Friday, but I was wondering if you could also shoot the dance on Saturday night."

"Gabby's assigned to that," I tell her, wanting to get the heck out of here.

"She's sick and can't do it."

"It's Wednesday. I'm sure she'll feel better by then."

"Why are you running away from me?" Noah says when he finally catches up, and I cringe because I just want to go.

"Well, if she isn't, can you do it?"

"Yeah, whatever." I dart around her, and Noah trails me.

"Thanks!"

"Can you stop for one second?" he gripes, but I keep going. "I feel like there's something you aren't telling me."

Finally making it to the doors, I head out into the parking lot and toward my car. "What's that supposed to mean?"

"You're never around."

A bunch of the lacrosse guys are hanging out at Brent's truck, which is a few spaces down from my car. Sebastian is with them, and when I go to open my door, Noah steps in between and blocks me.

"Move."

"I thought we were friends."

"We *are*," I say with exasperation. "Can we talk about this later?"

"I saw you with him the other day," he says, and I have no clue what he's talking about until he adds, "You were leaving the yogurt shop on Main."

Chills prick my skin at the truth he knows. Sebastian and I went to Revelations after school at the beginning of the week, I just had no clue anyone had seen us or that I had to worry about it.

"So, what? You're following me now?" I don't mean for my words to come out so sharply, but I'm freaking out.

"I'm not following you. I was taking my sister and her friend there."

My jaw tightens as he stares at me, but I don't know what to say. I just want to go home.

"Why are you hanging out with him? He's an asshole."

I want to defend Sebastian and tell Noah that he doesn't know what he's talking about, but that would only spur more questions on his end.

"Is what Kassi said true? Are you two . . ."

"Kassi's full of crap. I can't even believe you would ask me that."

"Trouble in paradise, losers?" Brent hollers, and from over the roof of my car, I see them all laughing at me, but it isn't until I see Sebastian shove Brent that I bolt.

Pushing Noah out of the way, I hop into my car, start it, and shift into reverse. As I'm backing out, I see Sebastian in my rearview mirror when he hollers, "Harlow, wait!"

Everyone is looking at the scene, and I throw my car into drive and get the hell out of here.

I can still feel all of their eyes on me even after I'm long gone from the parking lot. My trembling hands turn the wheel as I speed to get home, and when I hit a red light, I drop my head as I go into a panic.

They all know.

When I look up, I see Sebastian in the reflection of the mirror.

And now they all saw him chasing after me.

Panic spins into anger because he promised to keep his distance from me at school.

The light turns green, and he follows me turn for turn all the way into my neighborhood, which has me fuming mad.

As soon as I'm in my driveway and out of my car, I'm stalking toward him and screaming, "Why did you do that? Now they all know."

"Fuck them." He slams his door and steps in front of me. "Why do you even care what they think?"

"Because!"

"Because why?"

Balling my fists, I dig my nails into my palms as hard as I can and clench my teeth before I completely explode.

"Tell me why you want to hide the fact that we're friends."

Turning on my heel, I walk away, needing space to calm down, but things only get worse when a blaring horn sounds from the street. Brent's truck slows at the end of my driveway and a few other cars come to stop behind him.

"What the fuck are you doing, man?" Brent shouts as he hangs out his window.

I stare in horror as the guys from the other cars start shouting at Sebastian, but it isn't until they shift their focuses on me that I turn and run, trying to outpace their insults—parasite, freak, slut. Frantically, my fingers type in the code for the garage, and when it opens, I dart inside, close it, and run into the house. When I peek out the front window, I see the chaos before leaning against the wall and sliding to the floor.

Through my cries, I hear Sebastian yelling at them. I can't make out what he's saying, but I know he's only making the situation worse. There's nothing he can do to fix this, and by tomorrow, the whole school will be talking about it.

The door rattles when he tries opening it, and I startle.

"Harlow, open up."

"Leave me alone," I cry.

"It's only me. They all left."

"I don't care. Just go."

"Harlow, please."

I don't respond, and he doesn't say anything else. Picking myself up off the floor, I go straight up the stairs and into my room. Dropping onto my bed, I bury my head into my pillow and wail as loud as I can as tears spring from my eyes. My whole body constricts as I scream until I'm breathless and gasping for air. In a sudden shift, I go from hysterical to quiet, the only sounds in my room are my ragged gasps as I go still.

My heart hammers behind my walls, but my mind hushes. Sitting up, the tear tracks down my face remain but no new ones come. Braced on the edge of my bed, I hang my head as a current of numbness washes over.

The door cracks open, and when Sebastian steps inside, he's holding my keys.

"You left them in your car," is all he says as he cautiously walks across my room, drops them on to my desk, and sits next to me.

Instantly, I fall into him and let him wrap me in a consoling hug.

"I'm sorry." He's breathing heavily, and even though I'm furious, I still need him. "Harlow—"

"I'm mad at you."

"I know."

Lifting my head, I look at him, and there's no doubt he feels horrible, but behind that, I see he's hurt too.

Slumping my shoulders, I release a defeated sigh. "This is really bad."

"It doesn't have to be."

"That's easy for you to say. They all look up to you."

"I'm over it," he tells me, and when I shoot him an unconvinced look, he assures, "I'm serious. I'm sick of this."

"Of what?"

"Pretending that we're strangers."

I pull away from him, needing a sliver of distance. "I don't like them talking about me."

"They already talk about you, so what difference does it make?" When I turn back, he goes on to say, "Do you know how hard it is to listen to them tear you down and not say anything? It kills me, but I do it because you asked me to."

I never considered his feelings in this. Never did I think it would bother him as much as it is. It brings me so much guilt that I put him in this situation.

"At this point, they all know something is going on between us, so why hide it? It's only going to make them talk more."

"But what about you?"

"Like I said, I'm over it. I care more about you than what they think of me."

"What about Kassi?" I ask, thinking back to what she said in class about them hanging out.

He looks confused as he shakes his head. "What about her?"

I hesitate to tell him because something about it feels weird. "Nothing. Never mind."

"Did she say something?"

"Just that you guys were hanging out again."

"We aren't," he states bluntly. "I saw her at the docks a few weeks ago. She mentioned something about getting back together and then got pissed when I shot it down." He turns and faces me straight on. "You're all I have, you know that, right?"

I nod, because even though I still have my parents, he's the one I feel the safest with.

"Tell me we can be done hiding."

So many fears of how this is going to look tomorrow when we go back to school surface, but it isn't fair to him. It isn't fair to me either. He's my best friend, and I shouldn't have to hide that. If they're going to talk about me one way or the other, he's right, I'd rather them do it knowing he's got my back.

"Okay," I respond before asking, "Can we bide ourselves a little more time though?"

"What do you mean?"

"Can we ditch out for the rest of the week?"

"What do you want to do?"

When an idea pops into my head, I get a sly grin. "Maybe we can drive down to Seattle. I can show you the Fremont Troll."

"Dude, your painting alone was enough." He laughs, and it's crazy to think about how so much has changed between us since that day in art class.

Chapter Thirty-Four

SEBASTIAN

OTHER'S BURDENS PILE ON TOP OF MINE EVERY THURSDAY evening. When I leave AA meetings, I often feel worse than I did when I walked in. Sitting around and listening to people talk about how low they've sunk and the dark places alcohol has led them to is unsettling. Sure, some people share their triumphs, but tonight wasn't one of those nights.

I hit a wall of cigarette smoke as I walk outside. Everyone is lit up as they always are after a meeting. Addicts exchange one addiction for another—alcohol swapped for coffee and cigarettes.

"Sebastian?"

I turn to see Marcus of all people.

"Hey, I thought it was you," he says as he takes a drag and walks over to me, slowly blowing out a plume of smoke.

"What are you doing here?"

"I still come to meetings every once and a while," he tells me before asking, "How have you been?"

"Okay, I guess."

"It's good to see you in a meeting."

I shrug because I'm not exactly here by choice. "It's part of my probation."

"How often do they have you coming?"

"Every week for a year."

"Are they helping?"

"Yeah," I say, but he looks skeptical.

He should be, I'm a total fraud. The only time I make a conscious effort to stay sober is for the five days leading up to when I have to check in with my probation officer for my once-a-month urine alcohol test.

"You got a sponsor?"

"No."

He nods slowly, and I shift from foot to foot, wanting to leave before he calls me on my shit.

"Well, hey, I have to run, but . . ." He takes another puff before digging out his wallet and pulling out a random business card. After patting his pockets, he turns to the girl standing next to him and gives a nudge, asking, "Hey, you got something to write with?"

She rummages through her purse and retrieves a pen.

"Thanks." He scribbles his phone number on the back of the card and then hands it to me. "Here."

"What's this for?"

"Sobriety is full of pitfalls. That's my cell, just in case you ever need it."

Marcus was always cool with me while I was Hopewell. He was cool with Harlow too, bending the rules when he felt it was needed. It's easy to see that he cares and his job means something to him.

"Thanks." I shove the card into my back pocket.

"I'll see you around," he says, dropping the cigarette and smashing it beneath his foot.

We clap hands, and I watch as he walks out to the parking lot and gets into his car before heading over to mine. When I pull out of the space, a heavy yawn hits me hard. Yesterday was a shit day at school, so Harlow and I skipped today, and we'll be doing the same tomorrow. She promised me she would go back on Monday, but I know she's freaking out about it.

Today, we drove down to Seattle so she could show me the troll under the Aurora bridge. We took pictures of each other climbing on top of it. It wasn't nearly as scary as the version she had painted, which I made sure to give her crap about. She laughed, but it felt forced. None of the smiles she gave me today were real, and I know that what happened after school yesterday is really taking a toll on her. It was a conscious decision not to ask her about it and to give her space to talk to me when she was ready.

Kurt's car is in the drive when I pull in. It was no surprise that my mom posted his bail after he got arrested, but I made sure to stay away as much as I could for a few days after he came back to the house. When I do go home, I hide out in my room, but when nights get really bad, I sleep in my car. Even though Harlow told me I could stay with her, I've yet to take her up on it.

Kurt's riffling through the pantry when I walk in, and I make a dash for the stairs, but don't get far when he calls, "Seb, let's chat."

Tired and cautious, I stop on the steps. "About?"

"Something your mom told me."

If it were about anything other than my mother, I'd ignore him. Turning around, I go to the kitchen where he's leaning against the counter and digging into a box of crackers.

"Is she even here?"

"Nah," he says. "She ran to the store."

He shoves a cracker into his mouth and stares at me as he chews, irritating the piss out of me.

"What did you want to talk about?"

"Your mom was upset earlier, and I couldn't understand why." He sets the box down, pushes away from the counter, and takes his time as he strides across the kitchen toward me. "She said she was having doubts, but it didn't make sense because she's constantly on this," he says, grabbing his dick.

"Get to the point," I bite through my clenched teeth because I'm about to go off on this motherfucker.

"She told me you put those thoughts in her head."

I right my spine, but I'm folding on the inside. The fact that she would tell him what I said to her is yet another betrayal.

I should have expected it.

Kurt rounds the bar, and when he steps up to me, I flex my chest and meet him eye-to-eye.

"You got shit to say to me?" he taunts.

"I've got plenty to say to you, but you aren't worth the breath it would take."

"Is that so?" He runs his hand along his jaw, and that's when I see my father's wedding band on his finger.

My chest rips wide open, dumping burning acid down my ribs and into my gut. He sees me staring at the ring, and he cracks a cocky grin. I'm shaking—every inch of my body wants to murder this piece of shit. Bile rises in the back of my throat, and when I curl my fist and swing, I clip his chin, catching him by surprise. His eyes go black, and he barrels his knuckles into the side of my face, blinding me temporarily.

The impact knocks me back and into the barstools, but in the very next second, I'm launching myself at him, throwing punches. Falling to the ground, my fury erupts. Blow after blow, we take our shots as everything spins out of control. I manage to get on top of him and hammer my fist into his mouth, busting his lip open before he grabs my shirt and shoves me off of him, slamming my back against the edge of the bar.

Burning fire shoots up my spine, stealing the breath right out of my lungs. I hiss in pain, and when I open my eyes, he's standing over me.

"Kurt!"

My mother runs in, dropping a bag of groceries all over the floor and pulling him by the arm. She doesn't even acknowledge me as I push my chest off the floor and sit up. She's too busy inspecting Kurt's face and asking him what's going on.

As he gives her some bullshit answer, I cut in, yelling, "Why?"

She looks at me crumpled on the floor. "What has gotten into you?"

"Why did you give him Dad's ring?"

All she does is stare. She says nothing—*nothing*.

"Why?" is all that is left of me, and I hate myself for the tears that fall down my face.

She steps away from Kurt but won't come closer to me as I remain on the ground staring up at her, desperately needing her.

"I can't do this anymore." Her words are strangled in her pain, but I hang on to them because I can't do this anymore either. She begins crying and for the first time in a long time, I have hope that maybe she is coming to her senses. "I'm so tired of all this chaos."

"I am too."

"I want to move on. I need to heal and get on with life."

Her words are my very thoughts and I truly hope she is at her end with all of this so we can both escape this nightmare. She turns to look at Kurt, but when her eyes come back to mine, there's something in them that scares me. She's hesitant, but she goes on to say, "I can't stop living in the past when my past lives with me." Her voice cracks. "I've tried so hard, but it hurts to look at you when all I see is *him*."

Confusion has me shaking my head. "What are you saying?"

She stalls and then takes Kurt's hand. "This is me, trying to move on—*wanting* to move on."

"You're fucking kidding, right?"

Without another word, they walk out of the room.

The jagged edges of the love I used to feel from her dig into the core of my soul—the soul she used to take care of but has thrown away as if it never meant anything to her.

This must be what a broken heart feels like.

The sound of her bedroom door closing severs something inside me. I stand, unsure of what to do or where to go, but one thing is for sure, I'm not living here anymore. I go up to my room and take a look around at all the memories, but that's all they are—faded fractions of what life used to be.

I pull down a large duffle bag from my closet and start throwing things in. I'll come back for the rest after I figure out what I'm going to do.

Right now, I just want to leave, but not before tossing in the rest of the bottles from the liquor cabinet. There aren't many left, but I take them anyway before going out to my car. I wind up parking at the school and getting drunk. For hours, I sit and wonder where it all went wrong. Questions manifest, one after the other, and I drink to make them go away because I have no answers.

Flipping down my mirror, the tiny light shines on my swollen face. My eye is badly bruised and both of them are entirely bloodshot.

Drinking and crying.

Crying and drinking.

How is it that I'm left with just one person in my life when there used to be so many surrounding me? I'm so undeserving of her. After the years of shit I gave Harlow, she's found something in me worthy enough to put it all aside and forgive me. It's something that I will never stop being thankful for.

I don't remember starting my car, but I'm driving down the street, and when the light changes to green, I don't even recall it being red.

Was I even stopped?

When I pull along the curb in front of her house, I stare up at her window through the trees and wonder if she's asleep.

It's almost one in the morning, and there aren't any lights on inside her house. Still, I tap her name to send a text, but it becomes too much of a task to punch out the letters, so I call her instead.

Hope dwindles after a handful of rings, but then she answers.

"Hello?" Her voice is scratchy, and I bet her eyes are still closed.

"Hey." Mine is scratchy too.

I can hear her sheets rustling. "Is everything okay?"

A breath of a laugh finds its way out of me, but nothing about it feels good.

"Where are you?"

"Out front."

"Of my house?"

If I weren't drunk, I'd be ashamed. "Can I stay with you?"

She's quiet. Maybe she didn't really mean it when she made the offer.

"It's cool. Never mind."

"No, it's fine. Just . . . come around to the back door. I'll meet you."

I don't bother grabbing anything from my bag; I'm too eager to get to her. Walking along the edge of her house, I sway and then lose my footing before falling to my knees. Picking myself back up, I round the corner, bracing my hand on the wall to keep my balance, and when I reach the back door, she's standing there waiting for me.

"Hey."

She raises a finger to her mouth, warning me to stay quiet, and when I get close enough for her to see my jacked-up face, her eyes widen in disbelief.

"Come on," she whispers, grabbing my hand and pulling me through the dark house.

We make it up the stairs without a sound, and when I walk into her room and she locks the door behind us, I turn to her. She keeps her eyes glued to me as she takes in my bruises. Slowly, she slips her arms around my waist, and it's only then that I allow myself to fall into her.

She's the only one who cares about me, and although I'm so grateful, it still hurts. She holds me as I drop my head down to her shoulder, fighting hard not to cry, but a few tears slip out anyway.

We stand like this for a stretch of time, and I don't know how I've made it so long without her.

When I finally pull back, she takes my hand and leads me over to the bed. She crawls in while I kick off my shoes and undress down to my underwear. I slip in next to her, exhausted in every way possible.

Lying on our sides, she reaches over and gently drags her fingertips along my black eye. "What happened?"

I have nothing left to hide from this girl, so I let the words fall from my lips in a whisper. "Kurt's wearing my dad's wedding ring."

"She gave it to him?"

I nod. "I lost it, and we started swinging." Her fingers drift softly down the side of my face. "My mom said that I'm a reminder of the past she's trying to move on from. So I left, but I don't have anywhere to go."

With all my defenses down, I can no longer blink back the tears. Her forehead presses to mine, and I hold on to her as she brushes them away. The pain is intolerable, but her touch offers me comfort. I felt it when I kissed her last week.

We didn't talk about it, but I get the feeling that it was just as innocent for her as it was for me. That it was simply a way to connect. So, with no blurred lines, I lean in and kiss her again because I need the closeness, and she presses her hands into me, gripping me tighter, letting me know she needs it too.

It's a still kiss that I'm nervous to disrupt, but I do anyway because it isn't enough. When I begin to move my lips, I feel her hesitate and pull back.

Her eyes are downcast when she admits, "I've never kissed anyone before."

"Is this okay?"

It takes her a second, but then she nods before coming back to me. Gradually, I feel her tension slip away, and she relaxes in my arms. With her warmth pressed against me, I swear she heals some of these broken pieces of mine. The ache calms in my chest, and all the bullshit outside of this room dissolves into nothingness.

Eventually, our lips naturally fall from each other's, and she rests her head on the pillow next to me. "I'm scared I'm going to lose you," she whispers.

"You won't."

She sighs and drops her eyes.

"What?"

"I'm worried about your drinking," she reveals. "If you get caught—"

"I won't."

"You could."

I want to assure her that I'm fine and that she has nothing to worry about, but it would be a lie delivered on bourbon-tainted breath.

"Promise me the next time you drink that you won't drive."

The worry in her eyes is real and has me considering how bad it would be if I did get in trouble and I wasn't around for her when she needed me.

She doesn't talk about it a whole lot, but I know she's sad. It's impossible not to worry about her even though she told me I didn't need to. The fact that she felt safe enough to confide in me was huge. She trusts me when she doesn't trust anyone. Just the thought of what might happen if she were to lose that terrifies me enough to promise her whatever she wants.

She needs me, especially after what happened yesterday.

But I need her too. She's the only person who cares enough about me to be worried. Not even my own mother is worried—only Harlow. That alone has me caving.

"Just call me next time, and I'll come get you," she offers.

"Okay."

"You promise?"

"I promise," I tell her. "But I need you to make me a promise too."

"Anything."

"Promise me that we're going to get out of this place. That it isn't just us talking about it, but that we're actually going to do it."

Tucked in my arms, she rests her head on my chest. "I promise."

<h1 style="text-align:center">Chapter Thirty-Five</h1>

HARLOW

"**S**EBASTIAN." I GENTLY SHAKE HIS SHOULDER TO WAKE him. "Sebastian."

"Hmm."

He rolls onto his back with an exhausted sigh, and when his eyes finally open, I tell him, "You have to go before my mom wakes up."

"What time is it?"

"Six."

He cringes when he sits up, touching the side of his face, which looks worse than it did last night. "How bad is it?"

"It's pretty bad. I'll get you an ice pack before you leave."

He drags himself out of bed and slips his clothes back on while I crack the door open and peer out. There are no sounds in the house, and I wave him to come with me when I step out into the hall. With his shoes in his hand, he's as quiet as I am as I lead him down the stairs. When we pass through the kitchen, I grab an ice pack from the freezer and then follow him to the back door.

"Here," I murmur and hand it to him.

As silently as possible, I unlock the door, but the click sounds a thousand times louder than it should.

"Thanks for letting me stay with you," he says in a hushed voice as he steps outside before tugging me in for a hug.

"Will you come back tonight?"

"Is that okay?"

I nod, and he tells me, "I'll meet you at Marina later," since we're skipping school again today.

I watch as he shoves his shoes on and then makes his way down the side of the house. He rounds the corner, and when I go back inside, I close the door a split second before my mother walks into the kitchen.

"Good morning," she says as I walk over to the island as casually as I can. "You're up early."

"So are you."

"Homecoming." She pulls a coffee mug down and opens the fridge to get the creamer. "We have a bunch of orders this morning. Needless to say, I won't be around much for today and tomorrow; you know how it is."

"Yeah," I mumble. I'm supposed to be photographing the game tonight, but there is no way in hell that's going to happen.

I'm terrified to return to school, so there is no chance I'm going to the football game tonight, let alone the dance tomorrow night. I promised Sebastian I'd go back to school on Monday, but I don't know how I'm supposed to actually follow through on that.

Everyone will be looking at us—at me. I can't deal with that kind of attention, and no matter how much Sebastian tries to assure me that it'll be okay, it does nothing for my trepidation.

"What's that?"

Snapping out of my thoughts, I look over to my mom, whose eyes are locked on my wrist. I was mindlessly itching my tattoo and hadn't realized it. My stomach lurches as I shove my sleeve down.

"Are you marking your scar again?"

"No!" I spit out too defensively, folding my arms across my chest and tucking my hands beneath them.

"Harlow . . ." Her voice pitches in worry.

"Mom, stop. I'm not marking my scar, I promise."

It's a promise that falls on deaf ears as she sets her coffee down and walks over to me, holding out her palm. "Let me see."

She's bound to find out eventually, and the last thing I need is her panicking again, so with a sigh of annoyance, I hold out my arm.

Shoving my sleeve up, she literally gasps when she sees the tattoo. In disbelief, she turns my wrist until she can see the bow. Her eyes flick to mine. "Please tell me this is fake."

I pull my arm away.

"Harlow, is that real?"

"It's not a big deal."

Her mouth gapes. "Like hell it isn't! When did you get that?"

"On my birthday."

She exhales a hard breath out of her nose and perches a fist on her hip. "With Sebastian?"

"Mom, relax."

"Do not tell me to relax when you're hanging out with that boy and coming home with tattoos."

"It's just one, and why are you calling him *that boy?*"

"You know how I feel about him."

"You don't even know him."

Pressing her lips together, she pauses before asking, "Is there something going on between the two of you?"

"Oh my god," I exhaust, rolling my eyes.

"Answer me."

"No, Mom. There's nothing going on. We're just friends."

"Why is he your only friend?"

"Why does it matter?" I shoot back. "Why are you so against him?"

"Because he's a bad influence on you." I lock my jaw to keep myself from going off on her. She steps closer to me, taking my hand again, and glares at the tattoo when she says, "This isn't you."

Yanking it away, I snap back, "No, Mom. This isn't *you.*" My tone is sharp, alarming her. "He's my best friend. He's the only one who doesn't judge me for being who I am."

"I don't judge you."

"Yes, you do! You're constantly trying to change me and make me into someone I'm not because *you* don't like who I am."

"That is *not* true."

"You say you want me to have friends, and then when I make one, he isn't the right type of friend."

"You are fixated with him. It isn't healthy."

"He makes me happy!" I yell, my anger boiling over. "Isn't that what you want? For me to be happy?"

"Of course, I do. I just don't understand why you can't have a couple of girlfriends too. Why is it only him?"

"Because he understands me when no one else does."

Her brows sink in hurt, but it's the truth. "I'm trying," she says on the verge of tears.

Her pain softens my frustrations, and I lower my voice. "He was there for me this summer when I didn't have anyone."

"Harlow . . ." Her tears spill over her lashes, but I don't stick around to watch her cry.

I can't take on her pain when mine is beyond measure, so I go back to my room.

Shutting down, I take a quick shower, throw on some clothes, and pretend to leave for school, not saying another word to my mom before rushing out of the house.

She'll never understand me. And even though I claimed that Sebastian does, truth is, he doesn't. He gets me better than anyone else, but how could he possibly understand me when I don't even understand myself?

> Me: Instead of the beach, can you meet me at my dad's place?
> Sebastian: You want me to head over now?
> Me: Yeah.

I text him the address and then make my way there.

Normally, I'd be more upset after a fight with my mom, but oddly, I don't feel much of anything. In the two months since I was discharged, I've slowly been disconnecting from who I am. Or maybe I'm finally connecting.

It's hard to tell the difference when you're undefinable.

Last night scared me, but it hurt me too. The first time Sebastian kissed me, I felt so much. It was a comfort that slipped between my fractures and helped to fill some of the gaping holes—the parts of me that have always been missing.

I know it was merely an illusion, but it felt good, so I allowed myself to believe he was actually making me better.

But last night, I couldn't feel it. Something was missing, so I kept kissing him, hoping to find it again.

I couldn't.

I pull into the driveway only minutes before Sebastian arrives.

"You mind if I take a shower here?" he asks when we get out of our cars.

"No, it's fine."

He takes the duffle bag from his trunk, and we head in. After he cleans up, we spend the rest of the day in the room my dad set up for me. Lying in bed, we watch television and nap off and on, wasting away the hours. He only asks once if I'm okay, and when I tell him I'm fine, he simply lets me be. If it were anyone else, they'd be hounding me with questions, but he knows what I need, and he gives it.

Mom: About to leave the shop. You want me to pick up dinner?

"Who's that?" Sebastian asks when I start texting back.

"My mom. She's on her way home."

Me: I'm taking pictures at the homecoming game tonight, remember?

Sebastian reads the text and chuckles. "You're such a liar."

"I'm not ready to go home just yet," I say because I like hiding away with him and I don't want it to end.

"Are you going to get in trouble for not showing up to the game?"

I shrug. "I don't really care." I could easily text Jennifer to tell her I won't be there and that she needs to find someone else, but I don't. I can't even be bothered to make the effort. And it's true, I don't care. It's a stupid football game, played by stupid people, living out their stupid high-school dreams.

It's all stupid.

Mom: Have fun. I'll see you when you get home.

Tossing my phone aside, I tuck my head under his chin and soak up the time remaining before I have to go.

"You know, you could just stay here if you want," I offer.

"When does your dad get back?"

"Not for another two weeks."

"Are you sure it's okay?"

"He won't know, and it's better than you having to wait until my mom goes to bed for you to come over."

"Thanks," he responds.

After a few more hours, I tell him goodnight and head back home. When I walk in, my mother lifts her eyes from the book she's reading in the living room.

"How was the game?" she asks as if everything's fine and we weren't yelling at each other this morning.

"It was okay."

"Did you guys win?"

I hoist my backpack higher on my shoulder. "I don't know. I don't actually watch the game," I tell her. "I just take pictures."

"Are you hungry?"

"I'm tired. I'm just going to go to bed."

I'm still angry with her, but the emotion is muted.

Everything is numb.

Dragging myself to my room, I change out of my clothes and lie in bed as I stare out the window. The clouds glow silver, and I want so badly to believe there's a lining out there for me. A glimmering thread I could grab on to, something to pull me out of this nightmare.

I know there isn't.

I stopped looking for hope a while ago, but quietude has me contemplating that maybe I shouldn't give up on the possibility that there's something out there waiting for me, waiting to save me.

I watch the clouds drift across the sky; even in the stillness of the night, everything keeps moving.

Everything but me.

Picking up my phone, I realize how late it is and debate calling Sebastian. Instead, I pull up pictures of us on my phone—selfies we've taken since we've been home. When I land on the one I took of us at the beach, I stop. He's leaning in from over my shoulder and playfully biting my ear. The memory makes me smile, and I catch it. I don't want to let it go because I don't know if it'll ever return. There's an urge to cling to it and keep it forever, to spread it wider just to *feel*.

Without a second thought, I call him.

"Hey."

"Can you come over?"

"Yeah, why?"

"I just really want you here." Simple words that are pretty but empty and do nothing to stir the life I'm desperate to feel.

"I'm leaving now."

As I wait for him, I go back to the photos and scroll through a few more. Ten minutes later, my phone goes off.

Sebastian: I'm here.
Me: Meet me by the back door.

And just as I did last night, I sneak him up to my room. As soon as the door closes, my desperation shatters, and I sling my arms around him, hugging him tightly, needing my heart to wake up.

"What's going on?" he whispers in concern.

I want to tell him that I'm struggling to feel things, that I'm growing distant—too distant—and that I need him to help me, but I don't know how to say all that, so I hold him tighter.

My malfunctioning heart struggles to beat right. I want to cry, but my eyes remain dry. It's trapped for some reason, and I need to free it, free anything just to prove I'm still alive.

Sebastian slackens his arms and walks me over to the bed. As we slide under the covers, I need to know I'm not as lost as I think I am.

"Are you okay?" he asks, and I shake my head. "Will you tell me?"

Grabbing on to his shirt, I tug him closer, confessing softly, "I feel really alone right now."

"You aren't alone." He gathers me into his arms. "I'm here."

Our eyes tether, but it isn't enough. His words fall short when they fail to touch any of my senses, so I kiss him. When his lips move with mine, I become needy because I'm sinking.

And sinking.

"Hey." He's breathless when he pulls away. "Talk to me."

He's the only person I trust, and I'm scared not to be honest when I'm crying for help on the inside. "I'm struggling to feel things."

"What does that mean?"

"I don't know." My eyes fall shut, and I lean into him. "I've gone numb, and you're the only person I can connect to, but . . ."

"What can I do?"

I peer into his eyes, asking, "Do you have a condom?" The fact that I'm not flamed with embarrassment shows just how far I've slipped away from myself.

Sebastian, however, is shocked, but I don't care. I need a miracle. I'm freefalling and terrified, and if anyone will be able to catch me, it'll be him.

"What do you—I mean, are you . . ."

He stammers over his words, unsure of how to respond, so I simply ask again. "Do you?"

"Um, yeah. In my wallet, but . . ."

"Can we . . ." And now I'm the one who's fumbling over my words because I don't know how to actually come out and ask for what I want when I don't know what the hell I'm even doing.

"Are you sure? I mean, aren't you a virgin?"

I nod timidly, aware of how crazy this must sound to him. "I feel like I'm drowning, and I need to know that I'm not."

There's so much despair seeping out of me that I know he can feel it. How could he not? I'm drenched in it—the fear and hopelessness.

"Are you sure?" he questions with hesitation marking the lines in his forehead. "I don't want you to hate me for this or anything."

"Why would I hate you?"

"Because this is kind of a big deal for girls, and I don't—"

"I could never hate you." I take a moment before admitting,

"I'm so lost, and I just want to connect. You're the only one I can do that with."

With an understanding nod, he gets out of bed and pulls his wallet from his back pocket, takes out a condom, and drops it onto the nightstand. When he shrugs his shirt off and starts unfastening his pants, I shift to my knees and begin undressing.

Each movement becomes more awkward than the one before, and I wait until he's back under the covers with me before sliding off my underwear. When there's nothing left, we scoot in closer to each other. He's clearly nervous, but I don't want him to be because I need too much out of him right now.

"You don't . . . you don't have to make it romantic or anything," I tell him to help take some of the pressure off.

I just want to know that I'm still human.

He rolls on top of me, and I feel safe under his weight.

"You know I care about you, right?"

I nod.

"I just need you to know that before we do this."

"I know."

"You're the most important person in my life, and I want to be sure that we're going to be okay after we do this."

I pull his lips down to mine, give him an unmoving kiss, and then tell him, "You're my best friend. Nothing changes."

He kisses me, and just knowing that we're about to do this has my heart pumping. Uncertainty of how this is going to feel rattles my nerves, and I tense. I tell myself to calm down, but my body doesn't listen. Then I tell myself not to calm down because at least I'm feeling something—my pulse racing, my blood rushing, my skin burning.

His weight leaves me, and when I open my eyes, he's leaning over to the nightstand and picking up the condom. I try not to look at him, at his naked body as he slips on protection. This is all too new and too foreign and I can't stop my vision from going in and out of focus.

"You're shaking."

"It's fine." It has to be. This has to work. "I'm just nervous."

He comes back down to me, and I wrap my arms around him, pressing my hands against his back, feeling his muscles flex beneath his skin.

His head drops to the side of mine and he asks once more, "Are you sure?"

"Please . . ." It is the only word I can get out before my heart stops and everything silences around me—around us.

A wire is cut somewhere deep inside, turning me off. I stare into Sebastian's eyes as his chest moves against mine, but I can't hear him breathing.

I can't hear myself breathing.

I try to concentrate, to tune in when I'm tuned out. Closing my eyes, I force myself to focus on what's happening, but I have no clue where to start or how to find my way to being present.

I can't feel anything.

I reach for my heart, coming up empty handed. It should be on fire, bursting with adrenaline and expanding in emotions.

It isn't.

It's nowhere to be found in this hollow tomb of a body.

Opening my eyes, I look down on the two of us from a window above. My arms stretch around his body and everything appears normal, yet nothing is. I blink and am back inside myself. He's no longer moving as he braces himself above me, running a hand along my cheek.

"Are you okay?"

When I realize that it's over, I try to do my best to sound certain of myself when I tell him, "Yeah."

"Are you sure? You were really quiet."

"I'm sure."

He slides out of bed, and I turn my back to him as I rush to put my clothes on. After he returns, he tucks himself behind me and pulls my body flush against his so that I can feel his heart pounding wildly against my spine.

If only mine could too.

But it doesn't because it's missing. I'm missing.

And then the regret of what I just did washes over me.

We shouldn't have done that because it only exposed to him how incapable I am. Here he is, giving me so much while I give nothing in return. I'm worthless. He deserves to be loved by a friend in a way he can feel, but I'm dead inside.

I'm afraid that, by having sex with him, I just destroyed everything. I already know I ruined all his friendships at school. If I was never his friend, he wouldn't be in this situation. He'd still be hanging out with everyone, partying after the homecoming game tonight and taking Kassi to the dance tomorrow. Instead, he's in my bed, holding misery in its physical form.

What could I possibly be to him when I'm nothing to myself?

What am I to anyone besides a burden?

It seems all I do is complicate people's lives and make everything harder.

"Harlow," he says, tugging on my shoulder to turn me around, and I go.

"I'm sorry."

"For what?"

I don't bother trying to respond.

Dipping his head, his eyes catch mine. "I'm worried I did something wrong."

"You didn't." I rest my hand over his heart because I like the way it beats against my palm. "You did everything right. You always do."

Chapter Thirty-Six

HARLOW

MY NAME IS A WISP OF AIR, FEATHERLIGHT AS IT SWEEPS against my cheek and stirs me awake.

"Harlow."

The closer I inch toward consciousness, the heavier I become. Peace dissolves, and the massive anchor of despair plummets down on top of me.

I open my eyes to Sebastian sitting on the edge of the bed.

"Hey," he whispers as he pushes a lock of hair behind my ear.

"What's going on?"

"I'm going to head out before your mom gets up, but I didn't want to leave without telling you."

"Don't go." The words come without thought, but that's often where the meaningful things come from—out of organic instinct with no questions, with no whys—only need.

"I have to," he tells me. "I don't want us to get caught."

Our eyes lock, and as I stare up at him, I think about what happened last night. The fear that, somehow, I messed us up remains. "Are we okay?"

The corner of his mouth lifts slightly. "I was just about to ask you the same thing."

When I sit up, he scoots closer.

There's so much I want to say, so much I want to tell him, but whatever wire was cut last night severed something inside me that I can't describe. It's hard to talk when the energy needed to do so is incalculable.

So, I wrap my arms around his neck and hug him tightly, the

way a scared little girl would hug her father, as if the touch alone could heal.

His arms band around me, and I just want him to stay. It's as if he's the invisible thread holding me together when the entire world is ripping me apart.

The weight of despair is unbelievable today when there's no reason for it. I'm safe in this room with him, and yet, I'm sad. I've been awake for only a few minutes, and already, I'm done.

Sebastian draws back slightly and rests his head against mine. "I'll come back later, okay?"

"When?"

"In a few hours." He lifts his head and tells me, "Brent texted and wants to talk, so I'm going to hang out with him this morning."

"Oh."

"It's better if I talk to him now before we go back to school on Monday."

"What are you going to say?"

"That you're my friend and nothing is going to change that so he needs to cut the shit."

It's a bad idea, but the effort to care enough to tell him isn't present.

As he pushes off the bed, I stop him, grabbing his wrist and tugging him back. "Just another minute, okay?"

We sit and hold each other, and something inside me tugs. I wonder if it's his thread unravelling.

"Are you okay?"

I nod, and I hate myself for it because it's a lie.

I don't feel right. I'm off and unbalanced.

Pulling on his neck, I press my lips to his, but again, just like last night, the magic of his kiss is gone. It's meaningless even though I know it isn't because *he* isn't.

It's me, I'm the vacant soul who can't even feel.

Our lips part, and he presses his forehead to mine again before looking into my eyes.

He's worried.

From the inside, I cry for help, but my body is a silent vault.

"Call me if you need me," he says, and I nod before he stands and walks across my room. When he reaches the door, he turns around. "I'm serious, if you need anything, just call. I'll be back later."

The goodbye in my throat chokes me, so I nod again.

After he slips out of my room, I drop down to the pillow and hug it close. The smell of him saddens me because he's gone and I don't want to be alone.

I'm used to feeling empty, but this is more than that—it's vacancy in the negatives. My hand covers my heart, and I'm shocked I can feel it beating.

Lying still, I close my eyes and use the cadence thumping into my palm to pass the time.

I'm not sure what I'm waiting for when there's nothing to expect.

My breathing sounds louder in the silence of the room, a metronome I become hyper-focused on. As the gray sky brightens and the rain thickens beyond a gentle mist, my muscles slacken into a puddle of optical illusions. People stare down at me—a puzzle of misconception. They examine and dissect while I look hopelessly into their eyes, knowing all too well there's nothing to be discovered.

If they were to cut into me, they wouldn't find anything but an empty cavity, a chamber of depression, a crater of disenchantment.

There's a knock on my door, and when I open my eyes, I force myself to sit up. "Come in."

"Good morning," my mom says as she walks over and takes a seat next to me. "I was hoping we could talk before I left for the flower shop."

She typically doesn't work on the weekends, but tonight's the homecoming dance.

"Look . . ." She pauses as if to collect her thoughts. "I'm sorry." Her voice is soft, and through her makeup, I can see the red around her eyes. She's been crying, which makes *me* want to cry because I'm the cause of her pain. "I know you think I'm against you, but I'm not."

A tear drops from my chin; I didn't even realize any had surfaced.

"You are my daughter, and the urge to do everything in my

power to protect you is overwhelming at times," she says. "And you're getting older, which only makes me worry more." There's a smile that grows on her face, but it's a somber one. "It isn't easy watching you grow up and become independent. It's hard for me to let you go." Her last words crack, and she lets out a whimper as she takes my hand in hers. "I need to trust you more, I know that."

But she's wrong.

I'm the last person she should trust.

The one thing she *should* be trusting more isn't me, but rather, her instincts. Because as much as I hate to admit it, she has every reason to worry. She probably cares about me more than what I care about myself. Whereas she runs toward me to help, I run away, I avoid and deny and accuse everyone else around me. I made this last stint at Hopewell her fault, but I was angry at her for *everything*, when in actuality, I was angry at myself for being so screwed up. I'm still angry—I hate that I'm like this.

I've come to resolve that she did the right thing by sending me to Hopewell the first time, and she was right to send me this last time, and she would be right to send me back even now.

"I'm happy you've found a friend in Sebastian," she tells me. "I guess, in a way, I'm a little jealous."

"Why?"

She shrugs. "Because I'm sure he has pieces of you that I wish I could have."

Dropping my head, I crumble. Tears spill down my cheeks as she cries, and I feel guilty because she's right. I do give him more because I trust him more.

"I'm sorry," I weep. "I don't mean to hurt you, I just . . . I don't know how to talk to you. I don't know how to connect with you." Lifting my eyes to hers, I admit, "I don't want to fight with you, but I'm angry, and I don't even know why. It's just there, this constant annoyance."

She squeezes my hand, silently telling me that she loves me. I know she only wants the best for me and that she's trying, but still, it's all wrong, because I'm all wrong.

"It's all my fault," I confess, my words breaking beneath the heavy burden I carry.

"No, sweetie, it isn't your fault."

"It is." My shoulders hang, and when I look at her tear-stained face, I tell her, "I don't know how to be your daughter. I feel like all I am is a disappointment."

She pulls me into her arms and lays her cheek on top of my head. "You are far from a disappointment," she assures. "You're perfect. We're just on two separate pages, and we have to find a way to come together."

"I just want to be happy and normal like all the other girls, but I'm broken—too broken for you to love."

"I love you more than anything, and you are not broken," she states, pulling back and looking me straight in the eyes. "You've been doing so much better."

She's wrong, she just doesn't know it.

I'm far from better. It's my mask of abstraction that fools her into believing that I'm doing well. If she got close enough, she'd see the fractures, see the lies, see the truth. But only I can see them because I wear them all on the inside. Everyone else is simply blind.

Her hand runs down the side of my face before falling. When she gently pushes my sleeve up to expose the tattoo, her lips lift into an affectionate smile.

"Was this your idea?" she questions tenderly and without any judgment.

I shake my head. "It was Sebastian's." I smile weakly. "He told me I couldn't look."

"You didn't know what the tattoo was?"

"Not until it was already done."

She rotates my wrist face up and looks at the delicately thin bow that's tied over my scar. Tears swim in her eyes, and when she lifts them to mine, she's sincere when she says, "It's really beautiful."

We hug, and I wish I were different, something other than the girl I am—a disaster among people who never deserved my chaos. Perhaps I'm the cause of her straying from my dad. As much as I want to blame her, what if it was my fault? The fact that I couldn't make her happy, that I was this constant strain on her that made her feel as if she had to run to find relief from somewhere else.

What if I'm the root of it all?

I look around and see little fires everywhere, burning away at peoples' joy.

Am I the match or the gasoline?

"I have an idea," she says. "Let's spend this evening together, just you and me. We'll order in Chinese and watch a movie. I'll even let you pick. What do you think?"

"Yeah."

"Yeah?" She brushes away the last drop of sadness from my cheek, and I nod. "Okay then. Well, I should get going." With a kiss to my cheek, she stands. "We're going to be okay."

Are we?

"I love you, Mom."

She smiles, and this time, it reaches her eyes. "I love you too."

The door closes behind her, and the world drops out from beneath me.

I sit with myself for a while, unmoving, bones cold, lost—that's what I am.

Lost.

Malfunctioned.

Lying back, I zone out as I stare at the ceiling and then out to the clouds, out to heaven. I think about the peaceful souls, granted wishes, happily ever afters, the little houses with their little flower gardens.

My heart bleeds its last tear, and I'm done.

I can't do this anymore.

Here are your pills, show up to therapy, and don't forget about self-care. That's what everyone tells me.

But where's the cure? Where's the fix?

Where's the end?

I've spent years searching for the reason.

There is none.

I'm on a dead-end path, and I'm tired.

I'm so tired.

Listlessly, I pull myself out of bed, across the room, and down the stairs.

In the kitchen, I pour a glass of water and drink it all. Setting the empty glass on the counter, I turn and look out into the living room. Photos sit in frames, memories and smiles hide the dark truth.

They are all lies—exhausting lies.

My attention falls away, and I stare blankly at the island . . . and then the stovetop . . . and then the knife block.

Indifference is the scariest feeling I know. To have the ground crumble beneath me, to have the sky fall and the waters come in and feel nothing.

I pull one of the smaller knives from its slot and hold it in my hand. It isn't a knife I see, though, it's a key, a key to the lock that's held me hostage for far too long.

It's the key to my freedom.

I go back to my room, slip beneath the covers, and tuck myself into my warm bed. Resting my head on the pillow Sebastian slept on last night, I inhale his scent, wanting to connect the way all humans should, but I can't. I'm too detached.

I'm an inhumane atrocity this world has endured for far too long.

Why are you so sad?

If I could pull back these ribs of mine, they'd see the raw red wounds of vicious pain that hold no explanation as to why.

I grip the knife and touch the blade to my scar, the scar that leads to my deliverance from this ever-constant suffering. I trace the line gently as I nestle my head into the pillow.

This world has wrecked me so badly that, when I'm gone, there will be little pieces of me scattered everywhere. In the trees I climbed as a child. In the grass I ran barefoot on. In the sand I built castles with. In the Sound Sebastian and I jumped into just last week that will now carry me out to sea.

So take me, world.

Break me, shatter me, and toss my pieces into the sky.

Clutching the handle in my unsteady hand, my heart takes its last beats, my lungs their last breaths, my defective mind its last thoughts, and with conviction, I cut.

I cut deeper than ever before.

I cut until . . .

. . . until the ribbon breaks.

Epilogue

SEBASTIAN

Four weeks later . . .

D AMP EARTH SEEPS INTO THE KNEES OF MY JEANS, chilling my skin, chilling my bones. No matter how frozen they get, they will never be as cold as hers that now rest beneath me. I push my hand against the wet ground and dig my fingers into the dirt that separates us. Another tear rolls down my face, and when it drops off the tip of my nose, I wonder if she'll be able to taste it.

The irrational part of me wants to claw my way down to her because I can't accept that she's gone, even though I know she is.

How could I not?

I was there.

I saw her.

After I left Brent's house, I called, but she didn't answer. She always answered, so I called again and again and again.

I can still remember that morning. She kept hugging me because she didn't want me to go. It worried me, and I could feel it in my gut that something wasn't right.

But I left anyway.

When I got back to her house, her car was in the driveway, but when I rang the doorbell, she didn't answer. Panic had me running to the back door, which was still unlocked from when I had left earlier.

Fear stung as it lanced me because, when I called her name, there was no response.

I pinch my eyes against the memory that won't stop haunting me, and when I reach my hand out and press it over her name, I want to believe it's her I'm touching and not the headstone marking her grave. My eyes sting, swollen with misery as I try to blink them back into focus, but pain and alcohol have me completely bleary and weak.

Her bed was soaked in so much blood; it was horrifying, but it wasn't enough to stop me from gathering her into my arms. Her body was still warm. I couldn't let her go as I screamed and cried for her to come back to me. Everything spun into a complete blur, a fucking nightmare.

I was gone for only two hours.

Two hours.

"I should've never left you," I whisper, hanging my head as an unbearable ache rips through me—it's guilt, and it's been festering since I found her.

I look back now and see the warning signs. She handed me red flags, and I thought I was helping her, but it wasn't enough.

Picking up the nearly empty bottle lying next to me, I unscrew the cap and pour the vodka down my throat.

I have nothing left; I've lost it all—Harlow, my family, my home, my purpose. It's all gone. Yesterday was Thanksgiving, and I spent it getting drunk in the random hotel I've been staying at. Never have I felt so alone.

A heavy hand lands on my shoulder and squeezes. It's meant to comfort, but it doesn't.

"Are you about ready?"

I nod, and when Marcus kneels next to me, I break even more because I'm not sure I am ready.

"I don't know if I can do this without her," I admit.

"You can. I know it feels impossible, but it isn't."

I look at him, and his eyes are filled with tears as he stares at her grave.

"She told me not to go," I murmur. "Why didn't I listen to her?"

"You couldn't have known what she was thinking." He wipes a tear from his face.

"Why didn't she tell me? All she had to do was ask for help."

"We could ask a thousand questions, but none us will ever know what was going through her head or how badly she was suffering."

It hurts to think about the misery she must have been in to feel that hopeless, to just give up like she did.

"At least she's no longer in pain."

"I want her here. Selfishly, I just want her back."

"I know," he says, rubbing my shoulder, doing what he can to console me, but nothing will ever repair this.

She's gone, and my world is shredded.

He tightens his grip and then stands. "Take your last drink. I'll wait for you in the car."

After he walks away, I down another gulp before closing my eyes and trying to find her. I search for her all the time . . . in the mist and in the clouds and in the shadows.

"I still feel you," I speak into the air, believing she's here because she has to be. "I feel you every day, and I miss you." Hanging my head, I talk through the pain, my voice breaking against each word. "You were my best friend . . . you'll always be."

After another swallow, I stare at the bottle as if I'm going to find her in it. "I know how much my drinking and driving worried you. I honestly never thought it was a problem, and then you came along, and I felt like I didn't need it as much. But now . . . now you're gone, and it's all I have to help with this agony. I'm out of control, and I know it," I tell her. "Even though I was too trashed to hold a conversation last night, I called Marcus. I was scared—for the first time, I was truly scared of myself, of who I've become, of what could happen to me. He came with no questions asked, and when I'd sobered up enough to get coherent words out, I begged him to help me."

Tightening my coat around my body, I shiver against the bitter chill.

"I'm going back to Hopewell. Marcus thought it would be the best place since I could keep up with my schoolwork there and still graduate, but I want you with me." I pinch my swollen eyes shut, pushing rivers down my face. "I can't imagine how hard it's going to be to go back and fight this alone . . . without you. But I have to. I have to try. I have to keep living . . . for you."

I throw my head back and drink my last drops, making a

promise to myself that this is it, that I'm going to fight for my life and take it back. It's what Harlow would want me to do.

So, I'm going to do it—for both of us.

I set the bottle next to her headstone and reach into my back pocket.

Looking down at the turtle I folded this morning before Marcus picked me up from the hotel, another tear falls. I lay it on the ground and read the words I'd written across it: "I'm sorry I couldn't save you."

"I really am sorry." I sit for a moment, silently appreciating everything she gave to me and everything she was. As the mist starts to gather on the turtle, I think about the one she attempted to make and how proud she was of it. I'd teased her about it, and the memory causes me to smile, but it hurts so badly. "I still have your turtle, by the way."

I slip my hand into the pocket of my coat and pull it out. "See, I never got rid of it," I tell her as I hold it between my fingers, all misshapen. "It's my favorite because you're my favorite. And it's perfect because you're perfect. You never thought you were, but you were."

With a deep breath, I shove the turtle back into my coat pocket, wipe my face, and stand.

"I hope you found your peace." Then I turn and walk away, leaving the bottle behind but bringing Harlow with me.

"Are you okay?" Marcus asks when I get into the car.

"No." I'm empty without her.

"You will be. This is the first step."

And then he drives me to Hopewell.

Resources

If you or someone you know is struggling
emotionally or is thinking about suicide,
call or text 988 for help and support.
www.988lifeline.org

If you or someone you know is being abused or
needs a safe place to sleep,
call or text the National Child Abuse Hotline
1-800-4-A-CHILD (1-800-422-4453)
www.childhelphotline.org

Follow E.K. Blair

www.instagram.com/ek.blair

www.facebook.com/ekblairauthor

https://open.spotify.com/
user/1264681839?si=6df6a629ca9f4418

Acknowledgements

I must first acknowledge my assistant and dear friend, Sally, for without her, I'd be lost. She is my anchor in this crazy publishing industry. When I came to her six years ago with this story idea, she embraced it, and, for that, I am so grateful. Most would've shied away, but not her. She supported me and embraced my characters as they came to life. I knew this would be the hardest book for me to write, but she was with me every step of the way—through the tears and heartbreak—through every emotion I needed to go through to make this book a possibility.

It was Denise Moore's expertise that I relied on when writing the chapters at Hopewell. She's a superhero, and I am indebted to her for the hours she spent on the phone with me as she detailed and shared stories about her years working as a nurse in a juvenile mental health facility. She opened my eyes to the reality of what life is like for teens who spend time behind those walls.

My editor, Ashley Williams, worked tirelessly on this manuscript. Through late nights and stress-filled days, she is always there to help me improve my craft in order to be a better writer. She's the only one I trust with my words!

I couldn't do any of this if it weren't for the constant loving support of my family who allow me the time and space to follow my heart and write stories. I love my husband and children beyond measure, and I thank them for their patience.

What I have to say next is hard—terrifying even. You see, mental health and suicide is often veiled in so much shame. It's never easy to talk about, but I must say something. Suicide is not a selfish attempt for attention. It's quite the opposite. You should never deny a person who is struggling with suicidal thoughts or failed attempts of your love and compassion. Be there for them, let them know that they have a purpose, that they are worthy, and that there is hope. Because there *is* hope! I'm living proof of that.